THE HAVOC WE WREAK

THE FOUR - BOOK 3

BECCA STEELE

*To those who face their fears
and refuse to let them win.*

before

THE SECRETS WE HIDE
RECAP...

winter

B ack all together, minus Weston, who was busy digging for any data he could get his hands on, the mood turned deadly serious as the reality of what I'd discovered about Allan sank in.

"He's always been so quiet and unassuming. I never once would've imagined he'd be involved in any of this." Cassius rubbed his chin, deep in thought. "Nothing adds up."

Caiden nodded in agreement, his eyes on my phone as he scrolled through the photos I'd taken. "That's the fucking problem. Not even a hint of trouble."

"Except—" Zayde hesitated, and we all turned to look at him. The look in his eyes gave me chills. "I need to speak to Creed. I'll be back."

Caiden, Cassius, and I exchanged glances as he got up without another word, stalking out of the room.

"What was that all about?" Cassius wondered aloud. "Any ideas, mate?"

Caiden shrugged. "None. He's never said anything to me about Allan. Nothing suspicious, anyway."

"Is it worth speaking to your dad?" I leaned closer to

Caiden, and he gave me a quick smile, tugging me closer and putting his arm around me.

"Yeah, I could. But I'd rather keep that as our last resort, if we can't find out anything else. I don't think my dad's involved, and I don't wanna make him suspicious."

"You didn't think Allan was involved though, either," Cassius pointed out.

Caiden stiffened next to me, and I frowned at Cassius. *Don't*, I mouthed, and he grimaced, his thoughts clearly turning in the same direction mine had. Enough shit had happened for one day. I didn't want Cade stressing about his dad on top of everything else, questioning everything he knew.

"Nah, your dad's not involved. I'm sure of it." Cassius blew out a heavy breath. "I'm not convinced that all this shit with Allan is as it seems, either."

We sat in silence for a moment, Cassius motioning for Caiden to pass him my phone so he could look through the photos.

"You okay?" I stared up at Caiden, worried.

"I don't know."

Sadness filled me at his despondent tone.

"Cade..." I slid my arms around him, and he held on to me tightly, as if he needed me to support him. As much as I needed answers, and as strong as he was, he'd been through so much in his life, and to now have all this to deal with... It was enough to shake even the strongest person. "We're going to get through this, okay?"

He didn't answer me, but he placed a soft kiss on my forehead, pulling me into him.

"Winter's right. We're so close to putting these puzzle pieces together. Failure is *not* an option. We're gonna get the answers, fuck some shit up, then get back to our lives." I

the havoc we wreak

USA TODAY & WALL STREET JOURNAL BESTSELLING AUTHOR

BECCA STEELE

looked around to see Cassius holding out his fist, his expression resolute.

Caiden released me, reluctantly I think, and they bumped fists, a smile finally back on my boyfriend's face.

"C'mon, babe. You have to do it, too." Cassius held his fist out to me, and I was just about to respond when Weston crashed into the room, throwing a set of keys to Cassius.

"We need to go, right now. Cass, you're driving us to the docks. I'll explain on the way."

In the car, the second Cassius had started the engine, Weston continued, twisting in his seat to look at us, his leg bouncing restlessly, excitement in his eyes.

"Allan, nothing, total dead end, although I didn't have much time to look. But...call me a fucking genius. All the Alstone Holdings places other than AMC—the offices, warehouses, docks? Staff have an ID card they use to scan in and out with. I've been working on getting into their system for ages so I could match up the IDs to see if we could build up a picture of who was where and when. When I was searching for Allan, I had I guess what you could call an epiphany, and I managed to access the system. Finally! They had the strongest security I'd come across, as strong as Dad's." He paused in the middle of his speech, a thoughtful expression stealing across his face. "I wonder if it's the same as Dad's? If so, I might be able to hack his system at long last."

"Get to the point, will you?" Caiden stared at him impatiently.

"Yeah, sorry. I didn't dare to stay in the system for long in case I was detected, so I went straight to the date Winter was attacked, and the date she was rescued, on the off chance we might find an answer." Taking a deep breath, he met my eyes. "There's only one ID logged for the night you were attacked, which we have to assume was the guard. All the IDs are a long string of numbers, so I can't match them up to names yet. The night you were rescued? Same ID. But that wasn't the only one. Someone else was there, and the time they scanned in correlates with the rough time frame you were rescued, if we go by the time Kinslee got the phone call from the hospital."

"But how do we find out who—"

"Wait," he interrupted me. "I'm getting to that. That same ID has just scanned in at the docks. They literally did it as I was in the system, so they won't have been there long. There's one other ID already logged in, which I'm assuming will be the security guard, but that's it."

I gripped Caiden's hand tighter, my heart rate speeding up. Were we about to come face to face with my potential rescuer?

"Fuck!" Weston exclaimed, holding up his phone. "The answers are coming thick and fast. Not only are we about to find out who rescued Winter, or at least, find out who else was there at that time, but Mercury has info waiting for me. He says he's found out what Andromeda is."

What?

Hope soared in me. At last, we were going to get some answers.

We sped towards the docks, and Cassius threw his SUV into the layby I'd parked in way back when I'd first come here to investigate.

"Everyone stay together. Stay cautious," Caiden commanded in a low tone. "I've sent Z an SOS message, so he'll be here soon."

Moving stealthily towards the entrance, we fell into complete silence. Caiden kept hold of my hand the entire time but stayed in front of me, protecting me, while Cassius and Weston fell back in line behind me.

We could see the outline of the night guard in the hut, reclined in his chair, scrolling through his phone. It was easy enough to sneak past him and around to the long, low warehouse.

I sucked in a sharp breath, as all four of us stopped dead once we rounded the corner, staring at the figure that Caiden had almost run straight into.

My gaze travelled up, past the black boots, the jeans, the leather jacket, to the face, and our eyes met, mine widening in shock.

"*You!*"

the
havoc
we
wreak

Si vis pacem, para bellum.
If you want peace, prepare for war.

— VEGETIUS, *DE RE MILITARI*

1

winter

"You!" I repeated, unable to get my brain to work properly. I glanced over at Cassius, who looked as stunned as I felt. All of us shared the same look, in fact.

Cassius' jaw opened and closed a few times before he finally spoke, his voice hoarse and unsure. "Wh—what are you doing here?"

My eyes met hers, her initial shocked expression covered by a defiant gaze, piercing through me. Underneath her black beanie hat, wisps of pastel pink hair had escaped from her ponytail and were flying around her face, caught in the night breeze.

She was silent for a long moment, deep in thought, before she eventually turned to Cassius and spoke. "I'm here on behalf of someone else."

"Who?" Caiden asked sharply.

"I can't tell you that. Not yet, anyway."

"Lena...please. What the fuck is going on?" Weston strode forward, gripping her arm. "Talk to us."

She glanced around, and nodded. "Okay, but not here.

Try to get out of here as quickly as possible, then meet me back at your house."

"I'm not leaving you alone in the dark." Cassius glared at her. "No way am I letting my baby sister stay here. It's not safe."

"Not gonna happen," Weston chimed in, tightening his grip on her arm as if he expected her to try and make a run for it at any minute.

"For fuck's sake. You have to trust me. Please. I'll tell you what I know—what I can," she corrected herself.

I eyed her carefully, trying to work out what to do. The boys were so overprotective, but somehow, I didn't think Lena would listen to them. She had a stubborn slant to her brow, and she'd shaken off Weston's grip and crossed her arms in front of her chest, tapping her booted foot on the floor impatiently. I was worried about her myself, but whatever she was doing here, she seemed determined to carry it out.

"Okay." After carefully scanning the quiet, dark area all around us, I spoke up. "The only other person that seems to be here is the night guard. Right?" I cocked my head at Lena. She nodded. "Yeah. First thing I checked."

"Alright then." I turned to Cassius. "Come on. Let's compromise. What if we all meet her outside the docks, by the car? We can keep an eye on the guard hut, make sure nothing happens."

"Winter! You can't be serious right now." He stared at me in disbelief.

"I am. Come on. We'll be right outside if she needs us."

"Cass, please. I have my phone. Look, I'll pull up your number and have it ready to dial if there's any trouble. I won't be long. Promise. I'll even cancel my ride home and come back with you." Lena waved her phone at him, and he gave a frustrated growl.

"No. Way."

"Cassius. Let's go." I injected as much firmness as I could into my voice, and Lena shot me a small, grateful smile as I turned on my heel and grabbed Caiden's hand. Reaching up to whisper in his ear, I murmured, "Please? The others will listen to you."

His eyes met mine, and he sighed heavily, his gaze conflicted. "You're so fucking lucky I love you."

I watched as his lips tipped up at the corners in the barest hint of a smile as I replied, "I know."

"New compromise. Everyone except Lena, back to the car. Cass, get the engine running so we can make a quick getaway. I'm staying here to keep an eye on Lena." Caiden's tone was commanding.

"I don't need a babysitter," Lena hissed.

"Don't give a fuck. I stay, or I drag you out of here, right now." He narrowed his eyes, daring her to test him. "Don't worry, I won't cramp your style. I'll wait right here."

"Fine! I was almost done, anyway." Her shoulders slumped in defeat.

"Come on, let's do this," Caiden instructed. Lowering his voice, he leaned closer to me. "Watch out for the guard. Stay between Cass and West." He dropped a quick kiss on my forehead, before stepping back. Weston and Cassius gave him identical hostile glares, clearly unhappy with the whole situation, but they fell in line with huffs and angry sighs, Weston pulling me in front of him.

Back in the car, the tension was so thick you could cut it with a knife. I leaned forwards between the front seats and put my hand on Cassius' shoulder as he sat, staring straight ahead, making no attempt to start the car. "Cade will look out for Lena. It's going to be okay."

"She doesn't think about the fucking consequences of her actions," he muttered, finally starting the engine. "I don't know what shit she's got herself mixed up in, but it needs to stop right now."

We lapsed into silence, waiting. The only sound was the soft hum of the running engine and the distant crash of waves against the rocks below us.

"Where's Lena?"

I followed the direction of Weston's gaze to see Caiden jogging towards us, a dark shape blending in among the shadows, barely visible since Cassius hadn't yet turned on the headlights. He threw open the door, and Weston immediately turned to him. "Where's Lena?" he repeated, his tone urgent.

"She's right behind me—" Caiden's head shot around. "What the fuck? She was there a minute ago!"

Everything seemed to happen at once. I heard Cassius' *Oh, shit* and looked up to see another dark figure streaking towards us, closely pursued by yet another figure. A light bobbed up and down, the glow from the torch the pursuer carried dimly illuminating the ground as they ran, but too weak to illuminate Lena.

Caiden swung into the car, all business. "Go! Drive at them. When we get there, slow down. Get Lena in, turn your headlights on to full fucking beam and drive at the fucker chasing her."

Cassius nodded, already slipping the car into gear and moving, flying towards Lena and suddenly screeching to a halt as we reached her.

She wrenched open the door and threw herself into the car, landing in the footwell by Caiden's feet, and Cassius wasted no time in speeding straight back up again, flicking on the powerful headlights to full beam. I caught a glimpse of the horror on the night guard's face as he threw up his arm to shield his eyes from the sudden blinding light, and then he was diving out of the way as we drove at him. Cassius spun the wheel, sending the SUV skidding onto the road. The car shot across the tarmac, and we left the docks behind us, obscured by a cloud of dust.

Lena laughed wildly. "That was insane," she gasped out, clambering out of the footwell and sinking onto the leather seats, pulling a tiny backpack from her shoulders before she sat back, her phone in hand.

"What the fuck were you doing?" Caiden hissed at her, the fury clear in his eyes.

Her thumbs flew over the keys as she sent a message, ignoring the rest of us.

"Lena!"

She sobered up as she took in Caiden's expression and noticed the thick tension in the car, the adrenaline rush fading away. "I had to go back for my bag."

"You were almost caught." Cassius glanced at her in the rear-view mirror, grinding his jaw as he gripped the steering wheel tightly.

"I wasn't caught, though," she pointed out.

"That's beside the fucking point!" he roared, and even I shrank back in my seat.

Lena wisely shut her mouth, slumping back with her eyes closed. I was desperate to ask her questions—had she been the one to save me? Now was most definitely not a good time, though. My questions would have to wait.

Back at the house, the tension kicked up another notch, if it could possibly get any higher. Lena disappeared off down the driveway pretty much as soon as the car came to a stop, muttering something about needing to try and get hold of her contact.

We sat in the lounge, waiting. Tense, silent.

"What happened at the docks after we went back to the car?" I climbed into Caiden's lap, speaking low in his ear.

He bent his head, his breath hot against my skin, making me shiver, even though this most definitely wasn't the time or the place. "I waited, and watched her. All she fucking did was peer in the windows of that warehouse we were hiding behind."

"That was it?" I raised a brow.

"Yeah. I stayed back—I'm trying to learn from your example." He met my gaze, his stormy eyes boring into me. "I know you don't like me interfering. I'm...I'm trying, baby. But she's not you. Cass would've killed me if anything happened to her. I kept eyes on her the whole time."

"I'm glad you stayed behind," I told him honestly. I recognised a kindred spirit in Lena, but there was also a recklessness to her. I couldn't help feeling like she didn't take things seriously, and that worried me. A lot.

While we were waiting for Lena, Caiden tried to get hold of Zayde, but he wasn't replying to calls or messages. After the fifth try, he threw his phone down on the sofa in frustration.

I couldn't bear the tension in the room, and I turned to Weston and Cassius. "Let's trust Lena, okay? She knows what she's doing." Actually, for me, the jury was out on that one, but I wanted to give her a chance. "While we're waiting for her, let's talk about code names. I want mine to be Snowflake, since that was Caiden's original nickname for me." I laughed. "Even though it started out as a total insult."

His arms tightened around me. "Sorry, baby," he muttered in my ear.

"Good thing you came to your senses in the end, huh, King Caiden?" Smiling, I turned to kiss him again, sliding my hand up over his hard chest, feeling his muscles flex under my palm.

"That wouldn't work as a code name."

The tension in the room was suddenly broken at the sound of Cassius' voice. I smiled to myself. My plan for distracting everyone from their thoughts was working. "Why wouldn't it?" I stared at him, a brow raised, and he rolled his eyes.

"Oh, Winter. You have so much to learn about code names. The whole point is to use a name no one will recognise so they can't guess who you are. Everyone knows that Cade calls you Snowflake, so it would be obvious."

"I see." I smirked at him. "We'll just ignore the fact that you wanted to call this whole thing Operation Snowflake at one point, shall we? What would you pick, then?"

"For you?" He frowned, taking a moment to think. "You're gonna have to give me some time to think about that, babe."

"Well, don't keep me waiting too long."

"I already have a code name," Weston announced.

"You can't use the same one you use on the dark web. That's not allowed," Cassius told him.

"Says who?"

I tuned them out as they continued bickering about names, and Caiden bent his head, running his nose along my cheek. "Today has been so fucked up. I don't even know what to think right now."

17

"Forget the whole Lena thing. How are you feeling about Allan?" We hadn't really had any chance to discuss him yet.

He sighed. "Fuck knows. I need to talk to my dad. But I can't—not until we have some solid evidence for him."

"I know. He's going to have to find out at some point, but you're right. We can't go to him until we have proof."

Our conversation was interrupted by Weston, staring at the camera feed he'd pulled up on his phone. "Lena's on her way back."

2

winter

She came strolling into the room and threw herself down into an armchair, looking relaxed and carefree. Nothing to suggest any hint of stress, or guilt, or anything.

"I'm guessing you have questions," she began. Weston and Cassius sent her identical glares as she tapped on her phone, not meeting anyone's eyes.

Right. "Lena." I leaned forwards, injecting as much firmness as I could into my voice. I held her gaze. "Did you have anything to do with my rescue?"

"Rescue? What?" Her brows pulled together in a frown. "Why were you guys at the docks, anyway?"

"I think that's a question *you* need to answer," Cassius bit out.

"Oh, fuck it, why don't we just tell her what's going on?" I suggested. "Look, you know how I was in the hospital? Well, to cut a long story short, I was held captive at the docks. Someone got me out of there and to the hospital. I really need to know who it is. I'm trying to find out what happened with my dad's death, and I have reason to believe this is connected to it."

Her gaze assessed me, giving nothing away. She didn't seem all that surprised by what I'd just told her, which led me to believe that Cassius must have let more slip than I realised.

"West managed to, um, uncover some information," I added, unsure of how much to tell her about his hacking skills, or how much she already knew. Glancing over at him, I saw him shake his head almost imperceptibly. "We discovered that someone had used the same ID to swipe in to the docks both tonight and the day of my rescue..." I trailed off, giving her a hopeful look.

"No," she said, and my heart sank. "I can't tell you anything about that." She straightened up, her gaze never leaving mine. "But I might be able to tell you something that may be useful."

"Really?" My voice came out as an unsure whisper, as hope flooded me.

"Yeah. I think so." Closing her eyes, she rubbed her hand across her face. "Okay, I'll tell you what I can. Remember the party at the Cavendish house? The first time I met you?"

I nodded. "What about it?"

"I had an ulterior motive for being there. I wasn't only there for the party. I swiped someone's Alstone Holdings ID and made a copy."

We all stared at her in shock.

"What. The. Actual. Fuck, Lena?" Cassius sounded angrier than I'd ever heard him. "You'd better explain this, *right now*, or I'll make sure Mum and Dad ground you for life."

"Yeah, like that would happen." She rolled her eyes. "Look, I can't tell you everything. What I can say is that I was there for an unrelated reason, and I was given a task of getting hold of an ID card. We—I mean I—chose the Cavendish party, because I had it on good authority that a member of Arlo Cavendish's security team kept his within easy reach. Someone who had a high enough level of security clearance, but not so high that it would draw attention. And with my feminine charms, I was able to get hold of it."

What? What was Lena mixed up in?

"What feminine charms," Cassius muttered darkly.

Before he could say anything else, Caiden spoke next to my ear, his voice hard. "Who gave you the task? And why? And how?"

She glanced at him and shook her head. "I really can't say. Not yet, anyway. Sorry. But just think about it for a minute. If what you're telling me is right, that this same ID appeared at the same time Winter was rescued, then it must've been him. I mean, the person I was getting the ID for. It wasn't me; I can tell you that."

Weston stared at her. "Wouldn't the card have been deactivated once they realised it was missing?"

"Oh, that was an easy fix. My contact knew what to do."

He raised a brow, silent for a moment, before he nodded slowly. "Yeah. I guess if they knew what they were doing, and had the right equipment. Now, what were you doing at the docks today?"

Lena bit her lip. "I had to check something out for someone. I want to tell you the details, I really do, but I can't get hold of my—of them right now, and I can't say anything until I've spoken to them. All I can say is, there's something seriously shady going on down there."

"Well, that's just fucking brilliant." Cassius rolled his eyes. "Really helpful, sis."

"Fuck off." She threw her middle finger up at him, and he returned the gesture.

"That's sibling love, right there." I tried to ease the tension. Again. "Lena, can you tell us anything more? Anything at all?"

"I can't. Not yet, anyway. Look, if I could, I would. You have to give me time. I promise you, I'll have more answers for you as soon as I can."

Both of us ignored Cassius' low growl of disapproval. He wasn't about to let this drop, and I knew he'd be having words with Lena later.

"Okay. So you have to wait for someone to get in touch, before you tell us any details?" I probed carefully.

"Yep." She picked up her phone and started swiping at the screen.

"Why didn't you sneak in and out of the docks, like we did?" I wondered aloud.

Lena laughed. "That ID is like a golden ticket. I can get in and out anywhere, without wasting time sneaking around."

"But you're too recognisable! What if someone sees you and knows who you are?"

She waved her arm in the air, unconcerned. "I can talk my way out of anything."

I stared at her, open-mouthed, torn between irritation and concern. Was this how Caiden felt when I did something stupid? Probably. I groaned aloud.

"That's really fucking stupid," Cassius snapped at her. She ignored him, her thumbs flying over her phone screen.

"Okay, I can see we're not getting anywhere with this discussion." I sighed, trying to tamp down my frustration. "While we're waiting for Lena to hear from her contact, shall we get food? There's that all-night pizza place that delivers, if pizza's okay with everyone?"

"I'll sort it," Caiden murmured in my ear, then moved me off him. "I need a minute."

"You okay?" I glanced at him, concerned.

"Yeah. It's just a lot to deal with, y'know? All this shit with you and Allan, and now Lena, and the stuff that happened earlier with you and me."

"The 'I love you'?" I whispered, and he nodded.

"Yeah."

Fuck, I hoped he wasn't regretting saying it.

He must've noticed my expression because he stopped dead. Our eyes met, and he stared at me for a long moment, before he leaned over, kissing me fiercely. "Never doubt it. It was scary as fuck saying it, but I mean it. I love you, okay?"

My heart skipped a beat. I threw my arms around his neck, butterflies going mad inside me at his words. I loved that he was finally starting to open up to me and actually tell me how he was feeling, instead of keeping it inside. "I'll never get tired of you saying those words to me."

I suddenly noticed the silence that had fallen over the room, and I pulled away from my boyfriend to look at the others.

"So, King Caiden has a heart, after all," Cassius smirked. "Who would've thought it?"

"Leave them alone," Weston said, giving him a warning glare. "I'm happy for you both."

"Seriously, guys." I didn't miss how Caiden had gone all stiff and uncomfortable next to me. "Cade, you wanna get the pizza menus?"

He squeezed my hand, then got up, sauntering out of the room all casually, acting like it was no big deal that he'd told me he loved me in front of everyone. Was it the same for him as it was for me? Did everything else fade away, and I was the only thing he saw? He commanded my entire focus every time he turned the full force of his stormy gaze on me, every time he kissed me.

"When did this happen?" Cassius leaned forwards, propping his chin on his hands, his issues with Lena temporarily forgotten.

"That's between me and him, thanks. And don't go on about it in front of him. You know he doesn't like it."

"Sorry, babe. Didn't mean to."

"Sure you didn't." I rolled my eyes but softened the gesture with a smile. "It's okay. I know you don't mean anything by it."

"This has been fun and all, but I have things to do. I brought my homework with me," Lena interjected. "While I'm waiting to hear from someone, and before the pizza comes, I'm going to make a start on it." She jumped up and headed out of the room.

Weston stood, stretching. "Guess I'll go and see if Mercury has sent me the stuff on Andromeda." He followed Lena out, leaving me and Cassius.

Cassius sat back in his chair with a heavy sigh, closing his eyes.

"Cass? What's up?" I scooted over to the end of the sofa so I was next to him.

"Trying to get my head around my sister being possibly —no, definitely—involved in some shady shit. I'm gonna have to get Mum and Dad involved if she's putting herself in danger."

"Lena can handle herself. You have to let her make her own decisions. Her own mistakes." I put my hand on his arm. "I know you're her brother, and you want to protect her and look out for her, but if you're not careful, you'll end up pushing her away."

"Yeah, I guess," he muttered.

"Give her time. You want to tell me your code name ideas while we're waiting?" I suggested.

His expression brightened. "I have a list."

"Let me see."

3

caiden

F uck. Everything was moving too fast. I'd been blindsided by the bombshell about Allan, my girlfriend had put herself in danger, *again*, and the whole haze of anger followed by Winter telling me she loved me... My head was spinning.

I grabbed a beer from the fridge, popping the top, then opened the sliding doors that led out onto the deck. After flipping on the outdoor lights, I sank into one of the outdoor chairs. Balancing my beer bottle on the arm of the chair, I sat, thinking.

What the fuck were we supposed to do? How could we talk to Allan without Christine getting wind of it?

I clenched and unclenched my fists. I fucking hated being out of control, and right from the start, this whole situation had been a total loss of control.

The door opened and I looked up to see my brother staring at me hesitantly. "Uh, you got a minute? Mercury's sending me some stuff, but I wanted to talk to you while I was waiting."

I inclined my head towards the chair next to me, and he sank into it, his own beer bottle in hand. Taking a swig, he paused for a moment before he spoke, both of us facing forwards.

"This whole thing is so fucked up, huh?"

"Yeah. You could say that." I glanced over at my brother.

"Do you think Dad's involved?" He bit his lip.

"Honestly? I don't know what to think. I feel...fucking... betrayed by Allan, and it's blindsided me. Before tonight I wouldn't have thought him capable of being against us, so at this point? If Dad is, then that's just one more betrayal."

"He's been different lately, though, hasn't he?"

"Yeah."

"I can't help hoping he'll be on our side once we can pin evidence on Christine. Allan, though?" He let out a pained groan. "I can't get my head around it. He's always been the one to watch out for us when Dad was working all the time. I *trusted* him. I don't know what to do or think."

"You and me both."

We lapsed into silence, finishing up our beers.

"I'm proud of you, bro," Weston suddenly said.

A weird sensation filled me. The ever-present guilt was there, but now there was something else, too. Something I didn't want to examine too closely. I had enough emotional shit to deal with right now.

"I know you take on a lot of responsibility, but you know you don't need to, right?" His voice was soft. "I know you see me as someone you need to look out for and protect, and I appreciate that, but you need to share the burden. It's not all your responsibility. You scared me, when Mum died. You closed up, and for a while I felt like I'd lost my brother."

Shit.

This was the most honest conversation we'd ever had.

He continued. "I think that's why I grew so close to Cass, y'know? You were my best friend, the one person I looked up to more than anyone. But you pushed me away, and I felt like I didn't have anyone to talk to."

"Fuck...West." I took a deep breath, the words pouring out of me without censorship. The most honest words I'd ever said to him. "That wasn't my plan. I've always looked out for you, even when I was pushing you away. I did it because I didn't want you to be hurt anymore. We'd just lost our mum, Dad was off fucking the bitch Christine, and I didn't want to infect you with my darkness, so I stepped back."

Our eyes met, his determined. "I've got you back now. And yeah, we can credit Winter with a lot of that, but you're the one who started to open up and let people in again. I don't think you give yourself enough credit."

I shifted in my seat, and he must've sensed my awkwardness because he stood. "Anyway, that was all I wanted to say to you. Now come and give your brother a hug before you go back to being an asshole again."

"Fuck you," I muttered, but stood, a smile tugging at the corners of my lips. He pulled me into a brief hug before stepping back towards the door.

"Enough of that emotional shit. Let's get this sorted, then we can move on with our lives. I'm gonna go and see if Mercury's sent me the Andromeda stuff. And you need to get hold of Z."

I sat back down, relieved as fuck to change the subject. "Yeah, can't get hold of him. You know how he is, though; he'll appear when he's ready."

As Weston re-entered the house, I called after him, the

unplanned words flying from my mouth. "Proud of you, too, West. I'm lucky to have you as my brother."

He turned around, a huge grin on his face. "Yeah, and you'd better not forget it, either."

I returned his grin with one of my own, shaking my head.

Today had been a fucking weird day.

"Z!" Stalking down the hallway, I saw him enter the front door, pulling the motorbike helmet from his head. "Where the fuck have you been? I've been trying to contact you for hours."

"Around. I'll talk to you later." He took in my expression. "What's happened now?"

"Lena happened."

"Lena?" He raised a brow.

"Yeah. We ran into her down at the docks."

"What the fuck?"

"My thoughts, too. No fucking idea what's going on. My head's spinning, mate."

"Come on. Let's get this shit sorted. I can use my interrogation skills on Lena if necessary." He gave me a disturbingly evil grin.

"Maybe save that for another time." I shook my head at him, laughing, although I wasn't completely sure if he was actually joking or not. Hard to tell with him, as always.

"I think Cassius and Winter are in the lounge. I'll round up the others."

I found Lena in the computer room with Weston, laptop open and headphones in, while he used his own laptop opposite her, rather than one of his giant monitors. Guess he didn't want her to see anything he was doing on the screen. Trying to explain that he was essentially a hacker to anyone else, even Cassius' sister, was a massive risk. We'd told Winter because...I wasn't even sure why he'd told her, other than the fact she needed to know. And I think he'd trusted Winter from the beginning. She'd been completely open about what she'd been dealing with, investigating her dad, trusting us with that information, and in turn, he'd trusted her and knew she'd never rat him out to anyone. If only I could've been as trusting as him, maybe Winter and I wouldn't have had so many fucking obstacles in our relationship.

Of course, all this meant Kinslee knew as well, since Winter hadn't kept that shit from her, but Winter trusted her and that was good enough for me. Yeah, I had major problems with trust, but Winter's instincts were spot on—normally at least.

"Zayde's back," I announced loudly, and both their heads shot up. They glanced across at each other and looked away immediately, Lena's cheeks flushing. I narrowed my eyes, studying them both. I had my suspicions that West had a bit of a thing for Lena, but up until that point, I had no idea it was reciprocated. Not that it was surprising. Winter was the only woman that even remotely featured on my radar, so I rarely paid attention to anyone else.

"Gimme a minute, I'm just downloading the last of this file that you-know-who sent me," West told me, signalling me with his eyes that he didn't want to say anything in front of Lena.

"I'll just save my work, then I'll be there," Lena spoke at the same time. I nodded at them both and left them to it, making my way back into the lounge where Winter and

Cassius were deep in conversation, and Zayde was ignoring everyone, texting on his phone.

"You okay, mate?" I asked Zayde in a low voice, stopping by his chair.

"Yeah. All good," he assured me, his icy eyes meeting mine, giving nothing away.

"Good." I crossed over to the sofa and sat down, pulling my girlfriend onto my lap and burying my nose in her soft hair. "Miss me, baby?" I ran my hand down her arm, and she shivered.

"Always."

"Have a word with your girlfriend." Cassius was suddenly leaning forwards, his gaze fixed on mine. "Winter here thinks I'm winding her up. I told her that goats have rectangular pupils, and she refuses to believe me."

"What the fuck are you talking about?" I blinked, the sudden change of pace giving me whiplash.

"Goats. You know, goats."

"Yeah, I know what goats are," I said dryly.

"Their eyes have rectangular pupils. It's true, you can google it if you don't believe me."

"I'm not googling it because you'll laugh at me for being gullible and falling for your joke," Winter huffed.

"It's not a joke, babe. Guaranteed."

Whatever she was going to reply was lost as Weston and Lena walked in.

"I got the go-ahead to reveal a few key points about my reason for being down at the docks," Lena announced.

Finally.

She sat back, cool and collected. "I was sent down to investigate. My boss had reason to believe that—"

Cassius interrupted her. "Your *boss*? You're getting paid

to do some dodgy shit? You'd better explain yourself right fucking now."

"Cass, please." She rolled her eyes, clearly not taking it seriously. Fuck, if that was Winter, I'd... Yeah, best not to think about that.

"I'm investigating an illegal dog-fighting thing. Look, I don't know much myself, if that's what you're worried about. I only do the odd thing here and there. I get sent instructions from my boss, do it, then go. It's something I've been looking into for a while. You know I can't stand the thought of animals being mistreated. The other, unrelated reason I had for being at the Cavendish party that I mentioned earlier? Other than getting the ID? That was all to do with the dog fighting."

"Lena," Cassius groaned. "How did you even get into this shit?"

"That's a story for another day," she said firmly.

"Fuck. That dog fighting. I saw the video at the party," Winter said, her voice soft and sad. She exchanged a look of understanding with Lena, both of them communicating without words. As I studied Lena, suddenly she didn't seem like Cassius' little sister anymore. She looked like a woman on a mission. Determined, focused. Like my girl.

Fucking great.

I shook off that worrying thought and focused on her words as she continued. "The reason I was at the docks is because we had a tip-off that the dogs were being held at an Alstone Holdings location. All I was doing was sneaking down there to check it out. As it was, I found nothing. No evidence." Her gaze shifted slightly to the left, and I studied her closely. She seemed cool and collected, but I could see where she was digging her nails into her palm. There was something more she wasn't telling us, I'd bet money on it.

"Now you know, and that's it. Satisfied?"

"Not even slightly," Cassius growled. "I'll say it again, how did you get into this shit?"

"Save it for another day, mate." Weston frowned at him. "It's late, we're all tired and on edge. Lena? You want a lift home, or do you wanna stay here?"

"I'll stay," she said decisively. "I'm tired, and I already told Mum I wasn't coming home tonight. And yes, she knows I'm with you, Cass, before you ask." With that she left the room, with a final glare at Cassius, and I heard her stomping off up the stairs.

I exchanged glances with my boys, before speaking to Winter in a low voice. "Do you think she was telling us everything?"

Winter shifted, moving so she was sideways on my lap, and tilted her head to face mine. "No, I don't. Not for one minute." She bit her pouty bottom lip, deep in thought, and my gaze zeroed in on her mouth. Fuck me, she was sexy. I leaned forwards, running my thumb over her mouth.

"Enough of the lip biting, Snowflake. You're making my dick hard." I kissed her, unable to hold back, and she sighed, putting her arms around my neck, scraping her nails across the back of my neck and making me shiver.

"Can you not do that now? Please." We sprang apart to see Weston throwing us a pained look.

"Sorry," Winter said, although she didn't sound sorry at all. "Do you have anything from Mercury?"

"Yeah, and if you two would pay attention for one minute, I could show you. You wanna see it on the big screen, so we don't have to crowd around my phone?"

We followed him into the computer room, and he sat down in front of his giant monitors, typing madly on his keyboard.

A file appeared on the screen. A normal, innocent-looking file icon.

It was the name of the file that caused my breath to catch in my fucking throat.

Andromeda.

4

winter

Andromeda. I stared at the screen. "West? What's this?" My voice came out weak and breathless.

"We'll go through it now. We have a problem, though. Before we look at the file, there's something you all need to know." He spun in his chair to face us; his gaze serious. "I think Mercury knows who I am. Who *we* are."

"What?" Caiden hissed from behind me.

"The whole thing is fucking weird. I've never told Mercury the details of Winter's dad's death, or anything to do with that. But this file?" He paused, and his eyes met mine. "Mercury retrieved this file from the storage servers at the university your dad worked at. It was an encrypted file, in a folder full of all his university research. Pretty well hidden, but also hidden in plain sight, if that makes sense? Since it was in with all his other astronomy-related stuff."

"I-I don't understand." My heart was pounding, and I couldn't make sense of what Weston was saying.

Caiden's arms came around me, and he took my shaking hands in his. His presence bolstered me, and I took a deep breath. "So you're telling me that Mercury knew where to look for this file, without knowing about my dad?"

"Yeah." His gaze was full of worry. "I don't know what's going on. Unless Mercury somehow managed to hack into our own secure storage to get the stuff we saved on there and found out that way, but I've put so many layers of security on it, it would take him forever to hack into it. And I don't see why he would, either."

"So...the most likely explanation is that he knows who we are. Or who I am, at least." This was another complication, but at the same time... "Okay, I don't think we necessarily need to worry about Mercury's identity right now. He's always been reliable, right? Always helped you out?"

Weston nodded. "Yeah, I've never had any reason to doubt him."

"Well, then. Let's put that aside for now. Open the file."

He clicked the little folder icon, and a list of filenames came up. I leaned closer to see. There were audio files, documents, and images, all there to view. Weston clicked on the file at the top of the list, which was sorted in date order.

My dad's voice came through the speakers, and I fell apart.

I gradually became aware of Caiden's voice close to my ear. I was huddled into him, my eyes swollen from crying, my throat raw, my tears soaking his T-shirt. He held me tightly, stroking his hand through my hair, soothing me.

"I'm here, Snowflake. I've got you." I raised my face to meet his, and he gave me a sad smile. "I'm sorry, baby."

"I-it just hit me. Hearing his voice again after so long, it brought it all back..."

"You don't have to explain anything." He kissed my forehead, and used his thumb to carefully wipe away the remainder of my tears. Fuck, I loved him. He knew exactly what I needed.

"I'm okay." I repeated the words, my voice stronger, willing myself to make them become true. "I'm okay. West? You wanna play the audio?"

He nodded and clicked the file again.

I took a deep breath, hearing my dad's deep, rumbling voice coming through the speakers. Steeling myself, I pushed my emotions aside until I could deal with them.

"Voice memo," he announced. "I have reason to believe that my ex-wife may be responsible for plotting to overthrow Alstone Holdings." At his words, all of us gasped. He went on to detail how he'd overheard her meeting with Petr, which we'd seen the images of. There was no other new information.

Once the audio had finished, Weston turned back to me. "Are you okay to carry on?"

"Yes." I nodded firmly. "We need answers, and we need to go through every single one of these files."

He opened the second file.

It was another audio recording. The sound quality was awful, and I could barely make out anything that was being said, although my mother's voice was faintly discernible. There was the sound of clinking glasses and cutlery, and a low hum of conversation muffling her words.

"Let me try to enhance the sound." West opened up some software and clicked to add the file. He threw some headphones over his ears, intent on whatever he was doing on the screen.

"Baby?" Caiden's voice was worried, and I was startled to realise I was shaking.

"I'm okay. I just can't believe after all this time, we're finally getting some answers. And... Cade...I miss my dad so much."

"I know you do. You've got me, and I'm never gonna let you go, okay?"

"Thanks." I whispered the word, turning my head to meet his lips. When we drew apart, I met his concerned gaze. "After all the hurt that he suffered at her hands, with her turning her back on us and everything, he still wanted to see the best in her." I sighed. "How did it end up with him losing his life? Why did he always hold out hope? I so wish he was here. I wish I knew why. But more than any of that..." My voice cracked again. "I wish...I just want to hug him one last time. To tell him I love him."

"Fuck...Snowflake." Caiden pulled me even closer to him, running his hands up and down my back. I held on to him tightly, his body warm and solid against mine, his heartbeat calming me, until I could finally catch my breath again.

"Okay, I think I've got it," Weston said a few moments later, giving me a concerned look, identical to Caiden's.

I'm okay, I mouthed to him.

His gaze searched me, and eventually he nodded. He pulled out the headphones and clicked something. "I've managed to isolate the audio of Christine speaking. I can't seem to isolate the speech of whoever she's talking to, though."

"Play it," Caiden commanded.

Christine's voice came out of the speakers.

"The time frame is acceptable. Arlo is an inconvenience —but I need to keep him onside for as long as possible.

Alstone Holdings is expanding—there are rumours of a possible merger with the De Witts. It would be utterly pointless to act until the whole thing has been finalised. Our reward will be significantly higher if we wait." Whoever she was speaking to must have been replying to her because the audio went silent for a few minutes, before it continued. "Absolutely not. When I give the order, Arlo is to be taken care of in a discreet and timely manner. You know what to do. I'll leave the details up to you."

More silence, then, "The funds will be transferred tomorrow. More will come your way, for as long as you uphold your end of the bargain."

The audio ended, and we all sat, stunned, trying to process everything. The tension in the room was thick, heavy, and completely unbearable.

My stomach flipped. "Fuck," I croaked out. "This goes a lot deeper than we thought."

"*Taken care of*? Is she saying— She wants to murder my fucking dad!" Weston picked up a heavy-looking glass paperweight thing that was on his desk and threw it at the wall with his full force. It rebounded off the wall, leaving a visible dent in the plaster, and fell to the floor with a crash.

"West..." I began tentatively. I used everything I had to hide how I was feeling so I didn't fall apart, *again*. Anger, hot and savage, burned through me—I was only just keeping it together. My head was pounding, and all I wanted was to join him in his rage, but somehow, I managed to hold on to the thin thread of my control. Barely.

"Don't. Just don't," he bit out, putting his head in his hands.

I took a deep, calming breath. This wasn't about me. I jumped off Caiden and went to Weston, throwing my arms around him and stroking up and down his back. Some of the tension drained out of him as I murmured in his ear. "We're not gonna let anything happen, okay? She's already most likely killed my dad, and there is no fucking way I'm letting her take yours, as well."

"I already lost my mum," he whispered, his voice hoarse and broken.

"I know. We won't let her get away with this, West. I promise you," I vowed.

He pulled me closer to him, holding me tightly. "Thanks," he mumbled into my neck.

"Let's go through the rest of the files so we can work out what we're dealing with here."

"Okay." Blowing out a breath, he released me, composing himself, before returning his attention to the computer. I glanced over at Caiden, who was watching his brother. As my gaze held his, I watched the emotions play out on his face, as much as he tried to hide them.

Scanning through the other files, we found copies of the same information that had been in the paper file. There were a couple of additional photos, taken in the Crown and Anchor, when my mother had been meeting with Petr. Neither gave us any more detail—just my mother, sitting there, deep in discussion. Petr's hand hadn't been in either image, so I guessed that my dad had concentrated on the one image that showed him. I was glad he had, though— without that, we'd have no idea who she'd been meeting with.

The final file in the list had the same date as the text my dad had sent me, the night he'd died.

I steeled myself as Weston opened it, Caiden holding me tightly, reassuring me.

There were a few seconds of silence, then...

"Voice memo. My reasoning for visiting Alstone today

was to obtain further evidence on Christine's misdeeds. With Winter safely away at university, I believe it is the right time to step up my investigation. She's a strong, independent woman, but I need to shield her from this. She cannot get involved." He coughed, before continuing. "I managed to persuade Christine to meet me, and I confronted her. All along, I've been concerned that I was wrong, that she'd somehow got herself mixed up with the wrong kinds of people. I offered to help her, to hide her away..." His voice grew hoarse, and I wiped away the tears that were falling down my cheeks. Even after everything, after all the evidence stacked against her, my dad still wanted to see the best in her. He'd still loved her.

I listened as he cleared his throat, then began speaking again, his voice growing quieter. "She denied everything. Said I was deluded, a fantasist spouting lies, and walked out on me. I need...I need to warn Winter to stay away from her. If my ex-wife truly is mixed up in this whole business out of choice, then I need to keep my daughter far away."

The recording ended, and the room fell silent, all of us lost in our own thoughts. Once again, the pain and heartbreak of my dad's loss hit me, and I curled into Caiden, feeling so lost and helpless. Why did he have to die? Why was my mother like this? How could we even hope to stop her?

"Stop the negative thoughts. We won't let her get away with this. She'll pay for what she did." Caiden's resolute voice pierced through my dark thoughts, and I looked up to find all of the Four with the same determined expressions on their faces, glancing between one another.

He was right. "I fucking love you guys," I said, sitting up straight and wiping my eyes. "No more tears."

"That's my girl." Caiden kissed the top of my head, and Cassius held out his hand in a fist.

"You have to do it." He winked at me, and I stretched out my own fist to his, lightly bumping knuckles with him and smiling, despite myself.

I wasn't alone. I had my family right here, and together we were going to make Christine Cavendish pay.

5

winter

I woke with a heavy arm slung over me, and I wriggled backwards against a completely naked Caiden. "Morning," I mumbled sleepily. He didn't reply but kissed my bare shoulder, trailing his hand up to caress my breasts, swirling his fingers around my nipples until they stiffened, grinding his hardness against me.

"I love you in my bed." His voice was all husky from sleep. "How are you feeling this morning, after all the shit that happened last night?" I could hardly concentrate on his words as he kissed his way up to my ear and licked across the shell.

"I'm okay," I managed to say, arching back against him.

"Good." He flipped me onto my back, and I hooked my legs around him as he thrust into me, setting a slow, lazy rhythm. As he kissed down my neck, I ran my nails down his back and he shivered, his muscles flexing under my hands as he increased the pace. We moved together, harder and faster, until I was gasping his name and shattering around him.

"My favourite way to wake up." I reached up, pulling his

head down to kiss him and feeling him smile against my lips.

"Mine too. Shower?" He tugged me out of bed, and I followed him into the bathroom, where he turned on the water and proceeded to take advantage of the fact we were both naked and wet.

"What's the plan today?" Perching on a stool at the kitchen island a little later, I sipped my coffee, blowing across it to cool it slightly. I'd been hoping to question Lena a bit more, but apparently Cassius had driven her home first thing in the morning, before I'd even woken up.

"I've been thinking, a lot. Christine has a vested interest in this De Witt deal going through, doesn't she? Since it sounds like her aim is to take over Alstone Holdings. For that reason, I think we're safe to assume that she won't act until after that goes through." Weston's words were directed at us all, but his focus was locked on his brother's.

"I agree. And...fuck. I don't want to do this." Caiden's voice was reluctant, the words spilling from his mouth unwillingly as he pulled an expression of distaste. "But I think we need to get Granville involved."

"What?" My gaze swung to him in shock. "Seriously?"

"Yeah. Look, I don't know what the fuck is going on and how the Hydes and Granvilles play into all this. But from everything Granville said, and Hyde's behaviour at New Year's"—at that his jaw clenched tightly, and he gripped his knife as if he was imagining stabbing it through Joseph's neck—"I feel like it has to be connected, somehow. Granville is our weak link." He met my gaze, his steely. "*Your* weak link. He cares about you. It's time we took advantage of that."

"I can't use James like that," I protested.

"You can, and you will." His voice softened as I frowned at him. "Look, I know you care. But this is about finding answers about your dad's death, and stopping Christine from murdering anyone else, and taking Alstone Holdings out from under us. I'll die myself before I let that fucking happen."

I stared at him, his words whirling around in my brain, before I nodded slowly. He was right. James could be the key. At least we'd know whether or not to rule out a connection between the Hydes and my mother.

"Okay. Let's make a plan."

A couple of hours later, we'd come up with the basics, and I sent a text to James.

Me: I'm having a party for my birthday. Want to come?
James: Are you sure you want me there?
Me: Yes. We're friends, or at least we were. Please?

After holding my breath for what seemed like an eternity, I finally received a reply. Three words that filled me with both relief and unease.

James: Tell me where and when. I'll be there.

"I guess we'd better get ready for another party, then? Get the word out, or whatever you guys do?"

Caiden smirked at me. "Already done. No one can resist a chance to be seen at one of our parties."

"Of course not." I rolled my eyes at him. "Guess I'd better

start preparing. Remember that no one's supposed to know we're together. Other than our close friends, that is."

"I'm aware of that."

"Good. Ugh, I hope other girls don't flirt with you." I screwed my face up.

He laughed, shrugging. "Comes with the territory."

"Great."

Brushing my hair away from my face, his lips touched my ear. "You're the only one I want."

I smiled, turning my head to look into his eyes. "I know. Same."

He stood and dropped a hard kiss on my lips. "This mouth. Mine. This body—" He tugged me off my stool and into his arms. "Mine." His hands drifted lower, onto my ass. "This sexy as fuck ass. Mine."

"I get it." I laughed, even though I was kind of melting at the same time. I loved his possessiveness.

"Booze run, yeah?" Cassius waved his car keys in the air. "Anyone wanna come? Winter?"

"Got somewhere to be." Z stalked out of the door, his face as blank as always, but there was an air of menace surrounding him that gave me shivers.

I twisted in Caiden's arms to face Cassius. "Yeah, I'll come. If this is meant to be a party to celebrate my birthday, then I should at least have a say in what we get."

"You two go." Caiden dropped a kiss on my hair, before dipping his head to speak to me in a low voice. "I wanna make sure West is alright."

"Good idea."

He released me with one last kiss, and I followed Cassius from the kitchen.

"How are you feeling? Y'know, about everything?" Cassius' voice was uncharacteristically serious as we pulled into the huge supermarket car park.

I unclipped my seat belt and turned to face him. "I'm weirdly okay, actually. Knowing I have you four in my corner, and now we have all this evidence piling up, it makes me feel...hopeful, I guess?"

"Good. We've got your back, babe. You know you're one of us, now."

I smiled at him, but my smile dropped as I took in his face. "How are *you* feeling? About everything with Lena?"

His expression darkened. "I don't know how to feel. She's always been a bit of a wild card—she thinks she's fucking invincible, but she's not." He blew out a heavy breath. "I'm gonna be keeping an eye on the situation, that's for sure."

"I'll do the same, when I can. And you know West can track her phone or whatever."

"Yeah, true." The tension left his jaw, and his eyes lightened even as he let out a groan. "Why am I surrounded by so many stubborn women?"

"Guess you must attract them."

He grinned, back to his usual self, opening his car door. "Come on. Enough depressing talk." We exited his SUV and made our way into the supermarket, Cassius grabbing a shopping trolley on the way. "You're gonna love shopping with me."

Something told me that this was going to be an experience.

"Cassius Drummond! What do we need a piñata for?" I stood in the aisle that contained party supplies, hands on my hips, as he threw more random crap into the trolley. A huge packet of birthday candles joined the piñata, and he piled balloons and other party decorations on top.

"You never know. I like to be prepared." He added packs of paper cups, pretty much emptying the shelves, before he moved on to the next aisle, which happened to contain kids toys. "Water pistols, hmmm," he mused. "We'll get a couple of those." He pulled two huge water guns down from the shelf, both coloured in garishly bright orange and green.

"Uh, you do know it's January, right? Who's going to have a water fight in January?" I raised a brow.

"Babe. We need to be prepared for anything."

"Right." There was no point reasoning with him. Although, once he added the game Twister, I put my foot down. "Come on. Let's get some actual food and drinks, before we have no room left for anything else."

By the time we'd left the supermarket, the back of the SUV was pretty much full of bags.

"Cass? I think there's more stuff in here than there is in the shop."

He laughed. "Yep. It's your birthday party, babe. We've got to celebrate it properly."

"I'm surprised you didn't hire people to do all this shit for you," I told him.

"Now where would the fun be in that?" he teased. "You did have fun, didn't you?"

I smiled at him. "Yeah, I did."

"Then my plan to brighten up your day worked." He winked. "You're welcome."

"It did. Thanks." I leaned over the centre console and gave him a quick kiss on the cheek.

"You missed my lips." He smirked at me.

"Do you want Cade to kill you in your sleep?"

"It'd be worth it."

Rolling my eyes, I settled back into my seat. "You need to find yourself a nice girlfriend."

"Unless you can clone yourself, it's a no."

"I don't think we have that technology yet."

"Remember that sheep they cloned?"

"Not personally, no."

"I heard they tried to clone a mammoth."

"Mammoths are extinct. How can they do that?"

"They merged its DNA with an elephant, or some shit."

"Are you sure you aren't thinking of *Jurassic Park*?"

We continued our random conversation all the way back to the house, and by the time I got back, my stomach hurt from laughing and I'd forgotten all about my worries surrounding my mother.

"Cade, give me a hand with these bags," Cassius called from the back of the car, where he was unloading our shopping. My gaze followed his, to see Caiden standing in the doorway of the house in jeans and a thick hoodie.

"Better make it quick, then. I'm on my way out."

"Where are you going?" I asked him as he came to stand beside the car. He leaned into me, pulling me towards him and trailing his nose up my neck.

"Out. I've got to go into the city. Will you be okay here?"

I stared at him, curious. "Yeah, I'll be fine. Why do you have to go into the city, though?"

He kissed my ear before murmuring, "I have my reasons. Nothing to worry about."

"Alright. Be all mysterious," I mumbled into his neck.

He pulled back and gave me a wicked grin. "I'll make it up to you tonight."

"You'd better."

6

caiden

O nce Winter and Cassius had disappeared inside the house and I was in my R8, I pulled out my phone and shot a quick text to Zayde.

Me: You done?
Z: Yeah. You ready?
Me: Yeah.
Z: You sure about this?
Me: 100%
Z: Meet you there

Starting the engine, I pulled away from the house with a powerful roar, a smile spreading across my face as I felt the thrum of the engine responding to me. The rush that came every time I drove my car was better than any drug.

I put my foot down as I raced down the coastal road and onto the motorway that led to the city, the R8 effortlessly slicing through the traffic, leaving everyone else in my wake.

As I drove, I thought back over my earlier conversation with my brother. He'd been worrying about Christine,

53

replaying the voice memos from Winter's dad over and over, but there was a determination in him I'd never seen before. I knew if anyone could uncover more evidence, it would be him.

The buildings grew closer and closer together, tower blocks appearing on the horizon as I swung the car into the nondescript car park. I beeped the horn, once, and the graffitied metal garage door in front of me rolled slowly up, and I drove inside, parking next to Zayde's bike. I hit the button to close the garage door behind me, and headed through the small door that led into the tattoo shop.

Zayde was already in there, talking with the tattoo artist as he inked the skin of a bored-looking guy with a shaved head and pierced brow.

"Alright." I crossed over to join them.

"Rich boy." The tattoo artist spoke without looking up at me, intent on his work.

"Mack," I greeted him, admiring the design he was inking into the guy's bicep—some kind of scorpion, venom dripping from its stinger. "Nice work."

"Cheers. We're almost done here. Help yourself to drinks."

I gave him a brief nod. "Z? Want a coffee?"

"Black."

"Like your soul."

He smirked at me. "What soul?"

I laughed and helped myself to coffee, setting a mug down in front of Zayde. "Mack? You want one?"

"I'm good," he replied, turning off the tattoo gun and wiping the bicep of the guy he'd been inking. "Done. Let's get it wrapped, then you can go." They both stood, their low conversation fading as they walked over to the mirrors at the back of the shop.

"You sure about this?" Zayde asked me again. "This shit is permanent."

"Yes, I'm fucking sure, just like I was the other fifty times you asked me," I said irritably.

"Alright. Calm down." He flicked through the book of tattoo designs that rested on the table in front of us, deceptively casual.

"I've got another stop to make after this. You wanna come?"

"Depends. Where?"

I eyed him carefully. He was tense, again. Whatever shit he'd been doing this morning had left him on edge. "I've got to pick something up. A birthday present for Winter." He was opening his mouth to say no when I added, "It won't take long. We can grab a drink after, if you want." I'd been wrapped up in Winter and all this shit with her mother lately, but Z was my best mate, and he'd been disappearing more and more often lately. He needed this. Even if he didn't know it.

Abandoning the book of tattoo designs, he picked up his mug of coffee and met my eyes. "Yeah. Okay."

———

Sitting in bumper-to-bumper traffic in the city centre, I idly noticed the admiring glances of the tourists as they took in my car. At the risk of sounding arrogant, I'd say they were probably admiring me and Z as well.

Speaking of Z, I glanced over at him, needing to ask him the question that had been playing on my mind ever since the Allan bombshell. He reclined in the passenger seat, tatted arm propped up on the windowsill, and aviator sunglasses hiding his icy gaze. "You wanna tell me what happened when you disappeared when the rest of us went to the docks?"

He continued staring straight ahead. "Alright. I remembered Creed mentioned one of his boys had seen an older, balding guy when he was watching the docks. I had to check it out."

"Was it Allan?" I inched the car forwards, before coming to yet another stop. This traffic was a fucking joke.

"Yeah, think so—sounds like him, anyway. No fucking clue what he was doing, but he was seen talking to the security guy in the guard hut, then he disappeared inside the docks for about twenty minutes, then left."

"That's it?" I couldn't hide the disappointment in my tone.

"Yeah. If I knew more, I wouldn't keep it from you, mate."

"I know." I indicated to turn the car onto the side street that led to the private underground car park we used when we came into the city. Glancing over at him again, I chose my next words carefully. "Anything else you want to talk about? I know we've had all this shit going on, but I'm here for you, yeah?"

He was silent as I pulled up to the car park entrance and leaned out of the window to punch the entrance code into the pad mounted on a stalk in front of the entrance barrier. As the barrier lifted and I drove inside, he finally spoke.

"Nah, I'm good."

I didn't think so. I backed my R8 into a large space near the exit. "If you ever, y'know…"

"I know. Thanks."

After we'd picked up Winter's present and had a quick drink, I dropped Zayde back off at Mack's shop so he could pick up his bike. Once we got away from the city traffic and onto the open roads, we raced each other home. He only won because he cheated, sneaking between the cars on his bike when I got stuck behind the world's fucking slowest tractor.

Back at the house I managed to stash my purchase where Winter wouldn't find it, then went to find my girlfriend. She was playing darts with my brother, both of them doubled over laughing when she kept missing the target. Without making my presence known, I stood back and watched her, carefree, her dark hair falling over her back, her sexy little ass encased in yoga pants that looked borderline illegal. My dick stirred as my eyes raked over every inch of her hot body. Fuck. I needed to be inside her.

I didn't disturb her, though. My dick would have to wait. She needed this time to have fun and forget her worries for once. Weston, too, for that matter.

Not only that, but it was her birthday tomorrow, and I had research to do.

I left them to it and went to my computer.

7

winter

I t was my birthday. Anyone who had a birthday so soon after Christmas and New Year knew how much it could suck, but not this year. While I didn't have my dad, and we were in the middle of a shitstorm with my mother, I had the Four and my friends to celebrate with me.

My day began with being woken by soft kisses from Caiden, who was fully dressed already. "Happy Birthday." He gave me a heart-stopping grin, and I melted.

"Morning. Don't you want to start my day off with birthday sex?" I bit my lip, dragging the duvet down to expose my body.

He growled low in his throat. "Fuck, Snowflake. I've got a plan for today, but when you look like that..."

Suddenly he was pouncing on me, pulling the rest of the covers off my body and burying his head between my legs.

Oh. Yes. This was how all birthdays should start, in my opinion. I gripped his hair, holding his head in place as he worked magic with his tongue and fingers, until I was crying out his name and completely spent.

"Go and shower, then join us for breakfast," he commanded, raising his head and licking his lips, a satisfied grin on his face.

"Don't you want me to take care of you?" I sat up, running my hand over the bulge in his jeans.

A low hiss escaped his lips, and he crawled up my body to kiss me. "Fuck. You're impossible to resist. Not yet. We have plans."

He tore himself away, his eyes darkened with lust as he stared at me. "Go and shower now, before I change my mind."

"Aren't you going to join me?"

He shook his head, reluctance written all over his face. "I can't. Be quick. Come and find me downstairs." He disappeared out of the room, leaving me staring after him. What was up with his behaviour? No sex, and he never turned down a chance to shower with me.

After a massive breakfast with all of the Four, Weston pushed a large box across the kitchen island to me.

"This is from all of us. We all chipped in. Happy Birthday, sis." I tore open the wrapping paper to find a very expensive-looking laptop in a sleek white box.

I clapped a hand over my mouth in shock, clearing my throat to try and remove the sudden lump. "What? I wasn't expecting this. Seriously, I can't thank you guys enough." Hopping down from my stool, I went around the island, hugging them all in turn, before returning to my seat.

"We thought it would be useful. I couldn't stand seeing you use that old piece of junk you called a laptop anymore."

Weston grinned at me, then reeled off a list of specifications that flew over my head, but I appreciated the sentiment. So much. I still couldn't believe they'd bought me such a generous gift.

The birthday surprises kept coming when I was picked up by Lena and Kinslee. Apparently, we were going to a spa —Kinslee's gift to me, and she'd wanted Lena to come along. They'd hit it off at the New Year's Eve party, and the three of us were having a great time hanging out together.

As we drove, we talked about the upcoming party and the plan to talk to James. "You know, he isn't so bad," Lena said, gripping the steering wheel lightly as she manoeuvred her car onto the main road. "I know we have a rivalry thing with him, but he's been a good friend to me."

"I didn't realise you even knew him." I stared at her profile.

She nodded. "Yeah. I had a...guy problem once, and he helped me out. We hang out sometimes, and he's always been good to me."

"What sort of problem?" Kinslee leaned forwards from the back seat, her voice full of concern. Were her thoughts going in the same direction as mine?

"It was when I was younger—fourteen. I had some hassle, nothing major, but there was one time where these guys cornered me, and let's just say James was in the right place at the right time." She briefly glanced over at me. "Honestly, it was nothing huge, but James was there for me." A grin curved over her lips as she added, "No guy would mess with me, now. Ever since it happened, I've been honing my skills. I can handle whatever comes my way."

"I'm glad to hear it. Just don't take any unnecessary risks, okay?" She had an air of fearlessness about her, but I couldn't help feeling like she could actually get into serious trouble if she wasn't careful.

"I won't. Oh, don't tell my brother about any of it—about James helping me, or the fact we hang out sometimes. He doesn't know."

"More secrets," I muttered.

"What was that?"

"Nothing. Why don't you want to tell him?"

"He's so overprotective. He'd probably make me wear a tracker or something, and check in with him every five minutes."

"He's not that extreme," I laughed. "You know, though. It could work in James' favour if you do say something, since we need to get him to come around to our way of thinking at the party. If the boys know that he's helped you out, it might help his case with them."

"Hmm...you might be right. I'll think about it," she murmured. "Anyway, enough about all that. No more talk of anything depressing. Let's get all this girly stuff done, then we can go and do knife throwing."

"Knife throwing?" I raised a brow.

"That's one of the options on offer."

It felt a bit strange pulling up at a knife throwing range after a morning of relaxing with a massage, manicure, pedicure, and soak in the hot tub with champagne. But here we were. A huge, modern warehouse-style building with "Skirmish" printed in huge block letters on a sign above the doors. Underneath there was a smaller sign detailing everything the place offered—knife throwing, archery, axe throwing, paintballing, shooting, and various corporate team-building events. We parked next to Cassius' SUV and headed into the cool building to meet the boys.

They were standing by the reception desk talking to a tall figure that I recognised instantly. His head turned when he saw us, and his golden eyes glimmered with recognition. This time he wasn't dressed down in a hoodie but had on a shirt and tie that made him look even more powerful and imposing than the first time I'd seen him. "Winter. We meet again." He strode over to greet me, before he turned to Kinslee.

I watched, bemused, as Kinslee's gaze lowered as he looked her over.

"I'm Credence Pope, but my friends call me Creed. And who might you be?" he purred, taking her hand.

She stood there mutely, and I nudged her elbow. I hadn't ever seen her tongue-tied around anyone before. Maybe it was the aura coming off him—he came across as smooth and charming, but underneath you could sense how lethal he was.

"This is Kinslee," I answered for her, when the silence stretched. He smiled and lifted her hand, placing a kiss to the back of it, and I saw her flinch. What the fuck?

After one last look, he turned his attention to Lena, who had no such trouble with introductions, being her usual confident self.

Once the greetings were out of the way, he strode to the door, picking up a navy suit jacket from the hook on the wall and shrugging it on.

"Feel free to help yourselves to anything. Z knows where everything is. Happy Birthday, Winter." Then he was gone, and I spun around to face Kinslee.

"What the fuck was that all about?" I hissed under my breath.

"I don't know," she whispered. "He really scared me."

"*He* scared you, but Z doesn't?" I queried.

"Yeah. I mean, I can tell they're both cut from the same cloth, if that makes any sense, but...well, I know Z, I suppose..." She trailed off, shrugging, clearly at a loss for her own reaction.

"Okay." I decided to let it go. "Come on. What are you in the mood for? I'd quite like to try the knife throwing."

"Archery," she said decisively. "I want to be the next Katniss Everdeen."

"Of course you do." We walked over to join the boys, and I was immediately pulled into Caiden's arms.

"I missed you," he husked into my ear.

"It's only been a few hours."

"Still missed you."

I smiled and reached up to kiss him, threading my hands through his messy hair, loving the feel of his body pressed against mine.

We drew apart, and I turned around in Caiden's arms to face the others.

"Archery and knife throwing? Everyone agreed?" Cassius asked, and I nodded, seeing the excitement on Kinslee's face as she bounced on her toes, raring to go.

"Sounds good to me. Archery first?" I suggested.

Kinslee beamed, and I smiled to myself.

Zayde led us through the building to a large, spacious room where archery targets were set up, waiting for us. After the run-through of what to do, which in my case mostly involved Caiden using any excuse to get his hands on my body and aiming my bow for me, I was surprisingly okay at it. I managed to hit the target, at least, so I'd call it a win. Kinslee and Lena had an impromptu competition, both of them way better at it than I was, and I took loads of photos on my phone of them in action, posting a couple to my social media accounts and tagging them.

After the archery, we took a break before the knife throwing. "I have to say, this is not what I ever imagined doing for my birthday, not even close, but it's so much fun." I gulped down the water from my bottle, then wiped my brow with the sleeve of my hoodie, watching as Zayde and Weston compared knives, examining the blades under the bright overhead lights.

"Glad you're having fun. I've been wanting to bring you here for a while now, but y'know, life got in the way." Caiden tugged me closer. I was sitting on the floor in between his legs, leaning back against him while he leaned on the wall behind us. "And there's still more to come."

"You mean the party tomorrow?"

"No, not that. More today."

"More? What else could there possibly be?" I angled my head to look around at him, and he dropped a kiss on my nose.

"It's a surprise. You'll have to wait and see."

I pouted, trying not to smile. "Don't I even get a hint?"

"Nope." He smirked at me. "Your tricks won't work, so don't even try them."

"You're no fun," I huffed.

"Oh, but I am. I'm a lot of fun." His voice was suddenly low and rasping, and I shivered as he slid his hands under my hoodie, under my top, onto my bare skin, while he lowered his head to softly bite my ear.

"Fuck. If you want me to make it through the rest of the afternoon without dragging you off and making you fuck me senseless, you'd better stop that right now." My words were practically moaned, rather than spoken, thanks to the effect he had on me.

"Really," he drawled, nipping at my ear again.

"Let's make a bet!" Cassius' loud exclamation cut through our private moment, and Caiden released me with a sigh. "Whoever hits furthest from the centre of the target has to do a forfeit."

"Hang on, I've never thrown a knife before. The people who have, have an advantage," I pointed out.

Cassius pursed his lips in thought for a moment, frowning, before his expression cleared. "Okay. Everyone who's thrown a knife before has to throw it with their left hand, or with their eyes closed if they're good at throwing with both hands." He raised his voice, pointing first at Caiden, then at Zayde. "That's you two. Eyes closed. Everyone okay with that?"

"Sounds a lot fairer to me than your original idea. I'm ready!"

When it was my turn, I stepped up, holding the knife in my hand, trying to remember Caiden's basic instructions. "Ooh, this reminds me of playing darts. Hey, West?" I turned to him, and he gave me a blinding grin.

"Yeah, I guess it's kind of like that. You have to get the hang of balancing the knives, though."

I did *not* have a natural talent for throwing knives, it turned out. The boys were all pretty good, Zayde by far and away the best, hitting the target with unerring accuracy every time. Lena was pretty good, too. When I asked her if she'd done it before, she told me she'd had practice with weapons as part of her martial arts training.

Caiden was the last to go, and we'd definitely saved the best for last, in my completely biased opinion. My boyfriend throwing knives was sexy as fuck. He'd taken off his hoodie, and he was in one of his endless supply of tight black T-shirts that highlighted his muscles. He held a knife in each hand, and he was spinning them on his fingers in front of him, basically showing off, but it left me panting. A quick glance at Kinslee and Lena told me they were just as entranced with my boyfriend. Not that I could blame them, at all.

"Damn, girl, your boyfriend is hot," Kinslee murmured to me, and Lena nodded in agreement.

"He's always loved these," Weston told me, suddenly close to my ear, making me jump. I nodded distractedly, unable to tear my eyes from Caiden. As I watched, he threw them both in quick succession, and they embedded themselves in the target.

"Yes!" he shouted, fist pumping the air with a victorious grin, and I raced over to him, launching myself at him. He staggered backwards, unprepared, but caught me.

"What's—"

I cut off his words with a kiss, and he immediately responded, sliding his tongue into my mouth, sending a throbbing need straight to my core.

When I eventually pulled away, breathless, he lowered me to the ground, keeping his arms around me. "Wanna tell me what that was all about? Not that I'm complaining." His eyes were sparkling, and that sexy smirk was back on his lips. Yeah, he knew exactly why I'd jumped on him.

"I think you know." I rolled my eyes, but my voice came out all breathy. "And you'd better be prepared to make up for torturing me later."

His smirk widened into a grin. "I'm prepared. The question is, are you?"

After that, my concentration was non-existent, and I lost the bet. Cassius took pity on me, as it was my birthday, and since we hadn't agreed on a forfeit, he said my punishment would be to do a shot of his choice at my party. Shots at a birthday celebration? I wasn't about to argue with that—it didn't sound much like a punishment to me.

We decided to call it a day after the knife throwing, although Zayde and Weston both suggested having a go on the shooting range. At this point it was getting late in the day, and Caiden kept insisting we needed to get back to the house to get ready for the final part of my birthday.

When we arrived back, I headed upstairs with Caiden and flopped down on the bed, rubbing my aching arms. I pulled out my phone, looking back through the photos I'd taken during the day, when I suddenly remembered the birthday gift from Arlo.

Sitting bolt upright, I retrieved it from the drawer next to the bed and unwrapped it curiously.

A small note fell out, and I immediately recognised Arlo's handwriting.

Stay safe. Arlo

I opened the box with a shaking hand, pulling out a small silver cylindrical object, with a key ring at the top. It looked a bit like a pen, with grooves down the aluminium body, which tapered down to a pointed end. "What's that?" Caiden asked curiously from his position next to me on the bed.

I handed it to him with a shrug, along with the note, and he examined it from every angle.

"It's a kubotan." At my blank look, he explained, "It's a self-defence keychain. That could come in useful. Keep it close, with your keys, and I'll show you how to use it when we get a chance."

"For self-defence? I wonder why your dad decided to give me this particular gift." I frowned, slipping the object into my pocket.

His expression grew thoughtful. "I don't know, but we

need to speak to him. That, plus the message, is suspicious as fuck." He rose from the bed, pulling his hoodie back on. "We'll worry about it later, though. Dress warmly. Time for the final part of your birthday surprise."

I glanced at my phone clock. It was getting late, and it was dark outside. What was he planning?

8

caiden

I programmed the route into my satnav system, even though I was fairly sure of the way. It had been a long time since I'd been there last, though. My girl sat silently next to me, and I could feel the excitement thrumming through her as I steered us away from the house and onto the road, the R8's headlights cutting a swathe of light through the darkness. The weather conditions were fucking perfect—good thing since I didn't have a backup plan.

"You wanna put some music on?" I suggested.

"Remember that first time I was in your car, and you turned the music up really loud so I wouldn't talk to you?" I could feel her eyes boring into me, and I heard the smile in her voice.

"Yeah, I remember."

"Remember how you pretty much broke the speed limits so you could get to uni and get rid of me?"

I sighed heavily. "I remember that, too. Now do you wanna relive all the bad memories, Snowflake, or do you recall any good ones?"

"I remember how you stopped me from falling and caught me, before we went into the party at your dad's house. I remember your hand on me. When you touched my wrist, looking at my tattoo." Her voice grew so fucking soft. "I remember you holding on to me as we walked into the room. I was so intimidated and out of my depth, but even though you hated me, you gave me strength and support."

"Baby," I muttered. "I didn't hate you then. My head was so fucked up."

"I know." She placed her hand on my thigh, squeezing it lightly. "I remember the first time you kissed me. I'd never had a kiss like that before, and I thought I'd die if I never got to do it again. You made me feel alive, for the first time since my dad's death."

"Fuck." My voice was hoarse. I took my hand from the gearstick and trailed it up her leg, needing to touch her. "I wasn't even thinking straight that night—hadn't been since the first moment I saw you. But you have to know it was the same for me. You lit a fucking fire inside me, and when I finally stopped fighting myself, all I saw was you. You chased away my demons." I paused, gathering my thoughts, and admitted, "Yeah. I still have some. But you've smashed through all my defences and taken the one thing I've never given to anyone before."

"What's that?" Her voice was the barest whisper.

"My heart. You know you own every piece of me, Winter."

"You own every piece of me, too."

"Fucking right I do," I glanced over to her, grinning, and she returned my grin with a beaming smile. "Now, sit back and relax. We've still got another thirtyish minutes to go, and the road gets a bit dodgy up ahead, so I need to concentrate."

"Whatever you wish, King Caiden," she said.

I glanced over her to catch her smirking, noting her sarcastic tone. "None of that, or I'll have to make you get on your knees for me again."

"I think that can be arranged, regardless."

She turned her attention to the stereo as I shook my head, smiling, and turned onto the pitted, narrow, and winding road that would take us to our final destination.

"What is this place?" Winter stared around us curiously as I grabbed the large duffel bag I'd brought with me, heaving it over my shoulder.

"It's..." I hesitated. "Not sure, to be honest. All I know is, it's a dip at the top of the hill, and it'll keep the wind off us."

"Okay." She nodded, accepting my words, coming around to the front of my R8 as I carried the duffel bag into the large scooped-out area I'd parked in front of.

I glanced up, giving her a quick smile which she returned. She watched, sitting on the hood of my car as I spread out a blanket on the soft grass and laid out supplies on it. I didn't do romance, never had, but for her, I'd try my fucking hardest.

"Come here," I instructed, and she swung her long legs off my car and onto the ground.

I drank her in as she walked towards me. Even dressed down, she was fucking beautiful. She had a thick royal blue hoodie on over her top—one of mine, in fact—and she had pulled the ends down over her hands to keep them warm. I fucking loved her in my clothes.

She sank down onto the blanket next to me, and I leaned over, giving her a quick kiss before I resumed unpacking the bag.

"Lie back." I put a small pillow down behind her.

"Is that from your bed?" She turned around to stare at it, then back at me.

"Yeah. Now lie down on your back."

She eyed me, curiosity gleaming in her bright blue eyes. The night sky was studded with stars, and I had no problem seeing her. She lay down on her back, her pouty lips curving up into a smile. I couldn't fucking help myself—I leaned over her, kissing her soft lips, and she threw her arms around my neck, pulling me down on top of her.

"Mmm. I like this," she murmured, when I eventually managed to tear myself away from her mouth, my dick throbbing, needing to be inside her. What was I doing?

"You make me forget my own fucking name." My voice was hoarse as I looked into her eyes, our breaths mingling. "That wasn't what I brought you up here for."

"It wasn't?"

I had to laugh at the surprise on her face. "As much as I wanna be buried inside you right now, I am capable of other things. And right now, this is what I came here for." I climbed up to my knees, adjusting my hard-on, and moved over to the duffel bag.

"Here. In case you get cold." I handed her another thick, fluffy blanket which she arranged over herself, pulling it up to her chin so just her head was poking out, and she grinned happily at me. "Stay there and don't look."

Back to the car for the other thing I'd brought with me. I arranged it behind her so she couldn't see what I was doing. I took my time, wanting to get it just right, before I went over to her.

"Come here." I tugged her to her feet. "Do you trust me?"

Our gazes met, and held. "With my life." There was zero hesitation in her voice as we stared at one another.

"Close your eyes, and don't open them until I say." I led her to where I wanted her to be, putting my hands on her waist to manoeuvre her into position. Coming around behind her, I threaded my fingers through her silky hair and brushed it away from her face.

"Am I allowed to look yet?" I could hear the anticipation in her voice, her long lashes fluttering as she battled between obeying my command to keep her eyes closed, and wanting to see what was waiting for her.

I banded my arms around her waist, then skimmed my lips across her ear. "Open your eyes."

She stared in front of her silently for a long moment, and my stomach twisted. Shit, what if this had been a bad idea? Was it going to bring back unwanted memories?

"You know what today is, then? Not just that it's my birthday?" Her voice was small and shaky, but full of wonder as she reached out her hand to trace the cool metal of the telescope.

"I did some research. I remembered what you started to tell me before the party that night, and I figured that if it was important enough for you to tattoo a permanent reminder of it onto your skin, it was important to learn as much as I could about it."

"You remembered that?"

"Yeah."

"Cade. I love you so fucking much." She spun in my arms, crashing her lips onto mine. Fucking fireworks lit inside me, and I picked her up, holding her as she moulded her body against mine. I was lost. Lost in my girl.

I finally lowered her to the floor, and she looked up at

me, her eyes glassy with unshed tears, a huge smile on her face. "This is the best birthday ever."

My phone alarm beeped in my pocket, cutting off whatever I was about to say and reminding me why we were here. "Look through the telescope, baby. You don't want to miss the show."

She fiddled with the dials, peering through the viewfinder, and when the meteor shower began, I watched her watch the stars shoot across the sky.

"Cade, take a look." She lifted her head from the viewfinder, turning to look at me.

"This is all for you," I told her.

"But I want you to see." She grabbed my hand. "Look."

Wow. I wasn't into stars or any astronomy shit, but they looked fucking impressive through the telescope, it had to be said. I watched as the meteors appeared and disappeared, trails of light streaking through the sky. Next to me, my girl hugged me tightly, her head tilted to the sky as she watched the show.

"Your turn, now." I manoeuvred her into place, holding her from behind as she rested against me, engrossed in the view from the telescope.

After the shower was over, we lay back on the blanket, and I turned to face her, propping myself up on my elbow. Reaching out with my other hand, I pushed up her sleeve, tracing over her tattoo with my fingertips. "You wanna tell me the whole story about the meteors?"

A pensive, faraway look crossed her face as she stared up at the stars. "Okay," she said softly. Angling her body towards me, she met my gaze. "I was born by an elective caesarean. The way my dad told it, it was a cold January night. The snow had been really heavy that year. My mother phoned him at work to ask him to come and pick me up so she could recover—she'd refused to have him there for the birth. I'd been born early that morning, and she'd somehow persuaded the doctors that I could go home the same day—something to do with private hospitals and a donation." Her voice trembled, and her eyes filled with tears. "Basically, she wanted me gone. She never wanted me."

"Fuck, baby." I reached out and cupped her cheek in my hand. "That woman doesn't know how to love. She's got something missing inside her. She'd have to be, to not want you. You're fucking incredible."

"Thanks." She gave me a half smile. "I'm not trying to make this into a pity party. It...well, it just hurts. You know?"

"I know. You have me now, and you're never getting away." I tilted my head to kiss her. "I want you. I'll always fucking want you."

"Same goes for me with you." Her half smile turned into a full smile. "Okay, let me tell you the rest of the story." She took a deep breath. "So, my dad told her he'd get there as quickly as he could. When he got there, he filled in the paperwork, all the stuff he needed to do to let the hospital discharge me into his care. Then he put me in his car. He had to drive really slowly because the roads were so bad—away from the bigger roads, none of them were gritted. He was making a turn when his car hit a patch of black ice, and he said that he totally lost control of the car. It went spinning across the road, and we hit a snowdrift. Well, it was actually some kind of hedge, but it was all covered in snow." She waved her hand. "Anyway, that's not important. I'd started crying, and he didn't know what to do. He lifted me out of my seat and cuddled me into him. He was rocking me and singing to me, apparently, but nothing was working."

"Sounds familiar. There are times I can't get you to shut

up, either." I smirked at her, and she stuck her tongue out at me.

"Ha ha. I don't think you have a career as a comedian in your future."

"I can be funny. When I want to be."

"Sure you can." She rolled her eyes, smiling.

"Back to the story. What happened?" I asked.

"He'd tried all this stuff, and nothing was working. He thought I might be hungry but hadn't thought to bring anything to feed me—it was all back at the house." She huffed out a breath. "The way he told it was that he suddenly saw this shooting star out of the corner of his eye. He looked up and realised the Quadrantids meteor shower was starting, and he turned me around and I stopped crying, watching the meteors with him." A laugh escaped her lips as she continued. "I wouldn't have even been able to see them, probably. Can't babies only see things that are close to them? Still, it stopped me crying, and we sat and watched the whole thing."

"How did you get out of there?"

"Another car came along, a Land Rover or something, driven by a local farmer, and he got us out and back home."

"And you got the tattoo to remember that?" I reached for her hand, kissing the tattoo that was there on her wrist, following the meteor trail with my lips all the way up to her inner elbow.

"I got it to remember my dad. He'd always try and watch the meteor shower with me, every year, if he could." She shivered slightly. "Anyway, that's my story. It's getting colder, now, isn't it?"

Yeah, it was. My nose had gone numb. "Thanks for sharing that with me." I stared at her for a moment, and she shivered again. "Come on. Let's get back to the house so I can fuck you senseless."

"You're so romantic."

"I know."

I got her to wait in the warmth of the car while I gathered up the stuff I'd brought, shoving it back in the duffel bag, before carefully taking the telescope apart and packing it back into its box. I'd bribed Dave, a guy at uni who was a massive astronomy geek, to let me borrow it for the evening. It had taken a monetary bribe, plus a party invite to Winter's party, and the assurance I'd be seen speaking to him at said party so he could increase his "cool points." His words, *not* mine. He was more protective of the bloody thing than I was about my car.

I mentally shook my head, clearing thoughts of Dave from it, then sent Weston a quick text to say we were on our way back. I had champagne chilling in the fridge for my girl, and I wanted it in our bedroom ready for her when we got back. Neither of us were going to be leaving that room tonight if I had anything to do with it.

"Why did you bring me all the way up here, anyway?" Winter turned to look at me as I started up the car.

"Uh...reasons. I knew we could be alone. I knew the view of the stars would be great from up here." I cleared my throat, trying to get rid of the lump that had suddenly appeared. "And it was my mum's favourite place. She used to make us hike up here in the summer, and we'd always have a picnic at the top. Me and West would play tag, and she'd sit making daisy chains and watching us. Dad would come, too, sometimes." I frowned. "If he wasn't busy."

Her voice was soft. "We'll come back when it's warmer, then. Thank you for sharing it with me, Cade."

"I've never brought anyone up here. I wanted to share it

with you. To make it a place where we could both have good memories."

She sighed. "And you say you're not romantic. You're giving me all the feels, right here." She pointed at her stomach. "And here." She put her hand on her heart. We paused at the end of the track, waiting to turn the car back onto the road, and I placed my hand over hers.

Then I squeezed her delicious tit, and she squealed, batting me away. "Way to ruin the moment, asshole."

I smirked, sliding my hand up under her hoodie to caress her tits properly. "I think you like it, really."

She bit back a smile. "Sometimes."

I lightly pinched her nipple through her bra, and she moaned softly.

"Something you wanna say, baby?" I drawled.

"Take me home and fuck me senseless."

9

winter

He pushed me up against the front door, attacking my mouth, grinding his hardness into me. The time for romance was over. Now, all I wanted was for him to be buried inside me, and it was clear he was thinking the same thing.

"We need to get inside," I moaned, as he dragged his mouth down my neck, biting, licking, and sucking, sending waves of pleasure straight to my core.

"I want you so fucking much," he growled against my neck, as he somehow managed to open the door, holding me against him as he moved us inside.

We broke apart, breathing heavily, and I kicked my boots off. He followed suit, before he pounced on me again, picking me up as if I weighed nothing and stalking towards the stairs. "Careful," I cautioned, clinging tightly to him as he carried me up. As soon as we hit the landing, he lowered me to the floor.

"I need you so. Fucking. Badly."

He ripped my hoodie over my head, throwing it carelessly to the floor, and I moaned at the wild, feral look in

81

his eyes. "Get inside the bedroom. I don't want anyone else looking at you," he gritted out, his eyes drawn to my breasts where the outline of my nipples could be clearly seen through the thin material of my top and bra.

I stepped inside and he followed me in, closing the door with a crash, before stopping dead. A strange expression stole across his face as he looked at me standing by his bed.

"Cade?"

He bit his lip, his eyes dark as he raked his gaze over my body. "I need to give you your birthday present."

"I thought this was my present?" I unbuttoned my jeans, but he held his hand up.

"Wait. I can't think straight when you're like that."

"Like what?" I licked my lips, staring at him from under my lashes, and his restraint snapped.

"Fuck it." His words came out as a tortured rasp, and he launched himself at me, pushing me back onto the bed and ripping off my jeans. He pushed my legs apart, running his thumb over the silky material of my underwear. "Baby. You're so fucking wet for me right now." He leaned forwards and licked across my wetness, over the top of my underwear. I arched my back as his tongue teased me. "You taste so good," he groaned, sliding up my body, pushing my top up as he went, and tearing it off over my head. "I can't resist you."

"Do you want to?" I asked breathlessly, as he expertly reached around behind my back, undoing my bra with one hand and pulling it off me.

"I wanted to give you your present." He sank his teeth into my neck, sending a jolt of pleasure straight to my core as he ground himself into me, his jeans a delicious friction against my wetness.

"Don't stop," I begged, pulling at his hoodie, needing it

off him.

"Never." He lifted himself up, helping me out by tugging off his hoodie and T-shirt in one go.

In fact, I was the one to stop.

A shocked gasp fell from my lips as he uncovered his torso, and I went completely still. My eyes were drawn straight to the inside of his arm, to his tattoo of a skull wearing a crown. Directly above the peak of the crown was a new design I'd never seen before, the ink fresh, standing out against the other tattoos.

It was a tattoo of a snowflake, outlined and shaded in black. Swirls and pale shaded lines surrounded both the snowflake and the skull, making it look like they were caught up in a windstorm. It was gorgeous and perfect, and so him.

He followed my gaze. "I did this for you."

"For me?" I breathed. Hesitantly, I reached out to skim my finger lightly over it. "I probably shouldn't touch it yet, should I?"

He shrugged, and I looked up at his face. He bit his lip, suddenly looking unsure about my reaction.

"You did this for me?" I repeated.

"Yeah. Fuck, this sounds really fucking sappy and shit when I say it out loud...but the skull with the crown? That represents me. The snowflake is you, and the extra stuff I had added around both of them that kind of looks like the wind? That's supposed to represent the storms that we face and overcome. Together." He took a shaky breath. "And I had the snowflake inked above the skull to show that I put you above me. You'll always come first."

I had no words. None.

He slayed me.

Instead of saying something completely inadequate, I

ran my hands down the hard planes of his chest, down over his pecs, then his abs. Tracing my fingers over the top of his IV tattoo, I stopped at the top of his jeans. I could see his cock straining against the denim, and I was suddenly starving. For him.

I unbuttoned his jeans, stroking across the hard outline through his boxers. He remained completely still, his chest rising and falling, his eyes glued to my movements.

"These need to come off," I murmured. "Stand up." He obliged, his legs shaking slightly, as I dragged his jeans down, leaving him in his boxers for now.

"Have you ever had a champagne blowjob?" I asked conversationally, staring up at him as I knelt on the floor at his feet. He shook his head mutely, excitement clear in his eyes. He bit his lip, stifling a groan as I eased his boxers down, placing a kiss at the tip of his cock, the salty taste of precum on my lips. I moved away and over to the bedside table where the chilled bottle of champagne waited, placed there by Weston before we'd arrived home, ready for my birthday toast. Or so Cade had told me on the way home, at least. Whatever—fuck the birthday toast, I wanted him.

I grabbed the bottle, twisting it until the cork popped out, and tipped it into my mouth. With the cold, bubbling champagne swirling around my tongue, I took his cock into my mouth, letting the champagne slide down my throat as I did, then licked around the head before releasing his cock from my mouth.

"Fuuuuck," he groaned as I picked up the bottle with one hand. "Tonight was supposed to be all about you."

"I want this," I assured him, passing the bottle up to him. He placed the bottle to his lips and drank as I palmed his cock with both hands, my movements slow and steady. Bringing the bottle down, he dribbled champagne into my mouth, the bubbles fizzing on my tongue, and I lowered my head to take his hardness into my mouth again.

I was dimly aware of him putting the bottle down somewhere with a loud crash and hoped it wouldn't get knocked over, although to be honest, I was far more concerned with sucking my boyfriend's cock. I dipped my head, twisting my tongue in a corkscrew kind of motion as I moved up and down his shaft, until he was panting above me, his hands in my hair, gripping my head.

"Look at me." His voice was a low, desperate rasp. "I need to fuck your mouth now, baby."

"Mmmm," I hummed against his cock as I stared up at him, and he gasped.

"Do that again."

I hummed again, and he suddenly plunged his cock all the way to the back of my throat, and it was my turn to gasp. Tears filled my eyes as he fucked my mouth, and I shifted in my kneeling position, my wetness soaking my underwear. Seeing Caiden losing control from what I was doing turned me on beyond belief.

He suddenly wrenched himself out of my mouth, breathing hard, his eyes black and feral.

"Need. You."

The next moment he'd thrown me on the bed and ripped my underwear off, and thrust inside me in one powerful movement.

I was filled with him. His cock pulsed inside me, his muscles surrounded me, and his hot mouth was on mine as he kissed me fiercely before tearing his mouth away, moving to my neck. He moved lower still, kissing and nipping at my breasts, driving me wild with his touch. He ground himself against my body, withdrawing his cock almost all the way out, then thrusting back in. Repeating the motion again and again, he drove me insane with need, until I gripped his ass, holding him in place.

"Kiss me," I begged, my voice hoarse and breathless. He gave me a savage grin, before he crashed his mouth onto mine, his hand coming up to grip my throat.

That was my only warning before he was pistoning his hips in and out, hard and fast, our bodies slamming together. He'd completely lost control as he marked me with his teeth, his lips, his tongue, his hands; every part of me was his. And I marked him in return, both of us fucking wildly, sweat dripping between our bodies, drawing closer to an explosive orgasm.

All I could do was hold on to him as I came, crying out his name, starbursts of light bursting in front of my eyes. He followed me over the edge, my name falling from his lips while I was still trembling through the aftershocks, his cock shooting his cum deep inside me.

Collapsing down, his arms shaking, he twisted us so I was on top of him. He stroked my hair away from my face, holding me as we both recovered.

I could barely move, completely satiated, my head resting on his chest.

"Do you think it'll always be like this?" I wondered aloud, lifting my head slightly to look at him.

"Like what?"

"The fire between us. I want you all the time. It can't be normal."

His lips curved upwards. "If it's not normal, I don't want normal. I can't imagine not wanting you, baby."

"Well, if things get boring, we can always introduce some toys or something."

"Toys, hmm?" He kissed me, sliding his tongue against mine, before he rolled us back over so I was underneath him. "While you think about that, I'm gonna clean you up, then have my dessert."

He disappeared into the bathroom, returning with a damp towel. "On second thoughts..." He dragged his eyes down my body. "Let's get in the shower."

Standing under the running water, he took a washcloth, and pulled me to him so my back leaned against his chest. I could feel his cock hardening against me as he trailed the washcloth over my body with slow, torturous movements. When he reached down between my legs, my breathing quickened, and I moaned softly.

Turning me around, he angled the showerhead away from us and gave me a wicked grin. Then, he dropped to his knees and all other thoughts flew out of my head as he dragged his tongue across my wetness.

After he'd made me come with his fucking expert tongue, he was hard and ready for me again. We fucked in the shower, then in the bed, and eventually he made me put on one of his T-shirts so he wasn't tempted—or so he said.

I lay back on the bed, and he trailed his gaze down my body. "Fuck, Snowflake. You always look so hot in my clothes. This was a bad idea—I want you again, but I know you're sore."

"I am," I admitted. There was tenderness, and an ache between my legs that wouldn't go away, but it was the best kind of ache.

He crawled over me and gave me a soft kiss. "I can behave," he vowed against my lips, and I smiled.

"What if I don't want you to behave?"

He drew back, smirking at me. "Can't resist me, huh?"

"You know I can't."

"No. You need rest." He moved off the bed, grabbing the champagne bottle. "Have some of this. It's probably flat by now, but with the amount of money I spent on it, it's not going to waste."

I swigged from the bottle, because I was classy like that, while he padded over to the chest of drawers. I admired his body, just clad in black boxers, as he opened the top drawer and rummaged around inside it.

"Here." He climbed back onto the bed and put a small box into my hands. "Your birthday present."

I didn't look down at the box. Not yet, anyway. I looked at him. His stormy gaze was soft as his eyes met mine, and I couldn't help thinking again that I loved getting to see this side to him, that he hid behind a normally impenetrable facade.

"I love you." I leaned forwards and kissed him.

He gave me a huge smile, his eyes shining, and my heart skipped a beat. "I love you. Now open your present."

Tearing my gaze away from his, my eyes slid down to the box, wrapped in silver paper. I carefully opened it to find a rectangular velvet box inside. I stroked my finger over the soft, eggshell-blue velvet, before opening it. Lifting out the jewellery nestled inside, I examined it from every angle.

For the second time that night, he'd rendered me speechless.

"Do you like it?" he asked, a satisfied grin stretching his lips, clearly knowing the answer as my eyes flicked between him and my incredibly perfect, thoughtful gift. All I could do was nod, and pull him to me in a kiss.

"Oh, Cade. This is...wow. I wasn't expecting this."

He carefully took the bracelet from my hands. "I had it made for you, Snowflake. Titanium, because you're fucking strong. Then the boys picked out charms to represent them." Running his fingers over the dangling charms one by one, he explained. "A laptop from West. A knife from Z—"

"Of course." I smiled, interrupting him.

He grinned at me. "Yeah. I thought he'd pick a bike, but this isn't really a surprise." He moved to the next charm. "A jester hat from Cass. The rest are from me."

Moving closer to him, I leaned my head on his shoulder as he talked me through the others. "The snowflake is for you, the skull with the crown is for me, same as my tattoos." He hesitated. "This castle turret thing is...I thought it was significant."

I reached up, pulling his head down to mine and kissing him. "It is. It was the first time you admitted you wanted me. The first time you really saw me, I think."

"Yeah." His voice was quiet, contemplative. "So, y'know. I thought it was important. Then this last one—you're one of us now. Although it was always just the four of us until you, you're just as much a part of this as everyone else."

Stroking across the smooth silvery metal of the Roman numeral charm, I traced the IV, studded with tiny diamonds. "I love it. You've completely blown me away, Caiden Cavendish."

He fastened the bracelet on my wrist, and I shook it, the metal cool next to my heated skin. "Now you know how much you mean to me. To all of us." A glint appeared in his eye, and I prepared myself. "If you wanna show your appreciation, you can."

I glanced down at the growing bulge in his boxers, shaking my head. "You're seriously fucking insatiable today." Sliding my hand up his thigh, I gripped his cock through the material, swallowing his groan with a kiss. "I guess I could get on my knees for you one more time tonight, King Caiden."

"That's my girl."

10

caiden

I didn't want to brag, but Winter's birthday had been completely fucking perfect. Call me a selfish asshole, but I'd never really got the whole concept of putting someone else's happiness before my own. With my girl, though? All I wanted was to see that big smile on her face and know that I'd caused it. I never wanted to be the one to make her cry again. She'd cried enough over the stupid shit I'd done to her.

"Fried, poached, or scrambled?"

I looked up from my phone, meeting Zayde's eyes. "Any, mate. Whatever you wanna make. I'll do toast."

I added four slices of bread to the toaster and crossed to the fridge to grab the juice. "Ready for tonight?"

Zayde cracked eggs into a hot frying pan, watching idly as they hissed and sizzled. "I'm always ready. You?"

"I've got a bad feeling about it," I admitted. "I still don't know if bringing Granville on board is the right thing to do, but he knows way more than he's letting on. I'm sure of it."

"If you need my methods, I'm happy to oblige."

"You fucked up his cousin, he'd probably pass out if you got near him with your 'methods.'"

"True. It'll be awkward for you, too, remember. The last time you saw him, you put your fist through his jaw."

We smirked at each other. "Fuck, yeah. Punching him was so fucking satisfying."

"Punching who?" Winter's voice came from behind me. Shit.

"Uh, no one." I turned to face her. "Can you grab some plates, please, baby?"

She raised a brow at me, and I ignored Z's snort of laughter as I crossed over to the cupboard to pull down some glasses.

"I know who you were talking about, by the way," she said in a low voice as she came to stand beside me.

I did what anyone else would do in my situation. Took her mind off it.

"Do you, now." I chuckled darkly, pinning her up against the kitchen counter and trailing hot kisses down her neck. Keeping her caged with my arms, I ground myself into her, hearing her breathing hitch.

"What?" The word came out all breathy, and I smiled against her skin.

"Can you get the plates, please." I raised myself back to my full height, still caging her in, looking down at her as she stared at me, wide-eyed, her pupils blown.

"Uh, sure." She blinked a few times and I dropped a kiss on her head before moving away.

"Smooth bastard," Z muttered to me, a half smile on his lips as he added pepper to the eggs.

"Watch and learn, mate. Watch and learn."

The rest of the morning, I fucked off to the gym with Zayde and Weston, followed by lunch at an out-of-town, ancient pub that rested on the clifftops. Cassius was "helping" Winter and Kinslee decorate the house for the party, and fuck knows what I'd come back to.

"I spoke to Dad. Texted him, I mean." Weston eyed me over his pint of beer. "I asked him if we could meet up. You, me, and him. Male bonding."

"Let me guess. He said he was too busy." My words were flat. Yeah, my relationship with him had improved, *slightly*, but business always came first with him. Always had.

"No, he didn't," Weston said quietly, and my eyes widened. "He said...here, just read the message." He opened a message thread on his phone and handed it to me.

West: Hi Dad

Dad: Hello Weston. Did you get the email I sent you? I want you to be prepared for the new semester at university. The professors go easy on you in your first semester, but expect things to step up when you go back next week.

West: Yeah I did and I know. Do you want to get together with me and Cade before we go back to uni? Male bonding.

Dad: When would this be?

West: *shrug emoji* Whenever

Dad: What is the picture?

West: What picture? The emoji? It's a person shrugging

Dad: You know I don't approve of the use of emojis, Weston.

West: *eye roll emoji* *tongue out emoji* *crying laughing emoji*

West: Couldn't resist

Dad: I'll choose to ignore that. As for your original question, yes, I would like that. Very much. Could you clear it with my secretary?

West: OK. I'm on it. Thanks Dad

Dad: You're welcome.

"See?" West said when I finished reading the thread and looked up from his phone. I slid the phone across the table towards him and sat back in my seat.

"I'm...surprised. No, I'm fucking shocked. When was the last time the three of us did anything together?" Weston shrugged, and I swiped a chunky chip from his bowl, dipping it in ketchup as I thought. "Any ideas on what to do? Not golf. Anything but that."

"Get your own chips!" My brother glared at me, pulling the bowl out of my reach. Selfish bastard. I lunged across the table, tugging it out of his hands before he had a chance to react.

"You can be such an immature dickhead sometimes."

"Takes one to know one," I smirked at him, and he laughed.

"Fuck you. Gimme my chips back and you can share them."

"Take your dad to the shooting range at Skirmish," Zayde suggested, interrupting our potato-related negotiations. I swung my head around to look at him. I hadn't realised he was listening, not that it should've come as a shock. Z was a sneaky fucker, always there, silent and deadly, noticing everything and never giving anything away.

"That's not a bad idea. Dad likes clay pigeon shooting, doesn't he? We could book a shooting session, have a bit of friendly competition." Weston grinned at me, clearly liking the idea.

"Sort it and tell me when, and I'll get in touch with Creed." Zayde's attention dropped back to his phone, his part in our conversation over.

"What the fuck is going on in my life?" I muttered. For so long, things had been the same. Now, everything was changing so fast I hardly recognised my own fucking life. Not that I wanted anything to go back to the way it was before. No. Change was good, and once again, it was my girlfriend I had to thank for it.

Back at the house, Zayde threw open the door and stopped dead. "What the fuck?"

"Yeah."

"I'll repeat. What. The. Fuck."

We stared down the hallway. Streamers, balloons, fucking decorations everywhere in garish colours that assaulted my eyes. Never thought I'd need to wear sunglasses indoors. Until now.

An efficient-looking brunette woman holding a clipboard came striding down the hallway, her heels clipping against the floor.

"Who the fuck are you?" I asked.

"Cade! Don't be so rude," Weston hissed and shoved me out of the way.

"Weston Cavendish." He took her hand, kissing it, and she fucking giggled.

"I'll repeat. What in the ever-loving fuck is going on?" Zayde asked me under his breath.

"Ah." Her face cleared, and she consulted the clipboard

she was holding, flipping through the pages. She trailed a pencil down the sheet of paper she was studying, then tapped it triumphantly. "Weston Cavendish." She made a tick on the page.

"This is Caiden Cavendish and Zayde Lowry," Weston said, waving his hand in our direction, when neither of us made any attempt to say anything.

"Caiden...yes. Zayde...yes. Lovely." She made another two ticks, and gave us a bright smile. "Welcome to Winter Huntington's birthday party. I'm Maria, Ms. Huntington's party planner. Please let me know if I can be of any assistance." She glanced at her watch. "I'm afraid you're three hours too early. While you're waiting, please help yourself to refreshments in the kitchen." With that, she clipped off up the stairs, leaving us staring at each other.

"Did she just welcome us to our own house?" Zayde's voice was incredulous.

"Uh. Yeah, I think she did."

"This has Cass written all over it," Weston said, laughing as he eyed me and Zayde. "I can't believe you two actually seem shocked about any of this."

"Cassius Drummond!" I shouted, stalking down the hall. "You've got some explaining to do."

11

winter

After the boys had got over their shock of the last-minute party planner, which, by the way, I had no knowledge of, they became surprisingly enthusiastic about the whole thing. Mostly due to the fact that she'd had a fully functioning bar erected in the dining part of the kitchen, complete with staff who were busy showing Caiden and Cassius some complicated tricks that involved throwing glasses around. There was also a roulette table and a magician guy wandering around doing card tricks.

Kinslee and Cassius had arranged for the planner, and Cassius had forced the poor woman to include the stuff he'd picked up on our shopping trip alongside the professional decorations. This meant that it gave the whole thing a slight children's party feel, but it worked. Kind of. Caiden had been angry when he found out that Cassius had sneakily taken his credit card and used it to pay for the planner, but he didn't stay mad for long. Not when he saw how happy I was.

I changed into a short, tight black dress and added

sparkly silver earrings and my new charm bracelet. After finishing my makeup, I'd just stepped out of the bathroom into the bedroom when Caiden walked in.

He stopped dead, and his eyes licked me up and down, and just like that, I was suddenly breathless.

"Fuck. Look at you. I wish we had time for a quickie." His voice went all hoarse as he stalked over to me, pulling me to him.

Sliding my arms around him, I tried to sound firm. "Not now. Behave." I barely believed my own words. If it came to a choice of being with him or being at the party, I'd rather be upstairs with him, in all honesty.

"I don't want to behave."

"You have to. Don't mess up my lipstick." I stared into his stormy eyes, and my stomach flipped at the look in them. "At least, not yet."

"I want those lips around my cock, later." His lashes lowered as he stared intently at my mouth.

"I can do that."

"Good."

"By the way, you look insanely hot," I told him, running my hands down his strong back. He had on a black shirt with jeans, and his hair was all messy. Just the way I liked him.

"Stop eye fucking me."

"I can't help it."

"I know." He gave me a smirk, and I pressed my lips softly against his, then wiped away the small smear of lipstick with my thumb. Smiling, he glanced at his watch, before he reached down for my hand and tugged me towards the door. "Come on, birthday girl. You can't be late to your own party."

Yeah, like any of these people were here for me—other

than a small percentage, anyway. The majority of them just wanted to be seen here, to be at one of the Four's parties.

The music was pulsating, a dark, heavy beat that made me want to dance as we made our way downstairs. The lights had been turned down low, and the house was already full of people talking, laughing, and drinking. Caiden led me to the temporary bar area where the bartender mixed me a cocktail—something fruity and delicious that I knew I'd drink way too quickly.

After my cocktail was ready, Caiden pulled me into a dark, quietish corner of the room and slid his arm around my waist, kissing my neck as I sipped my drink. He trailed his lips up to my ear, and I shivered at the feel of his mouth on my skin.

"Listen, baby. I know we said about the whole Granville thing—him coming here so we could get some answers from him. But I want you to have fun, as well. This is your party."

"A party we're having for the specific purpose of getting answers from James."

He laughed. "Yeah, okay. But we *are* celebrating your birthday."

"My actual birthday was the best birthday I've ever had. Anything else is just a bonus."

"Good." He kissed my cheek and then released me with a frown, glancing over my shoulder. "I'm not sure who's here, but we'd better cut down on the physical contact."

I nodded. I wanted to speak to Arlo about what was going on between me and Caiden, but at the moment our primary concern was Christine. As much as I wanted to shout about the fact that Caiden was mine, we had more important concerns. Like the tiny fact that Christine was most likely planning to have Caiden's dad killed.

How the fuck did I end up being related to this woman? She'd actually done us the biggest favour by leaving my dad when I was little. If I'd been forced to grow up near her, or even worse, with her, things might have turned out differently. I might have turned out differently. And not in a good way. To be a cold, heartless bitch? No, thanks.

My mind wandered as Jessa and Portia entered my head, against my will. Why were some people like this? What made them so bitchy and rude to me?

"What are you thinking about? You were miles away." Caiden studied me from where he was now casually leaning against the wall, drink in hand.

"Portia and Jessa."

He raised a brow. "Not the answer I was expecting. Why the fuck are you thinking about them?"

"Oh, I was just wondering why they have such a problem with me."

He snorted, shaking his head. "It's obvious, isn't it? They're jealous of you. They were used to being the ones who had the most attention from us, until you came along. You managed to work your way into our group without even fucking trying, and they've always been hanging on the edge."

"It's not just that, though," I mused. "Their personalities are... It's like they actually enjoy acting that way."

"Yeah. I don't know, Snowflake. Women are fucking crazy." I raised a brow at that comment and saw him trying to suppress a smile, which quickly faded. "I've grown up with these girls, but I don't know them like that, you know? We weren't friends. Just..." His voice trailed off, and I knew what he was saying without him putting it into words. Just fuck buddies, or whatever. "Can we not talk about them anymore? I don't even see them. All I see is you."

"I know. Same."

"That's a given. Have you seen me?" He gave me that smirk again.

"Yeah, and unfortunately, so has every single girl in this place." I pouted, making him laugh.

"I love your jealousy."

"I love yours."

We stood grinning at each other.

"Go find your friends and dance. That's an order."

"Yes, Your Highness." I gave him a mock bow and turned on my heel, hearing his low chuckle from behind me as I strutted away to find Kinslee.

She wasn't hard to spot, over by the bar having a cocktail mixed. A huge smile spread across her face when she saw me, and she pulled me into a hug.

"Looking good!" She looked me up and down. "Totally approve of the dress."

"Same. It looks like we planned this." I admired the tiny black dress she was wearing—so similar to mine, but looking totally different on her thanks to her curves. "Your boobs look amazing."

"I know." She flicked her hair over her shoulder, striking a pose, and we both laughed. I turned to the bartender, holding up my empty glass in a silent request to make me another cocktail, as Kinslee continued speaking. "Do you know who's coming tonight?" She stirred her cocktail with her straw, the ice cubes clinking inside the glass.

"Thanks, this looks delicious," I accepted my new drink from the bartender with a smile, before returning my attention to Kinslee. "I think most of the usual crowd, plus whoever else managed to get into the Four's good graces. I invited Lena, although she wasn't sure if she could make it or not."

We looked around us, and I saw Caiden talking to a tall, thin guy with blond (or was it bronde) hair that kept flopping into his eyes. "Who's that?"

"Who?" Kinslee placed her glass down on the bar. "That went down far too quickly."

"The guy Cade's talking to."

She glanced over. "Oh, he's in one of my classes. I think his name is Dave? Not sure. I didn't realise he was friends with this crowd, though."

Our conversation was interrupted by the magician, who proceeded to do some complicated card trick that ended up with Kinslee's chosen card inside her empty cocktail glass. I watched her, smiling as she examined her glass from all angles, completely enthralled.

"How did he do that?"

I shrugged. "Magic."

The Four were all sitting on the sofa as Kinslee and I walked into the lounge a bit later in the evening, giving me a sudden flashback to the first time I'd ever laid eyes on them. This time, though, there was no hostility. Just Caiden's slow, deliberate perusal of my body, and the fire in his eyes that told me he wanted to do bad, bad things to me.

I swallowed hard, my throat suddenly dry, as I was held captive by his darkened gaze. A slow smirk spread across his lips as he watched me watching him, and he cocked his head in a silent invitation.

Stepping closer, I stared down at him.

"Hi."

"Hi." He slid the tip of his finger up my bare leg, out of

view of everyone else, and goosebumps broke out over my body.

Casually perching on the arm of the sofa, I turned to the others, my voice rising an octave to be heard above the music. "Uh, can I say something to all of you?" It took all my focus to ignore Caiden's finger trailing across my skin. "Can you stop teasing me?" I hissed out of the corner of my mouth, aware of everyone's eyes on me.

I heard Caiden's low chuckle, but he stopped the torturous movements. I curled my finger around his, a subtle, hidden touch, and he mouthed *later* to me, when I met his eyes.

"What is it?" Weston's voice interrupted the moment.

"Oh, sorry. I was miles away." I turned back to the boys, taking in the amusement on their faces. "I just wanted to say thank you. For this." Holding up my arm, I jingled the charm bracelet on my wrist. "It...it means a lot to me."

Cassius gave me a grin. "All Cade's idea, wasn't it, mate? He just asked us each to pick a charm for you."

I glanced back at Caiden, who shrugged, a small smile playing across his face. *I love you*, I mouthed, and his smile widened.

"The jester hat's perfect for me, right? I know I'm the most hilarious guy you know."

"Well...I don't know about that, Cass." I held his stare, keeping a straight face, and his smile disappeared. "Course you are," I said eventually, and he threw me another blinding grin, pretending to wipe his brow in relief. "Anyway, I just wanted to thank all of you. So. Thanks."

"You're welcome." Weston leaned over and squeezed my hand, his finger brushing against my bracelet. Zayde gave me a wink, and I smiled at him.

"Winter." Kinslee's voice cut through the music, and I spun my head to see her beckoning at me.

"See you all later." I extracted my fingertip grip from Caiden and headed back over to Kinslee.

"James is here," she murmured discreetly in my ear, and subtly indicated her head to the left. I saw him standing with a group of his friends, looking completely relaxed and at ease. Okay, maybe this wouldn't be as bad as I'd imagined.

"I'm going to talk to him. Why don't you find a dance partner?"

"I've sworn off men," she sighed.

"Since when?"

"Since New Year's Eve—it was my New Year's resolution. I've decided I'm going to focus on my studies and let the right man find me."

"Um. Okay. That sounds...sensible, I guess?" I shrugged.

"It is." She gave me a huge smile. "This is the new, improved Kinslee."

"You don't need improving."

"Whatever. Go to James."

"Okay, okay. I'm going. Have fun." I gave her a quick hug, and made a beeline for James.

Straightening up, he watched me coming towards him, and his jaw set, the air of relaxation gone. "Can we talk?" He studied me for a moment, then nodded. I gave him a small smile. "Thanks. Come on, let's go somewhere quieter." I felt eyes boring into my back, and I knew wherever I took James, Caiden wouldn't be far behind.

We headed into the kitchen to grab drinks, and then I opened the sliding doors and took him out onto the back deck. No one else was there, the coldness having chased people away. I grabbed some blankets, throwing one to him, and patted the seat next to me. "Have a seat."

"I know what this is about." His expression was resigned. "I knew you'd work it out, eventually."

Work what out? This was unexpected. I decided to just go with it. I could feel Caiden's presence behind me, lurking in the doorway, and I knew he was listening to everything that was being said.

"You had to realise you couldn't keep it a secret," I said, hoping he'd say more.

"I had to. I told you before, at the ball, there are things about my family..." He shrugged, leaving the sentence unfinished.

"Why didn't you say anything sooner?"

"How could I? I was trying my hardest not to get involved. This whole situation is a fucking nightmare."

I eyed him carefully, taking in his tortured expression, the way he was biting his lip and clenching and unclenching his fists.

"It is a nightmare. But if you knew I'd work it out, why keep it from me?" My stomach was churning as I waited for him to reveal whatever it was he thought I knew.

"Like I said. I was trying to stay out of it. And Joseph would have killed me."

"Like, actually killed you?"

His expression lightened a tiny bit. "Probably not." The lightness disappeared. "He would've beaten me half to death, though, then knowing him, he would've done his best to have me disowned from the family. Or at the very least, made life incredibly difficult." He stared at me, apprehension all over his face. "You're not going to tell him, are you?"

"Joseph?" My blood boiled, thinking of what he'd done to me. "I'm not going to tell him anything. Did you know he hit me on New Year's Eve?"

"He *what*?" James' shocked gasp cut through the still night air. "I'm going to kill him!"

"I think Cade and Z took care of that."

"So that must be why he disappeared," he mused. "Haven't seen him for over a week now. I've heard from him plenty of times, but haven't actually seen him face to face. I imagine they fucked him up pretty badly?"

I shrugged. "I haven't asked them, and I was kind of out of it at the time, to be honest. In shock, you know?"

He nodded. I left him with his thoughts for a while as I slowly sipped my drink, thinking through what he'd said. *I knew you'd work it out, eventually.* What did he mean by that?

I bit the bullet and took a gamble. "James?" I waited until his eyes met mine. "Just to be clear, so I know we're on the same page. When you said you knew I'd work it out, what did you mean by that?"

He held my gaze steadily. "The docks. I was the one who rescued you."

12

caiden

A shocked gasp slid from my girlfriend's lips as she stared at Granville.

Fuck!

My stomach dropped.

Why did *he* have to be the one to rescue her? Of all the fucking people in the world, it had to be him? Now I had to be grateful to that fucker. Yeah, so I was fucking glad that he'd done it, but now I owed him, and the last thing I wanted was to owe a Granville anything—especially not one who had an interest in my girl. He'd saved her life—I could never repay shit like that.

Swallowing the nauseous feeling, I stepped onto the deck, followed by Z. "Tell us what happened," I commanded.

"I should've known you'd be close by." Granville sighed heavily, looking resigned.

"Yeah, and do you blame me? Shit keeps happening when she goes off on her own. Isn't that right, Snowflake?"

She had the audacity to roll her eyes at me, and I really

wasn't in the fucking mood. My head was spinning with Granville's revelation. After giving her a warning glare, to which she blew me a kiss in return, I crossed over to the railing. Pushing my feelings down, letting my face become a blank mask, I leaned against the railing, arms folded, waiting to hear what Granville had to say. Z took a seat in one of the outdoor chairs, his sharp gaze laser-focused on Granville.

"James." Winter's voice was soft, as she leaned forwards to touch his arm. "Ignore them. They're just...overly protective. Please can you tell me how it all happened?"

Her hand on his arm? I dug my nails into my palms, still outwardly calm, but I was so close to storming over there and ripping her away from him. Zayde looked pointedly in my direction, his expression cautioning me, as I inwardly battled to regain control.

Why? Why did it have to be him?

Granville nodded, looking all smug. Yeah, maybe that was just me projecting, but I was still pissed off about him being the one to save my girl. "I guess since you know it was me, there's no harm in me telling you how. Can you promise this won't get back to my family, though? Or my cousin's family?"

He glanced up at me, waiting, and I nodded. Yeah, no fucking chance was I having any interaction with those assholes. I was going to have a hard time not kicking the shit out of Hyde next time I saw him. "You have my word."

"Mine too," Z added, and Granville gave a sigh of relief.

"Thanks. Okay. I'll tell you how it happened."

He sat back in his seat, looking far too fucking comfortable next to my girl, who still had her hand on his arm, and I tried to hide my irritation as he continued.

"First thing you need to know is that I've been looking into something for a friend. It's nothing to do with Alstone Holdings, nothing to do with our family rivalry. I want to make that clear. I'm not working against you."

"Except for the whole video thing, but let's not mention that, yeah," I growled.

"Cade! Please," Winter hissed, frowning at me.

Granville suddenly rose to his feet and strode across the deck to me. "I let you hit me, because I know I messed up. I'm apologising. I'm sorry, okay?"

I stared at him in disbelief. "Let me get one thing clear. You didn't 'let' me do anything."

"Cade."

Winter's voice came from behind Granville, and I swallowed my pride for her. "I accept your apology," I gritted out, even though the words tasted like ash in my mouth.

"Thank you." A hesitant expression crossed his face, but he held out his hand, and I groaned. I had to shake hands with this fucker? Feeling my girlfriend's eyes on me, I sighed and gripped his palm. For Winter's sake.

He turned to Z, who shot him down with one look. "Don't even think about it."

Granville lifted his hands in surrender and sat back down next to Winter. "Back to the story. I was at the docks because I was looking into this...thing, for a friend. I overheard—"

"Wait a minute," Winter interrupted, the wheels turning in her head. I could guarantee her thoughts were along the same line as mine. "Does this 'thing' have anything to do with dog fighting, by any chance? And is the friend Lena?"

Granville's mouth fell open. "H-how did you know?" he stammered.

I rolled my eyes. "Not important at the moment. Get to the fucking point, will you?" Winter glared at me, and I added, "Please." She blew me another kiss, then smirked at me. *I'm gonna punish you later*, I mouthed at her, watching a wicked gleam come into her eye.

"Yes, to both of your questions." He met Winter's gaze. "When Lena told me you'd caught her at the docks, I asked her to keep my name out of it. I didn't want any more trouble, you know?"

"I knew she was hiding something," Winter muttered under her breath, then raised her voice. "Yeah. I get that. What happened?" She cocked her head, staring intently at him.

"I was hiding round the back of one of the warehouses, waiting for the guard to finish his patrol, when I heard him on his phone. He was talking to someone, who he referred to as 'madam,' saying he was holding someone captive. As soon as I heard that, I moved closer so I could hear better. When he asked whoever was on the other end if he should dispose of the captive, I—"

He immediately stopped speaking when Winter gave a small, agonised whimper, the sound stabbing right through my heart. I was straight over to her, scooping her up and sitting down with her body curled up against mine. "I've got you, baby." I held on to her tightly, kissing her head.

"Thanks," she whispered, before she turned back to Granville. "What happened next?"

"Well, once I'd heard that, I couldn't very well leave without checking it out, could I? Anyone would have done the same."

I looked at him with new interest, and he shuffled in his seat uncomfortably when he noticed my stare.

"It sounded like the guard had arranged for whoever he was speaking to come down to the docks the next morning, and I knew I didn't have long. I didn't know where you were —" He looked at my girl. "—so I had to follow him."

"Were you scared?" Winter breathed, completely caught up in his story.

"More scared than I've ever been," he admitted with a shrug. "I was jumpy enough being down there in the first place. I wouldn't have been there if we hadn't received a tip-off, and Lena was supposed to meet me, but she was running late. Couldn't sneak out of the house, which turned out to be the best thing that could've happened. She...she's more fragile than she realises."

"Sounds like you know her well," Zayde commented. His voice was flat and emotionless, but I knew he was just as curious as I was.

"It's not like that. We hang out sometimes, and we've been working together to look into something. That's irrelevant at the moment, though."

Yeah. It wouldn't be, once Cassius found out Granville was hanging out with his sister.

"Back to it. I picked up an iron bar from the junk that was round the back of the warehouse, and I followed the guard as closely as I could. He entered the building I'd found you in, and I went in after him. He disappeared into a room and left the door open, but I didn't know whether to follow him in there or not."

He stopped to take a drink, while I not-so-patiently waited for him to continue. Fucking finally, he stopped, setting his cup down on the arm of the seat with a loud thump.

"Sorry. Dry throat. Anyway, the guard had been gone for

a while, so I peered into the room. I suddenly saw his head appearing out of the floor, and I jumped backwards, hiding further down the dark corridor so he wouldn't see me. He came out of the room and I—" He buried his face in his hands.

"James?" Winter's voice was soft and concerned. "It's okay. We know what happened."

He raised his head, fucking tears in his eyes. "I panicked, and I hit him as hard as I could with the iron bar and he fell. He knocked his head on the stone wall as he went down. There was so much blood..." He trailed off, his hands shaking.

"You've got a good swing on you." What the fuck was I saying? Had I just complimented Granville?

"All those years of playing golf." He gave a wry smile, then scrubbed his hand across his face with a heavy sigh. "With the guard knocked out, I didn't waste any time. I ran straight into the room he'd been in, found the hatch, and opened it. I was in shock when I saw you down in that basement, Winter. You were unresponsive, completely out of it, so I guessed he'd given you some kind of sedative. I got the fuck out of that place as quickly as I could. Lena turned up when I was trying to get you into the car."

"Why didn't she say anything to me?" Winter spoke quietly. I could hear the hurt in her tone, and I stroked up and down her arm, trying to comfort her. "We've hung out a lot, and I never had a clue."

"Seeing you like that scared her, I think—you were in a pretty bad state. We didn't know what you were mixed up in. I didn't want to know, in all honesty, so I decided to take you to Lansdown General Hospital rather than the local one, where there was less chance of you being recognised. Lena and I made sure the hospital knew to contact Kinslee, and after that...we left." His hands twisted together. "The whole thing shook me up, scared me half to death. I couldn't let myself get involved. I've stepped back from everything since. Tried to stay out of it all."

Fucking hell. This evening was *not* going down the way I'd expected.

13

winter

"Okay, I get what you're saying." I watched him closely. "I understand you wanting to stay out of it."

"I just couldn't believe I actually knocked someone out. I've been having nightmares every night about it. I hope there was no permanent damage. I couldn't live with that on my conscience."

I exchanged glances with Z, feeling Cade stiffen behind me, pleading with my eyes.

"No permanent damage done," Caiden unexpectedly said, and I collapsed back against him, seeing the look of total and utter relief that came into James' eyes.

"Thank you," I whispered to Caiden, mouthing the words carefully so Zayde could see them, too. I wasn't okay with keeping things from people, generally, but in this case, the whole situation had clearly messed with James' head.

"I'm only doing this for you," Caiden muttered in my ear, and I turned my head so I could kiss his jaw, the stubble scratchy under my lips.

"I know."

"Is there anything else?" James looked at me.

"Yeah. James, I need—no, I want to thank you for saving my life. What you did was incredibly brave, and I can never repay you."

He gave a small laugh. "Like I already said, I was only doing what anyone else would in that situation. You don't have to worry about repaying me." Then he looked at me closely. "Am I allowed to know how you got there in the first place?"

"I—yes. Long story short, I moved to Alstone to investigate my dad's death. He, uh, passed away under suspicious circumstances." I paused to grab my drink, letting the cool liquid soothe my suddenly dry throat. "I had a lead that something may be happening down at the docks, and I went there to check it out. You know what happened next—I managed to get myself caught."

"You need to be more careful, Winter. Seeing you out of it, with those bruises all over your face—that really scared me."

"That's what I keep telling her," Caiden agreed, his voice low and disapproving.

"Ugh," I huffed. "Yes, I was irresponsible and all that, but that's in the past now. We need to concentrate on what's going to happen next." I took a deep breath. "Do you know if Joseph Hyde or his family are working with my mother?"

"Your mother?" He stared at me, taken aback. "What's she got to do with it?"

"I have reason to believe...actually, no, I have evidence, that she had something to do with my father's death."

"*What*?"

"Yeah, and when Joseph attacked me, he mentioned something about how I'd fucked up for a lot of people, and how his life was getting back to normal until

Cade showed an interest in me. Originally, I thought it was all a coincidence, but now? I don't think it is."

He sighed, pinching his brow. "Fuck. This is a lot to take in."

"Any information at all, no matter how small, could help us. Nothing you tell us will get back to the Hydes, I promise you."

"Remember what I told you at the ball? That sometimes we have to do things for family reasons? That—that kiss," he began, and Caiden growled next to me, his arms tightening around me. James looked startled, his eyes darting to my boyfriend's face. He swallowed hard, noticing Caiden's murderous gaze.

"Cade, please," I murmured softly.

"The kiss," James began again. "Joseph refused to give me details, but he was paid to do that. The idea was to break you and Caiden up. I guess you may as well know the rest. I didn't want to go along with it, but he can be persuasive when he wants to be."

"Paid? By who? And what do you mean by persuasive?"

He groaned. "The black eye I had when I kissed you was courtesy of him. He's got a mean right hook."

"Yeah, that's true." I stared at Zayde in surprise. What had gone down between him and Joseph? I couldn't help feeling like there was some history there that I wasn't aware of.

James narrowed his eyes but shrugged it off. "As for who he was paid by, I don't know. But he's been very secretive lately. You know how we have the rivalry. He's been talking about 'finally getting what he deserves' and..." He trailed off, looking apologetically at Caiden. "He's been saying about how you guys are going to get what's coming to you."

"I'm going to fucking end him." Caiden's voice sliced through the sudden tension.

"Don't shoot the messenger."

"He won't," I assured him. "I trust you. Maybe I shouldn't," I admitted. "Since we're on separate sides of this situation. But fuck it, I do."

"I don't." Caiden's voice was hard, and I groaned.

"I wouldn't expect you to," James said quietly.

"But my girl trusts you, so I'm willing to put that aside, *for now*. If you know anything that can help us," he added begrudgingly.

A smile curved across my lips, and I squeezed his forearm lightly.

There was silence for a while, before James stood. "Thank you. I'll see if I can find out any information from my family, any proof that they're involved with this. Unless there's anything else you want to discuss?" He shuffled his feet, looking like he was ready to make a break for it. I didn't blame him.

I moved Caiden's hands off me and got to my feet. "Thanks," I murmured to James, pulling him into a hug.

He smiled when I released him. "You're welcome. Stay safe." He inclined his head briefly towards Caiden and Zayde, and then he was gone.

"Did you have to hug him?" Caiden scowled at me, and I rolled my eyes.

"Yes, I did." I pulled him to his feet. "What a night, huh? I feel totally blindsided by James, and I won't lie, I feel a bit hurt that Lena kept this from me."

He gripped my face, caressing my cheek. "Same for me. I need time to process all this shit." Lightly brushing his lips against mine, he released his grip on my face. "Fucking

Granville," he muttered under his breath, his tone full of disbelief.

He was right. We all needed time to process this information, and for now, the best thing to do was to attempt to salvage the rest of the evening. "Come on. Let's enjoy the rest of the party and pretend that we're normal students, having a perfectly normal time with our friends."

"Oh, baby, there's nothing normal about you." He grabbed me around my waist, dipping his head to kiss up my neck, walking us towards the door to the kitchen as he continued to rain kisses all over me.

"Z, you coming?" I managed to ask, breathless and smiling widely.

"In a minute." He stayed seated, staring at nothing.

Caiden glanced back at him, stopping in the doorway. "Go and have fun. I'm gonna keep Z company for a bit."

I nodded, and he gave me one last kiss before giving me a gentle push into the house and closing the door behind me.

"Everything okay?" Cassius was at the kitchen island, a pretty blonde tucked under his arm, watching me carefully.

"Yeah." I smiled at him. Now was not the time to discuss what we'd found out. "I'm ready to enjoy this party."

He gave me a long, searching look, before nodding. He grinned, raising his cup of whatever he was drinking in a salute. "That's my girl. Have you played roulette yet?"

I shook my head, and he tutted disapprovingly. "Let's go." Dropping his arm to the blonde girl's waist, he pulled her around to where I was standing. She giggled, reaching up to kiss his cheek, and he grinned. Stretching out his free hand towards me, he passed me his drink. "Hold this, will ya?" I took it from him, and he slid his arm around my waist.

"There. Now everyone else will be jealous when they see us. Two of the hottest women at the party, with me."

"Sure they will." I laughed, rolling my eyes playfully. Right now, I needed to put aside James' revelations, to allow my brain time to process everything. Cassius had read me perfectly, and he was ready to take advantage of the fact that all I wanted at this moment was to enjoy the rest of this party. Simple, uncomplicated fun, forgetting about my worries for the rest of the evening at least.

"Stick with me, and you'll have a great time." Leaning down, he spoke in my ear, his voice too low to be overheard by anyone else. "If you want to stop, or go, or talk, or whatever, just say the word."

"Thanks, Cass." I gave him another smile. "Right now, all I want is to enjoy this party."

"Say no more." He walked us over to the roulette table. I eyed it with interest, excitement building within me. The music swirled around us, and everywhere I looked I could see people enjoying themselves. This was going to be fun.

"Fuck! The piñata!" Cassius suddenly shouted.

"Later. Roulette first," I insisted, and he grinned down at me.

"Whatever my lady desires."

"You're so weird."

"You love me."

"Doesn't stop you being weird though, does it?" I jabbed him in the ribs, tickling him, and he screeched, making the girl under his other arm double over laughing.

"Stop that right now!"

"Never."

14

winter

The last few days had been quiet. We were still trying to process everything, and as it stood, we had no more answers. I was waiting to hear from James, but so far he'd been silent, other than a quick text to say he was going to attempt to contact Joseph.

Monday morning, lugging my ridiculously heavy backpack, I climbed into Caiden's car, ready to drive to university for our first day back after the Christmas break.

As we started the drive, I glanced over at Caiden and noticed the tight set of his jaw, and the way he was gripping the steering wheel.

The soft whoosh of the wipers on the windscreen did nothing to break the unbearable silence, and eventually, I had to say something. "Cade? What's the matter?"

"Hyde."

"Hyde? What about him?"

"I don't know if I'm gonna be able to control myself when I see him."

Oh.

"Cade. We have to think of the long game. Let's trust

James to do what he said he was going to do—see if he can find out any information. It's only been a few days."

"I know that. But it's three more days without any more fucking answers!" He slammed his hand on the wheel suddenly, making me jump.

"Cade..." I began hesitantly, putting my hand on his arm. His muscles were taut, tension rolling off him in waves.

"She wants to destroy everything I love." His voice came out hoarse and broken.

Fuck, I couldn't stand it.

I glanced at the clock on the dashboard, noting the time.

"Pull over," I instructed, injecting as much firmness into my voice as I could.

"What?" He glanced over at me, startled.

"Just do it."

He manoeuvred the car off the clifftop road, pulling onto the grass verge. Up ahead I could just about make out Alstone Castle, tall and foreboding against the deep grey of the skies. The rain fell softly around us, the sea mists enveloping the car so it felt like we were in our own private bubble.

The road was silent, no other cars passing us at this time of the morning, but at this point, I didn't care either way. As soon as the car came to a stop, I unsnapped my seat belt, and climbed across the centre console to straddle him.

"Snowflake..."

"Shhhh." I hooked my arms around his neck, then leaned forwards to kiss him. He instantly responded, sliding his mouth against mine, and bringing his arms around me, pulling me closer to him.

I lost all sense of time as we kissed. He lowered his head, skimming his teeth down my neck, and I let out a groan, rolling my hips against him as much as I could in the cramped space.

"No," I managed eventually. "This wasn't what I stopped us for."

His eyes met mine, wide and confused. "No?"

A smile spread across my face. "No. I want you. So, so badly. But I wanted to tell you that I'm here for you." I stared at him, his stormy gaze holding mine. "You're amazing. I want to make the most of it tonight."

"I love you so fucking much." He kissed me softly. "Never leave me."

"Never."

Our lips met again, and I couldn't get enough.

This man.

Pulling away from him, fucking reluctantly, I looked into his eyes. "Do you want to talk about it?"

He stared at me, his gaze conflicted.

"No," he said at last, his voice a low sigh. "Not now. Just... Just stay with me?"

Caiden.

"You're never gonna get rid of me." I attacked his mouth with kisses, feeling him respond to me, his body pretty much melting against mine as we kissed, totally wrapped up in one another.

All good things had to come to an end, sadly.

Climbing off him carefully, I fell back into my own seat. Stretching my cramped muscles, I smoothed down my hair, wiping under my eyes as I looked at myself in the mirror, before glancing over at him. His whole demeanour was relaxed, most of the tension in his jaw gone. I smiled to myself.

"How do you know just what I need?" He looked over at me as he turned the car back onto the road. The rain had slowed to a dull drizzle, the sea mist clearing away as we continued the drive to Alstone College.

"Because I know you. Like you know what I need."

He smiled at me, finally, and I decided to try and lighten the atmosphere further. "Plus, you're a man. Your basic needs are food, fucking, and—" I paused. "Fighting? Fun? I'm trying to think of another *f* word."

"Fame? Fencing? Fishing?"

We were both laughing by now. Caiden laughing? It was like the sun coming out. I still wasn't used to seeing this fun, relaxed side of him, but I couldn't get enough of it. I'd do anything to see him happy.

I watched his profile, drinking in the smile curving over his lips, his eyes lit up with amusement as I continued our playful discussion. "Flamin' Hot Cheetos? Actually, no. It can only be a one-word answer."

"One word, huh?" His brow furrowed in thought. "What about...football?"

"Family?" I suggested. "I'm including myself in that."

"Family. Yeah." He smiled at me, before returning his gaze to the road.

As it turned out, we didn't have to worry about running into Joseph Hyde. When we were pulling into the uni car park, my phone buzzed with a text from James.

James: Thought you might want to know that Joseph's taking some time off from his TA position.
Me: Do you know why?
Me: Also, good news. It means I don't have to worry

about Cade murdering him and then me having to dispose of the body.

Caiden snorted, leaning over to read the messages.

James: He didn't say. Can we meet at lunch? I have some info.
Me: Yes! Where?
James: You pick. 12pm?
Me: Meet in the library. Less chance of being overheard.
James: Will your shadow be there?

"Fucking prick," Caiden muttered under his breath.

James: Caiden if you're reading this, that was a JOKE
Me: *laughing emoji* Best not to provoke him
James: I'll try. See you in the library at 12. Top floor?
Me: We'll be there

"Are you okay to meet at twelve?" I undid my seat belt, opening the car door. The rain had stopped, but a cold wind blew into the car, making me shiver.

"I'll be there." We got out of the car, and Caiden came around to my side, pressing me into the door and kissing me. "Stay out of trouble. I mean it."

"I will."

It felt so strange to be back at university, getting back into the swing of lectures and taking notes. So much had happened since the previous semester, that I could barely get my head around it all. The morning dragged as I sat through a business seminar, taking notes on autopilot. I couldn't even say what it was about afterwards. My brain was at least aware enough to get the notes down, but I'd have to make an effort to read through the materials properly later.

"Did you understand any of Professor Mulligan's lecture back there? I found it a real struggle to concentrate." I sighed, turning to look at Cassius as we pushed through the doors that led outside, carried along by the crush of students.

"I've got you covered." His voice reassured me. It may have seemed like he didn't take life seriously, but he took his studies seriously and was one of the top students in the whole university. "You've had a lot on your mind, babe," he continued. "It's no surprise you're struggling to concentrate."

"Yeah, I guess," I sighed.

"I'm always happy to give you extra tutoring, if you know what I mean? A helping hand? Or two?" He nudged me, grinning down at me.

"Cass, please," I groaned. "I'm not sure Cade would be down for that."

"He could join us."

"You ask him, see what he says. I bet you a tenner he gives you a black eye."

"Not the face!" He clasped his hands to his cheeks dramatically, before he laughed. "I'd like to see him take me on." His brows creased. "On second thoughts, maybe not. I reckon I could take him, but he'd fuck me up badly enough in the process."

"Maybe keep your thoughts to yourself, then, huh?"

We walked across the quad towards the library building

and he left me at the doors. "Meet you here at four? If you still want a lift home?"

"Please. See you later." I waved him off. Caiden and Weston were meeting Arlo after university for some male bonding thing, so I couldn't get a lift home with Cade. It had been the only time Arlo's secretary could fit them in, and I was so glad that they were finally starting to build bridges. I hoped with everything in me that Arlo wasn't involved in any of this shit with my mother.

On the top floor of the library, I found a quiet table towards the back corner, next to the windows. The sky outside had darkened again, black clouds rolling in, and the first drops of rain hit the windows. It turned into a downpour, and I watched as students ran between the buildings, trying to shelter from the sudden onslaught of rain.

"Hi." I looked up to see Caiden, his hair all wet, water droplets still clinging to his lashes and running off his body.

"Hi." I licked my lips, staring up at him. "Has anyone ever told you how good you look all wet from the rain?"

He smirked. "Once or twice. You know who else looks good all wet?" He dropped into the seat next to me and leaned close to my ear. "You."

Fuck me. His husky tone, full of promise—

I was suddenly jolted out of my haze of lust by the pointedly loud thump of a leather messenger bag being thrown on the table.

My gaze flew up to meet James' unimpressed face. He sat down opposite me and Caiden, pulling a sleek silver tablet out of his bag. No one said anything, the boys giving each other wary glances.

I rolled my eyes. This wasn't at all awkward.

"Just so you know, I don't like you." Caiden narrowed his eyes at James.

"The feeling's mutual, Cavendish."

I huffed loudly. "Can we not, please?"

"Fine," Caiden muttered, folding his arms and leaning back in his seat, stretching out his legs in front of him and splaying his palms over his thighs. Deceptively casual, but I could feel the tension from his body. I lowered my hand under the table, threading my fingers through his, and he squeezed my hand, some of the tension leaving him.

"Okay. What's going on, James?" I turned back to him, desperate to find out the reason he'd called us here.

"I couldn't get to see Joseph. He's 'gone away,' whatever that means, but I don't think there was anything nefarious in his plans. I did some subtle digging and invited myself round to my uncle's house for dinner." He swallowed nervously. "I hate being caught up in all this shit. I said I needed to get some textbooks that Joseph had promised I could borrow, and his dad didn't even think twice. I went to his room, and I-I turned on his laptop. No idea what I was looking for, but I figured that emails were a good place to start. I found this email in his trash." He slid a tablet across the table to us, and Caiden bent his head close to mine, both of us studying the words on the screen.

FROM: cliff442@gomail.com
TO: j.hyde@alstonecollege.ac.uk
SUBJECT: W H

As agreed, proceed with the plan. Winter and the Cavendish boy need to break up. Do what you must. Payment will be deposited once the plan has been carried out satisfactorily.

I expect regular photographs and updates on Winter to ensure your end of the bargain is being upheld. Drive a wedge between them, at any cost. Further payments will follow.

Regards
C C

We sat in stunned silence. "So...she was the one who wanted us to break up?" I said eventually. "But why? Maybe it was something to do with the deal."

James shrugged. "My guess is as good as yours. I don't know how she got to Joseph, but I do know that he hates you and your family, and with monetary reward involved, he'd jump at the chance." He sighed. "He wasn't always like this. He was...better."

My mind went back to the photo I'd seen, of James, Joseph, and his brother and sister. "Better?" I prompted.

James exchanged glances with Caiden, unspoken words flying between them. Regret, apology, anger—I looked between them, fascinated. "Before the rivalry between our families stepped up, and his brother paid the ultimate price. He was...maybe not a good guy, but he was less..."

"I get what you're saying." I leaned forwards, still grasping Caiden's hand. My aim, now, wherever possible, was total honesty. I was sick of all the lies and secrets. "I saw the photo and I heard about his brother, and his sister being sent away. I know words aren't enough, but for what it's worth, I'm sorry."

He nodded. "Thank you. Our family has never been the same since then. But now isn't the time or place to talk about it."

"Yeah." One word from Caiden, packed with so much

meaning and intent that the subject was immediately dropped.

A thought pushed its way forwards from the back of my mind. "My mother mentioned something at that gathering thing at your dad's house. Something about me dressing more appropriately day-to-day. I bet you anything that this is what she meant. I bet Joseph was sending her photos of me." I frowned. "I haven't noticed anyone following me."

James' lips flattened as he gathered his thoughts. "It probably would've mostly been around the university campus, when he had access to you. He wouldn't risk going near your house."

"And you didn't know anything about this? Because it would've been quite easy for you to feed back information to him, with us being friends."

He shook his head emphatically, his gaze open. "I swear to you, that the extent of my involvement was the kiss. Joseph came to me and said that I had to do this, and when I voiced my concern, he..." He swallowed hard. "He used other methods of persuasion. I never wanted to hurt you, you know that."

Maybe I was being stupid and naive, but I believed him.

"I believe you," Caiden suddenly said, and both James' and my eyes widened in shock. "I think you've proven that you have Winter's best interests at heart, with saving her and all." He growled the words out through gritted teeth, as if they pained him. "If you fuck anything else up..." He let the words trail off, his threat hanging heavy in the air.

"I get that. I won't let Winter down." James glanced at me, his lips turning up at the corners in the barest hint of a smile, before he opened his bag, shoving the tablet back inside. "Thank you for giving me a chance." He took a deep breath, visibly composing himself. "Anyway, I need to get going. Is there anything else you wanted to discuss?"

"Just keep an eye out, and if you hear anything relating to any of this, I'd appreciate it if you let us know."

He nodded, his eyes meeting Caiden's. "I'll have to stay away from you on campus. Can't have anyone thinking we're hanging out and Joseph getting wind of it."

Caiden snorted. "We're not friends, not even fucking close. No danger of that."

"Course not," James muttered, before adding something else under his breath that wasn't very complimentary, if Caiden's hostile glare was anything to go by.

"Thanks, James," I said, squeezing Caiden's hand warningly. "I appreciate everything. And I can't get over the fact you saved my life."

He stood, shrugging off my thanks. "You're welcome. See you around." Then he was gone, leaving me with my brooding boyfriend, my head spinning.

15

caiden

I pulled my R8 into the car park of Skirmish, seeing my dad's car already there. He climbed out at the same time Weston and I did, still in his suit, looking every inch the successful, confident businessman that he was.

"Afternoon. Caiden, Weston," he greeted us. "I have to say, this wasn't exactly what I had in mind when you suggested we get together. I assumed we'd be playing golf."

Golf.

Weston screwed up his face. "No, thanks, Dad. You know I don't like golf."

We headed into the building, the automatic doors opening with a soft whirr as we neared them.

"Do you want to know a secret?" My dad turned to Weston conspiratorially. "I used to hate golf, too. But I'll give you the same advice my father gave me. Some of the most important business deals are made on the golf course, not in the boardroom. Remember that."

Weston eyed him with all the care of someone for whom business didn't even feature on their radar. "I see."

"You have to understand, it's an important part of business. My initial De Witt negotiations were hashed out over a round of golf."

Bored of their discussion, I stalked up to the reception desk, signing us in, leaving them talking together. The blonde girl behind the desk pouted and batted her eyelashes as she tried to flirt with me, but I ignored her advances.

"I'm free, later," she purred, leaning closer to me.

Why wouldn't she get the fucking hint? "Not interested. Try him. He's single." I pointed with my thumb over my shoulder in the direction of my brother, barely sparing her a glance.

"Two of you?" She practically salivated. "Is that your dad?" She continued talking, still not getting the hint that I wasn't interested in making conversation. "He's seriously hot for an older man."

I grunted, not bothering with a reply. Undeterred, she tossed her hair over her shoulder, batting her lashes even harder as my dad and brother joined us at the reception desk.

Weston gave her one of his cheeky grins, then he just had to throw in a wink, and she gripped the edges of the desk, swooning.

"For fuck's sake," I muttered under my breath.

"Everything ready?" My dad, with perfect timing, distracted them both from the sickening flirt-fest that was going on.

She straightened up, professional at last. "Yes. You can go on through, now." She pressed the button under the desk that opened the automatic-locking gate that led into the rest of the building, and we pushed through.

At the gun range we were handed heavy pistols and ear defenders.

"We thought we could have a bit of a friendly competition." West looked over at my dad, who was examining his gun, weighing it in his hand. "Dad?"

He glanced up from the pistol. "What did you have in mind?"

"Loser buys dinner?"

"You do realise who pays money into your bank accounts each month, don't you?" He raised a brow, a small smirk crossing his lips. "Come on, then. Let's see what you've got."

He raised his gun, ready to go. The wall at the bottom of the range lit up, a set of spotlights indicating the prime targets, and the buzzer sounded to indicate our time had begun. No hesitation, he shot in quick succession, coolly and cleanly taking out the targets one by one, before pulling off his ear defenders and turning to me.

Tugging my own ear defenders off my head, I stared at him, open-mouthed. "That's fucking impressive. Since when can you shoot? Other than clay pigeons, I mean."

"Language," he said, but there was no heat in his words. In fact, there was a sparkle in his eye, and he was...was he actually grinning at me? "I have plenty of skills, son. Maybe your old man can teach you a thing or two."

I shook my head, a smile tugging at the corners of my lips. "I think I can beat you," I said confidently. "Maybe I'll be the one teaching you."

"Do your worst." He indicated towards the target.

As it turned out, he beat both me and Weston by a narrow margin. As the lights dimmed, indicating our time was up, I glanced at my watch, surprised to see how much time had passed. This was...unexpected. Really fucking unexpected. We'd spent hours together, and yeah, we'd had a good time. Fuck, I wanted to do it again.

Shaking my head internally at that thought, I followed West and my dad down the corridor towards the exit.

We headed out of the building, the sky outside now dark and dotted with stars, and paused by the cars.

"I had a good time, boys. Speak to my secretary to arrange dinner. Bring Winter. We can have a family meal."

Weston groaned, under his breath, but my dad caught it. A thoughtful expression stole across his face. "Christine goes to play bridge most Wednesday nights. Why don't the three of you come over on a Wednesday, and we can order food?"

"Like we used to do. Before..." Weston said softly, his voice cracking. I stepped closer, placing my hand on his shoulder.

My dad nodded. "It's about time we restarted some of our old family traditions, don't you think?"

I was fucking floored. All I could do was nod in agreement.

"Wait, before you go. I have something for you." My dad unlocked his car, reaching into the back and pulling out a bag that he handed to me. "I believe these belong to your stepsister."

Shocked, I stared into the bag, seeing Winter's shoes and then back at him.

"What?" was all I managed to say, hearing Weston draw in a sharp, surprised intake of breath next to me.

"I'm not as ignorant as you believe, Caiden." With those words, he climbed into his car, wasting no time in starting the engine, before backing out of the space. He left us with a toot of his car horn, leaving us staring after him open-mouthed.

"What the fuck?" Weston eventually said.

"Yeah." What the fuck, indeed.

That wasn't the only shock of the evening.

16

caiden

What did my dad know? I sat in the lounge, sharing a joint with Winter, everyone talking at once. Whatever it was, he hadn't seemed angry or stressed, so I was pretty sure he had no clue about Christine's plotting against him.

"Christine's car's on the move," Weston suddenly said, holding up his phone. "Where's she going this time? It's late."

Yeah, it was fucking late, and there could only be one reason she'd be heading out at this time of night. She wasn't going to slip through my fingers again.

"I'm going after her." I stood, and my girl immediately jumped to her feet.

"I'm coming, too."

"No, you're not." I slid my hands up her arms, gripping her chin and rubbing across her pulse point. "You're staying here. No arguments."

"But—"

I slanted my mouth across hers, kissing her protests away. "No, baby." I softened my voice. "Please."

She stared at me, but resignation entered her gaze when she saw how deadly serious I was. "Fine, but stay safe. Please."

"Always." I kissed the tip of her nose and gently pushed her back down onto the sofa. She picked up the joint and took a long drag, still looking unhappy.

My eyes moved to Cassius, and he nodded, understanding me instantly, moving across to Winter. "I got those notes from Professor Mulligan. Wanna go through them with me?"

Looking between us, her eyes narrowed, and then she shrugged, lifting the joint in the air.

"I didn't understand them the first time, but maybe this will help."

"Doubt it will, babe, but let's give it a go." He fished around in the bag at the side of the sofa, pulling out his laptop. I left them to it, my attention returning to the immediate situation.

"We'll take the bike." Z was already standing by the door. "West, do that shit with the GPS so I can follow her."

Weston nodded, tapping at his phone screen. "Take the drone with you," he suggested. "Just in case. I charged it this morning."

Good idea.

After a quick detour to grab the drone, I was jamming the bike helmet on my head and climbing on the back, and we shot away from the house, hot on Christine's tail. Luck was on our side, for fucking once. She was passing near our house, and we were only around five minutes behind her.

Zayde slung the bike into the turns, and I leaned with him on autopilot, my mind racing, adrenaline pumping through my body. Whatever was going on, it couldn't be good.

We slowed down as we entered Highnam. I knew where she was heading, and so did Z. The Crown and Anchor.

Zayde pulled off the road before the car park, turning the bike into a narrow alleyway, bumping it over the rough cobbled surface. He came to a stop in a small area filled with huge rubbish bins and piles of wooden pallets, easing the bike into a shadowed corner.

"We'll leave the bike here and sneak around the building."

I nodded, climbing off the bike, focused on our mission, alert to our surroundings. We moved stealthily around the side of the hotel, silent shadows in the night.

I halted, hearing the sound of voices.

"They're in the car park," I hissed to Z, inching around the corner, staying low. From our vantage point we had a clear view of the car park, lit in opposite corners by two dim lamps on tall stalks. I saw Christine standing by the car, leaning back in through the window, speaking to someone inside. The other occupant climbed out, and my stomach flipped, nausea filling me. Up until this point I'd been hoping Winter had somehow made a mistake about Allan's involvement, but there was no fucking mistaking it now. He came around the side of the car, his face pulled into an unhappy frown, looking older than I'd ever seen him.

A tall, hulking figure came into view, and I held my breath. Petr.

"We should be recording this." Zayde's voice was almost inaudible, but I heard him perfectly. Lifting my phone, I hit the video button, just in time, as Petr started to speak.

"The boss is concerned. Vasily is gone, and we know nothing about his disappeared captive. He is...how do you say...spooked, and talking of pulling the operation, and switching to a new location."

"No, no, no. That is not acceptable." Christine was agitated, pacing up and down in front of the car. Even for this clandestine meeting, she'd still dressed in heels and some kind of tailored wool coat. "This is mutually beneficial. I offer you unfettered access to the docks every week. Where else will he get that? Does he want to get caught? I know how much this trade means to him, Ivanov."

Petr's jaw set as he stared down at her, towering over her small frame. "He is displeased. You cannot guarantee safety any longer. It is no longer worth the risk to him."

"Don't family connections mean anything to him?"

Family connections? What the fuck?

His lip curled into a sneer. "*Your* family connections? You are no family of the Strelichevos."

She straightened up, her hand whipping out to slap him around the face, and both Zayde and I gasped, immediately trying to silence our reactions. "How dare you speak to me that way? Do not forget, without me, your gang of thugs wouldn't have half of the business you do here in England."

He stared down at her, unfazed. "You greatly overestimate your importance. This arrangement will be terminated, unless you can guarantee our safe passage to and from the docks, and no more disappearances."

Allan stepped closer to him, placing a hand on his arm, and they spoke in hushed tones, in what I assumed was Russian. Both their voices were low, too low to make out, their tones agitated.

"What the fuck do you think is going on?" Z hissed in my ear. I shrugged, shifting on my feet.

As soon as I shifted, I wished I hadn't.

My foot dislodged a small stone, sending it skittering towards a metal roller door, and it reverberated off it, making the loudest fucking sound known to man. All three of their heads snapped up towards the corner we were hiding in.

"Run!" We backed away as fast as we could, then raced around the corner. Zayde started heading in the direction of the bike, but I pulled him in the opposite direction. The bike would be too loud, and there was the danger of either Allan or Christine recognising it if they saw it. Instead, we ran, hugging the hotel wall, rounding the corner and ducking down between two of the cluster of large bins that stood outside the back entrance to the hotel. My heart was fucking pounding as we crouched there, tense and waiting.

Zayde reached down and fished out something from his pocket, and handed it to me.

I felt the cool, smooth metal of the flick knife handle in my palm, and my breathing slowed. We had weapons. We could call for backup if we needed to. Yeah, Petr could be a problem due to his sheer fucking size, but we could take him. Allan wouldn't be a problem, and unless Christine was a secret ninja, she wouldn't be, either. But the best thing to do was to remain hidden and hope to fuck that they didn't find us. Being discovered at this point was the worst outcome.

"We don't reveal ourselves unless we have to."

Zayde nodded in agreement, his eyes glinting in the moonlight. He fucking loved this. Guaranteed, if it had only been Petr here, he would've been tempted to go after him and fuck him up. Which wouldn't help our cause, not while we were still searching for answers.

Soft footsteps sounded, close to our hiding place, and I saw the top of a shaved head come into view. For a big guy, Petr seemed to be able to sneak around really fucking quietly, which wasn't good for us.

I settled into a crouch, ready to spring out and jump him

if he reached us and found us hiding between the bins, when there was a screech that went straight through me, reverberating through my skull.

"What the fuck is that?" Zayde winced, putting his hands over his ears. Petr's head swung towards the noise, and his whole demeanour relaxed. He stepped back, then turned away in the direction he'd come from. There was the sound of scuffling, and as we left our hiding place, I found what I knew I would as soon as I'd heard the sudden noise.

Foxes. Two foxes. Under the glow of the streetlamps, they snapped and pawed at each other, teeth bared, the high-pitched screeches sounding from their jaws as they scuffled.

"Never saw foxes fighting before. Thought they would sound like dogs. But this is fucking ear-splitting torture," Z muttered.

"Yeah. Come on, let's go."

We left the foxes to their fight, creeping back around to our original hiding spot. I'd accidentally left the video recording, so there would be a whole load of the view of the alleyway and the inside of my pocket.

"Urban foxes are disease-ridden vermin that should be eliminated," Christine was saying as we got within earshot, her tone haughty.

"She needs to be fucking eliminated," Zayde whispered to me, and I laughed.

"Yeah, you got that right, mate." We fell silent, listening as Christine ranted on about her dislike for all animals.

Eventually she ran out of steam, and the conversation fucking finally got back onto matters that concerned us.

"I want your assurances, Ivanov. Either you're in, or you're out. There are others who can replace you."

"Others?" He raised a brow in disbelief.

"Yes. Do not overestimate Strelichevo's importance."

"Do not underestimate his importance. You do not want him as an enemy, Christine."

Allan finally spoke with a heavy sigh. "Let me speak to him. As his *dyadya*, he may listen to me." He turned to Christine. "Blood ties cannot be denied. I may only be his uncle, but with his father gone, my words may carry some weight."

I fucking gasped in shock, throwing my hand over my mouth. *Uncle?* My dad's butler was the uncle of some Belarusian crime lord? What the actual fucking fuck?

"Uncle?" I hissed to Z, my voice shaky.

"Shhh. Listen," he cautioned.

Allan gestured to Petr, and they began speaking again in low, rapid-fire Russian. What the fuck was going on? Petr eventually stepped back, and they shook hands. Throughout the whole exchange, Allan had an unhappy frown on his face, worry in his eyes.

"It is done," Petr said to Christine. She nodded, and she and Allan climbed back into the car, the engine starting a moment later. Petr moved to lean against the building, lighting up a smoke and taking a long drag before sending the smoke curling through the air. We stayed, frozen in place, until he finished smoking and disappeared inside after grinding out his cigarette stub under his boot.

"Did you stop recording?" Z pointed at my phone, which was flashing a low-battery alert at me.

"Fuck, I forgot." I turned it off.

We made our way silently back to the bike. Before he dropped the visor on his helmet, Zayde met my eyes. "What do we do, now?"

"We get back, get West to work his magic, then we bring the bitch down."

17

winter

Caiden had been subdued since he'd followed my mother and learned the information about Allan being related to the Strelichevos. From everything I knew, Allan had always been around for him and Weston when they were younger—much more than Arlo had, at least, since he'd always buried himself in his work. The betrayal was hitting him hard; he'd seen Allan as a trusted figure, and now that trust was shattered.

What we couldn't work out was the connection between Allan and my mother. I kept thinking back to the box of letters and the photo of Christine as a child. What did it all mean? At the moment, we had no clue. There was clearly some connection between them, but Petr had specifically mentioned that Christine wasn't related to the Strelichevos.

Still, we were finally building up a dossier of information that we could present to Arlo, once we'd filled in the missing pieces of the puzzle. Well, Weston was. Everything was online, stored securely under layers of encryption. Although I had to take West's word for that, since all that computer stuff went way over my head.

My last thought before I went to sleep, was that I had to get Caiden out of his own head. I'd watched him brooding ever since he'd come back from following Christine, the storm clouds gathering in his eyes, the way he flexed his jaw, tension radiating from him. This whole thing with Allan was fucking with his head. I had to distract him.

Phone in hand, I went in search of him the next morning. Rubbing sleep out of my eyes, I padded down the stairs in a cami and shorts, my hair an attractive bird's nest of tangles. Mornings were not my favourite time of day. As I reached the bottom of the stairs, I noticed the door to the basement gym was ajar, and immediately knew where he'd be.

They were all there.

It was too much to deal with this early in the morning. Bodies glistening with sweat, muscles for days as the four of them punched, pounded, lifted, grunting, the testosterone filling the room and making it hard to breathe. I enjoyed the sight, drinking it in, before I backed quietly away.

I took a quick picture before I left, though. The view was too good not to.

I made myself busy cracking eggs and preparing omelettes, ready for when they'd finished their workout. Eventually they entered the kitchen, one by one, while I was on my second coffee of the day, but still feeling half-asleep.

Cassius' mouth broke into a huge grin when he saw what I was doing, and he sidled up to me. "How did you know I was in the mood for omelettes?"

I laughed. "When are you not in the mood for omelettes? Or some kind of food?"

He winked, grabbing one of the plates from the pile I'd placed on the island and scooping some out of the pan.

"Cass." I glanced over at the others, who were discussing

something to do with their workout, by the sound of it. Caiden's face was still brooding, the light gone from his eyes. "Can you do me a favour?"

He tilted his head, his brow creasing in a frown when he took in my serious expression. "Course I can. What's up?"

I lowered my voice. "I think the stress of everything is getting to Cade. He hasn't been himself since he saw Allan with Christine, and I feel like it's hit him harder than even he originally thought."

"Yeah, I noticed the same. What do you need?"

"Can you maybe take him out somewhere with the boys? Do something to take his mind off everything? Something that he won't associate with anything to do with this whole situation?"

Cassius leaned back against the island. He was silent for all of two seconds before he gave a decisive nod. "Strip club." I gave him an unamused look, and he grinned. "Just kidding. Football." Pulling his phone from his pocket, he raised his voice, waving the phone in the direction of the others. "Boys, I'm booking the uni football pitch. Who's up for a friendly five-a-side match?"

I squeezed his arm in a silent thanks and picked up my own phone from the island, scrolling to my messaging app. I tapped out a quick message to Lena.

Me: Free today? Want to do something?

Her reply was instant.

Lena: Yes *grinning emoji* What? Want to come out on the boat again?

I glanced out of the window, noticing the grey skies and wind whipping through the trees.

Me: Looks a bit windy for that. I could come over if you want to just hang out and chill?
Lena: Wimp! Come over anytime, and bring snacks.
Me: I'll text when I'm on my way. Yes to snacks!

While I'd been texting Lena, the boys had filled their plates with omelettes and were digging into the food, talking about football. All except for Caiden, that is. He was leaning against the island, watching me. I took in his inscrutable expression, the way his mouth was set in a flat line, and I didn't hesitate. Moving over to where he stood, I met his eyes and slid my hands up his arms to hook around the back of his neck.

The tiniest smile flitted across his lips before it was gone, but I'd take it. I pressed a kiss to his mouth, and his arms came around my waist, holding me.

"Cade," I began. "This whole thing... Look, we're gonna get through this, okay? I'm not trying to force you to talk about it, and I won't. But I'm not going to let you forget that we're in this together, and we *will* find out what the fuck is going on and sort it. You're a fucking Cavendish—you own this town. There's no way anyone else is taking that from you."

This time he smiled properly. "Fuck, I love you." His arms tightened around me as he blew out a harsh breath. "This whole Allan thing is messing with my head."

I kissed him before he could say any more. "I know. Eat, go play football and take your mind off everything."

Moving aside, I picked up his plate and handed it to him.

"What are you gonna be doing while I'm out? I don't like leaving you alone, especially not with all this shit happening." He frowned as he took the plate from me.

"I'm going to pay a visit to Lena."

Reclined on Lena's bed, I tore open the bag of Skittles, grabbing a handful and throwing them into my mouth. Shuffling into a more comfortable position, I watched Lena, busy arranging the huge computer monitor on her desk so we could view it from the bed and binge-watch Netflix. "Thanks for inviting me over. I've been meaning to speak to you for a while."

She nodded, before grabbing a remote from her desk and throwing herself on the bed next to me. "I've been expecting it. Let's get the show started, then you can ask me what you want to know." She scrolled through the list of options, and as the episode began playing, she spoke again, her eyes on the screen. "This is about James, right?"

Good. She wasn't going to avoid the subject. I'd been meaning to get her alone to speak to her about it ever since James' confession that he'd saved me, but I wasn't sure if she'd try to hide the truth from me again. Not only that, but I figured that without the boys around, she'd be more likely to talk, and I'd hardly been away from them since the party.

"Yeah. He told me what he did, about him rescuing me at the docks. And...you." She twisted to face me, and I met her eyes. "Why didn't you say anything? Why did you act like you didn't know what had happened to me?"

"I couldn't." She stared down at her hands, collecting her thoughts, before raising her gaze to meet mine again. "This whole thing is so fucking complicated. I couldn't say anything without telling you that James was involved, and he was adamant that he didn't want you to know."

"Why, though?"

She shrugged. "You know. He wanted to keep it quiet. All the shit with him kissing you..." Trailing off, she stared at me. "Do you know how bad he felt, doing that? Don't get me wrong, we're not like BFFs or anything, and we don't tell each other much more than the necessary shit, but he was so... I dunno how to describe it exactly. Guilty, maybe?"

I sighed. "Yeah. Well, that's all in the past now. It still doesn't explain why you didn't tell me."

"He asked me not to say anything. You have to understand—he feels caught in the middle. He's not friends with the Four, he fucked you over, he has all this pressure from his cousin...and no, I don't know what's going on there. All I know is, he got me out of a really bad situation when I was younger, and I trust him. He's been looking into this dog fighting stuff with me...both of us have a personal interest in it. Anyway, he asked me not to say anything, and I had to respect that. I couldn't say anything without implicating him, you know?"

"Yeah. I guess so." I thought back through everything James had told me. What kind of pressure must he be under, to feel so torn?

"Another thing." Lena chewed her lip. "Uh, so I turned up at the docks just when James was putting you into his car. You looked...you were so... It scared me, yeah?"

I stared at her, before giving her a wry smile. "Yeah. I scared myself, the first time I looked in a mirror. I get it, I do. I just can't help feeling that if only everyone had been a bit better at communicating, we might have been able to piece everything together by now."

She nodded, picking up a handful of Skittles, lining

them up on her palm. I scrutinised her face closely, seeing the conflict she wasn't bothering to hide. What could I say? "It's hard. We only have our own perception of a situation, and we can only make our decisions based on our own experiences. I want you to know that I don't blame you for anything, or hold anything against you. James, too, for that matter."

"Good. And thank you."

"Have you spoken to Cassius yet? I haven't said anything —I was giving you a chance to."

She groaned. "No. I'm not looking forward to that conversation."

"You have to tell him, though. Soon," I warned her gently.

"I know, and I will."

We lapsed into silence, both watching as the group of girls on screen searched for answers. Ugh. I needed to watch something else. Something that didn't involve people being just as frustrated as I was.

A thought suddenly occurred to me. "The ID card you took from the security guy... West mentioned that he only saw it log in and out that one time when James rescued me, plus the time we found you down at the docks. How come there are no other login records from that card?"

She sat bolt upright. "The card? Um. My boss... I guess we forgot to say that the record needed to be erased after we found you. You have to understand, we were panicking. Finding you was way beyond anything we'd imagined or were equipped for. The whole thing really shook me up. Shook us up."

I thought it through. "Yeah. I guess that makes sense." Rolling onto my side, I grabbed the bag of tortilla chips sitting on the table next to the bed. "Let's forget all that shit for now, and you can tell me what's going on between you and West."

"*What*?" she screeched. "I don't have time for boys. Can we just watch Netflix? I didn't invite you here for an interrogation."

Her face made me collapse back against the headboard of the bed, laughing until I was breathless. "Yeah. Sounds good to me," I said, when I finally managed to compose myself. "No more talk about subjects you're determined to avoid."

The sky had grown dark outside when my phone buzzed with a message. I'd heard from Cade earlier, and he'd said the boys had finished football and were going for drinks with the other guys they'd been playing the game with, but nothing since.

I swiped the screen to see Zayde's name appear, and I sucked in a breath.

Zayde: You done? Cade needs you.

My stomach flipped.

Me: What do you mean by that? Is he OK?
Zayde: Yeah he's OK but think you should get him home.
Me: On my way. Where?
Zayde: Student Union bar. Call me when you're here and I'll come out and meet you.
Me: OK see you soon

I stood, brushing the crumbs off me, wincing. Tortilla chips were so bloody scratchy.

"You're leaving?" Lena looked over at me, her expression knowing.

"Yeah. Cade... He needs me." I shrugged, hoping she'd understand. "I can't—"

"I get it, Winter. It's all good. No need to explain." She glanced at her phone. "We've spent hours together, anyway. Not that I'm complaining, I've had a great time." A smile lit up her face. "We need to do this again."

"We will." I returned her smile. "Call or text me anytime, okay?"

Outside the Student Union building, I tapped out a quick message to Zayde to say I'd arrived.

He turned up a few moments later, indicating for me to follow him inside. As we descended the stairs, pushing against the crush of students ascending, he grabbed hold of my hand, which was unexpected, but reassuring, his cool grip anchoring me.

As we entered the doors to the bar, someone stumbled into me, and I knocked into Zayde, who used his other arm to steady me, pulling me against him protectively.

"You've moved on quickly," the girl slurred, staring pointedly at our joined hands, taking in the way Zayde was gripping onto my arm. I looked into her eyes and groaned aloud. Portia. Great.

"Get some fresh air, and stop making a fool out of yourself," Zayde clipped out, steering me around her and into the bar. He leaned closer to me, raising his voice to be heard over the music. "Get him home if you can. He's been drinking, but I've been keeping an eye on him. I don't want him getting wasted and doing anything he'll regret later. Last year he ended up getting us kicked out of a pub for trashing the place."

I glanced up at him and nodded once, letting him lead me in the direction of the pool tables, where he let go of my hand.

The crowds melted away, and I saw Caiden.

Thankfully, he didn't seem to be drunk, not at first glance, at least. He was leaning against the wall, his eyes lowered, a beer in hand. My gaze raked over him, taking in his bottle-green T-shirt, ripped jeans, and his raven hair that was all over the place on his head. I came to a standstill, just watching as his tattooed arm brought his beer to his lips, and he tipped it up, his throat working as he swallowed.

I dug my nails into my palms, trying to stay focused on the reason I was here, and not how good he looked. How was he mine? Shaking the thoughts from my head, I moved closer, past Cassius and Weston, who both looked worse for wear, it had to be said. I made a mental note not to get up early in the morning—I did *not* want to be dealing with their hangovers.

Coming to a stop in front of my boyfriend, I plucked the bottle from his grip, and swallowed his sound of protest with a kiss. He melted into me, sliding his tongue against mine, before he drew back.

"I fucking missed you." His words were a little slurred, but he wasn't drunk, as far as I could tell. Maybe a bit tipsy, yeah, but he was aware enough to know what he was doing.

"How was football?" I kept the conversation light to begin with, while I tried to gauge his mood.

The corners of his lips tipped up in a tiny smile. "Good."

My eyes met his, and I watched his pupils dilate as he looked down at me. "Are you okay?" Stupid question.

He tugged me into his arms, leaning his head against mine. "I am now. Didn't realise how all this shit would affect me."

I held on to him as tightly as I could. "I know."

Before I could say anything else, he gave a heavy sigh. "Today helped. Kept thinking of what you said to me this morning. I'm not gonna let her win, and I'm gonna try my fucking hardest to get answers for you; for your dad."

"Cade." I drew back and looked into his eyes, seeing the fire I loved simmering in them again. "You wanna come home with me?"

"Yeah."

Breathing out a sigh of relief, thankful that he'd been in agreement, I took his hand and led him out of the bar.

18

winter

Time to visit Arlo, and maybe get some answers. Ever since Caiden had returned with my shoes, and even before that, when I'd read the note Arlo had left me with my gift, plus the gift itself, I'd been trying to guess how much he actually knew.

As we stood, waiting for the door to open, I mentally prepared myself to face Allan, knowing that he was working with my mother. Caiden and Weston were both on edge, too.

The door swung open, but it wasn't Allan who was behind it.

"Evening." Arlo smiled at the surprise on our faces.

"Since when do you open the door?" Weston said what we were all thinking, as we followed him inside.

"I am capable of opening a door, Weston." His dry tone made me laugh, but I covered it with a fake cough.

"I know that, but you have staff to do that for you," Weston countered, as we headed down the hallway and stopped outside a door I'd never noticed before.

"I gave the staff the night off." Arlo took a small, ornate

key from his pocket and twisted it in the lock. As he turned the door handle, I heard both Caiden and Weston's identical shocked intakes of breath, and I frowned. What was behind the door?

I looked around me with interest as we entered the small room. Small for Arlo's house, at least. It was cosy, all dark wood panelling and thick, soft carpet on the floor, with lamps providing soft light, and a group of squashy sofas and armchairs clustered around a large coffee table. A huge bookcase covered one wall, overflowing with hardback books.

"I haven't been in here since..." Weston's voice trailed off, and I knew what was left unsaid.

Arlo crossed to a large cupboard next to the window. "I thought, since we're resurrecting old traditions, we should have the food in here. Like we used to." He crouched, opening the sliding door, and pulled out a slim rectangular box. "Remember this?"

"My old Monopoly set. I didn't realise you still had it." Caiden's voice was quiet. He stepped closer to me, and I squeezed his hand, letting him know I was there for him.

"I have all your old games. There's more in the attic, too."

Both boys fell silent, and I suddenly felt like an intruder in a private family moment. "Bathroom," I whispered, slipping out of the room and heading down the hallway to give them a moment of privacy. I paced up and down, trying to gauge how much time to give them, knowing that Caiden would come looking for me if I stayed away from him too long.

As I re-entered the room, the three of them were seated, Arlo and Weston deep in conversation, a takeaway app open on the tablet that rested on the coffee table.

Caiden indicated the space next to him on the sofa with a tilt of his head. I sank down next to him, and he leaned over, brushing a strand of hair away from my face. Turning to him with a smile, I leaned forwards to press a soft kiss to his lips.

The sound of a throat pointedly clearing made me realise where we were. Caiden and I jumped apart to see Arlo staring at us and Weston cringing next to him.

Fuck.

"Do either of you have something to tell me?"

"Ah…" Caiden groaned, scrubbing his hand across his face. "Oh, fuck it," he muttered, before he reached over to grasp my hand and met Arlo's eyes.

Okay, we were doing this.

"I'm in love with Winter." His voice rang out, clear and sure, and I almost fell off the sofa in shock. I didn't know what I'd been expecting him to say, but a declaration of love hadn't been it.

"I see." Arlo took off his reading glasses, taking his time folding them and placing them on the coffee table. He finally looked at us both, his inscrutable gaze boring into me, and I tried not to fidget in my seat. "Do you feel the same way?"

"Uh…yes?" I croaked, mentally slapping myself when my words came out sounding like a question. I took a deep breath and tried again. "Yes, I do. I love your son."

He was silent for a long while, eyeing us both, his face giving nothing away. Then he sat back. "Okay."

"Okay? That's it?" Caiden stared at him in disbelief.

He sighed. "I won't tell you that it fills me with joy. Not the two of you together—of all the people that you could have fallen in love with, Caiden, Winter is head and shoulders above the others." I blushed at his praise. "If only you weren't stepsiblings. There are people that would seek to drive a wedge between you."

"I—" Caiden began, but Arlo held up his hand.

"Let me finish, son. I had an inkling that something has been happening between the two of you for a while now. More than an inkling, in fact. The first time you were here, Winter, I knew that there was something there between you."

Really? I thought back to that first awful meal, where Caiden had insulted me and stormed out of the house. Maybe there really was a thin line between love and hate.

Arlo was still speaking, and I came back to the conversation to hear him saying, "There were one or two other incidents, but I hadn't realised it was anything more than a minor infatuation. Caiden...well, you haven't been known to have serious relationships. It's...surprising. But I'm happy for you both." He gave me a smile. "If you could keep this quiet until the deal has gone through, I would appreciate it."

"We already are." Caiden's voice was firm and reassuring, as he caressed the palm of my hand with his thumb. "We've been careful."

"Does anyone else know?"

"Our friends. Some of the people at university, but they wouldn't say anything. This deal is important to a lot of people, not just us."

"Then we'll say no more." He picked up his reading glasses, placing them back on his face, and pushed the tablet towards us, the conversation over. "Choose whatever you want to eat on the app, and we'll order it."

There was silence for a moment as we scrolled through the menu on the tablet.

"By the way, it's best that you keep this quiet around

your mother. I'm assuming she doesn't know?" Arlo watched me carefully from behind his glasses.

I shook my head, although it wasn't true. She had known, but I couldn't tell him about her paying Joseph to split us up. Not yet. Not until we had more evidence of everything.

Food eaten, I was comfortably curled up on the sofa listening to the others reminisce about a time they'd had a massive snowball fight in the castle ruins as kids. I couldn't even imagine Arlo doing anything like that, but I guessed he hadn't always been like this. He was changing, I could see it. I highly doubted that an evening like this would have happened even a few months ago. Caiden seemed to be willing to give him a chance, and that was all I could ask for.

I debated whether to mention the whole thing about Arlo finding my shoes, and the note he'd given me, but in the end my curiosity won out.

"Arlo?"

"What is it, dear?"

"My shoes," I began, not exactly sure how to word this.

"Ah, yes. I wondered when you would mention those. Funny story. Imagine my surprise when I was in my office, the morning after our gathering, and one of my security team brought them to me when he was doing his morning patrol." His eyes glinted with amusement as he regarded me. "At first, I wondered if a couple of guests had wandered off to...well, you know. It wouldn't be the first time. I reviewed the security footage, and what did I see? You, sneaking around the side of my house, barefoot, then being tackled to the ground by your friend Zayde and driving away."

Oh fuck. How were we going to explain our way out of this one? Thank goodness he hadn't seen me climbing out of Allan's window. There was no way I'd have been able to come up with a believable excuse. I was so glad there had been no cameras pointed at Allan's room, although I guessed they would be mostly facing away from the house, anyway.

"Would you like to tell me what you were doing?"

I shook my head. "I can't. Not yet." I took a deep breath. "But I will. I just need..."

"Time," Caiden finished for me. "Dad, there are things we need to make you aware of. But we can't yet. Not until we know for sure."

Arlo looked intrigued, and he nodded. "Okay. I trust you both. Now, speaking of security footage..." A smirk crossed his face. "This relates to my earlier comment about knowing there was, or had been, something between the two of you."

Oh no. What now?

He continued. "I had some interesting footage to erase. I keep a couple of discreet cameras in my office, here, not that I expect to need them. They're really only there as a precaution—they don't pick up sound or anything."

Next to me, Caiden groaned, already knowing what he was about to say. "We didn't mean for that to happen."

"What to happen?" Weston stared at him.

"Uh. I kissed Winter in Dad's office, when we came for that meal. Y'know, when I arranged to have her car resprayed."

"Why didn't I know this?" He frowned.

"Do I want all the details of your love life? You don't need to know all the details of mine."

"Sorry, Arlo." My face heated for the second time

tonight. Ugh, it was so awkward. We'd basically attacked each other in Arlo's office, and the thought he'd seen that...

He waved a hand. "All taken care of. Now, while we're clearing the air, is there anything else you want to talk about?"

I didn't want to bring up the note and gift he'd given me, not yet. To be completely honest, I was feeling so awkward about him finding my shoes and knowing I'd been in his private office kissing Caiden that I didn't want to draw any more attention to myself.

I hesitated for a moment. No. I needed to know why. "Um, I do have one question." I bit my lip as Arlo gave me his full attention. "It's about my birthday present. I just... why that gift, and the note?" He looked at me thoughtfully. "Don't get me wrong, I'm very grateful and I appreciate it—I guess I just wondered why you'd choose that."

"It's nothing sinister. You, ah, come across as a headstrong young woman. Not that there's anything wrong with that; it's an admirable trait in fact," he hurried to add. "I couldn't help but feel that your—" He coughed. "—way of handling things had the potential to land you in hot water. I spoke to one of my security team about discreet self-defence items suitable for carrying around day-to-day, and he suggested the kubotan. It was merely something I thought would be helpful to have as a precaution, although, of course, I'm hopeful that you would never need to use it."

"Oh. Well, thanks."

A small smile played across his lips, as he repeated the words he'd written on the gift note. "Stay safe."

"I'll try." I shrugged, pulling a face, and he chuckled.

"That's all I can ask. Now, was that all, or shall we play one of these games?"

"Actually, Dad, there's something I need to talk to you

about. In private." Caiden straightened up next to me. Was this about his mum? I was guessing so, if he didn't want Weston to be a part of it.

Weston raised a brow, and I knew it was up to me to distract him as Arlo nodded and stood, murmuring, "Let's go to my office."

"West? You wanna play a game of cards?"

caiden

I followed my dad into his office and closed the door behind us. He took a seat at his desk and indicated towards the chair that sat perpendicular to it. Leaning on his desk, he steepled his fingers, assessing me with his gaze. "What is it?"

This was going to be so fucking awkward. "I want to tell Weston the truth about Mum's death."

He reared back in shock, clearly not expecting me to say those words.

"W-why?" he stammered. He was never flustered, and it unnerved me.

"Because he deserves to know the truth. Because I'm fucking sick of carrying around this huge secret all the time. It's killing me. All this fucking guilt? I feel like I'm drowning."

At my admission, his gaze cleared. "Caiden? You know you don't have anything to feel guilty about. Your mother... she wasn't well. None of this is your fault. You couldn't have stopped it happening. She was determined." He dropped his head into his hands, his voice coming out muffled. "I've been a terrible father, haven't I? I should never have—" He cut himself off and raised his remorseful gaze to mine.

"Yeah." Fuck it, I was going to be honest. If there's one thing I'd learned from my girlfriend, it was that honesty was usually the best policy. "I hated you, you know. When you started sneaking around with Christine. Mum got worse and worse, and you were never there. *She* was here, making excuses to come over, taunting Mum and throwing your affair in her face."

"She what?" he whispered hoarsely, his face creasing with anguish. "Why didn't you say anything?"

"Would you have listened?"

He closed his eyes, pinching his brow. "No, probably not. I was...blinded. I have no excuses, Caiden. Your mother and I weren't getting along. She was ill, and although I paid for the best psychiatrists, nothing seemed to help her. Christine came along and swept me off my feet. She was beautiful, and full of life, and told me everything I wanted and needed to hear."

"You abandoned Mum when she needed you most! Abandoned us!" I roared, slamming my hand down on his desk. Fuck, that hurt.

He flinched. "I know. If I could take it all back I would. I did everything wrong. I know I did." His voice grew quieter, his expression defeated. "I know you'll never forgive me. But I hope we can rebuild our relationship. I'm trying, here, Caiden, I really am. What can I do to make it up to you?"

My anger dulled to a simmer as I took in the expression on his face. Yeah, he'd done a lot of things wrong. Saying you could forgive someone might be easy, but in reality, to actually forgive? That was one of the hardest fucking things to do. I honestly didn't know if I could forgive him for all of it, but I *did* know that I wanted to move past it. I wanted to mend our relationship, and he *was* trying. The biggest workaholic I knew was making time for his sons, and that was huge for him.

"Leave Christine, for a start," I muttered.

"What was that?"

"You heard me."

He sighed heavily. "My relationship with Christine isn't up for discussion. However, in the interests of transparency between us, I will tell you this. I have reason to believe that she may be involved with someone else. She's...she's been acting strangely. There's a strain on our relationship that was never there before." He picked up a fountain pen from his desk and started spinning it in his hands, an internal debate playing across his face. "I can't deny...the way she speaks to you boys, particularly you... I should never have allowed things to get so bad."

"Yeah."

"I don't have any answers for you, Caiden. All I can say is that I'm re-evaluating things." He placed the pen back on the desk, and it rolled towards me. I grabbed it before it could roll off the edge of the table.

"Okay. That's good, I guess." Fuck, I wanted to tell him what was going on with Christine. He was so off track thinking she was having an affair. "I don't think all is as it seems. I don't trust her, Dad. I think she's hiding something. Do you trust her with Alstone Holdings?"

I probably shouldn't have said that, but I needed to warn him, somehow.

He frowned at me. "Let's not talk business, now. Back to the reason we're here. If you want to tell Weston, if it will help ease some of the unwarranted guilt you feel, then go ahead. I want you to consider it carefully, and to be prepared for the fallout. Weston...well, we've always tried to shield him from the worst aspects of life. He's not like you."

"What's that supposed to mean?"

"You're..." He paused. "Yes, you haven't always handled things in the best way, but when I look at you, do you know what I see?"

I shook my head, not trusting myself to speak.

"I see a man that will one day become a powerful leader. A man I'm proud to call my son."

"Uh, thanks," I managed to croak, shocked by his words. Was that really how he saw me?

"Now, I don't know about you, but I need a whiskey after this conversation." He stood, rounding his desk and looking expectantly at me.

Fuck, yes. "Bring the bottle."

19

caiden

Tray in hand, I scanned the cafeteria for my boys. Looked like I was the first to arrive. I stalked over to the table by the window that we always sat at. "Sorry, mate. You need to move," I told the guy sitting there, and he jumped up, gathering his tray and slinking off to another table. Yeah, I was a dick sometimes, but if I didn't assert my control, then others would try to take my place, and I wasn't about to let that happen. "Thanks," I belatedly threw out after him, hearing my girlfriend's voice in my head, berating me, and he responded with an angry huff, sliding into his new seat.

I tried.

Eventually, Cassius walked in with Zayde and joined me at the table.

"This burger is fucking gross," Cassius complained, pieces of said burger falling out of his mouth as he spoke.

"Do you mind? I don't wanna see your half-chewed food, thanks." I pulled a face at him, and just because he was Cassius, he opened his mouth even wider.

"C-Cassius? Zayde?" Cassius immediately closed his

mouth, as a girl I'd never seen before stood at the edge of our table, swallowing nervously as she took us in. She held a pile of books in her arms, and...was that a pencil tucked behind her ear? Did people even do that in real life?

Shaking my head, I turned my attention to my phone as she mumbled something to them about an assignment they were partnered on or some shit, scrolling down to my text conversation with my girl.

Me: Where are you?

I saw the three dots appear straight away, and I smiled, waiting for her reply.

Snowflake: On my way. Waiting for Weston. Kinslee's coming too. Is there space for her?

I looked around the table. Only two seats were available, since some fucker had taken the others.

Me: Yeah, but you'll have to sit on me
Snowflake: I think I can deal with that *kissing emoji*

I threw my phone on the table and turned to my boys. The random girl had disappeared, and we fell into an easy discussion about football. I was so engrossed I didn't even notice Weston sliding into the chair next to mine until he was already sitting.

"Alright, bro?" He cocked his head at me.

"Yeah, you? Where's Winter?"

He nodded in the direction of the food counter. "There."

I forgot about him as my girl appeared in my eyeline,

and I raised my head to watch her strolling over, looking sexy as fuck in the tightest jeans known to man and a thin knitted blue jumper that showcased her tiny waist and perfect tits. Her hair was up, swinging in a long ponytail, and I had a sudden vision of gripping that ponytail and bending her over the table while I fucked her from behind.

I adjusted my dick, trying to stop my wayward thoughts. Getting a boner with my brother sitting next to me, in a crowded cafeteria full of students, wasn't ideal.

"Hi." Winter smiled at me as she came to a stop next to my chair and placed her tray on the table, before her face fell. "I just thought, I can't sit with you because people might see."

"Fuck them. Hyde isn't here, Granville won't say anything if he knows what's good for him, and if anyone else says anything, I'll make sure they regret it." I tugged her down onto my lap. "You're mine, baby, and I want you here with me." I trailed my nose down her neck, her skin soft against mine. "I think Dad's making way too big a deal out of the whole thing. I doubt anyone here even cares."

She twisted open the cap on her bottle of water. "Yeah, you're right." Glancing around us, her voice lowered. "Actually, you might be wrong about that. If looks could kill, I'd be dead."

I snorted. "Yeah. I can't help being a catch. You know all I see is you."

"I know." I could hear the smile in her voice.

"Anyway, you're not the only one getting jealous looks. Look at the guys." I moved my mouth to her ear, and she shivered. "They're all wishing they were me. Wishing they got to have you sitting on them. Knowing that later you'll be riding my dick, while they go home to their sad little lives."

"Caiden!" She pretended like she was outraged, but she couldn't stop the smile spreading across her gorgeous face.

I shrugged. "Just saying it like I see it. It's all true."

She shook her head. "I'm just gonna eat my food while you sit there and let your head grow even bigger."

I laughed and picked up my drink. She fell into an easy conversation with Kinslee, and I sat back, holding her with one hand, sliding my fingers under her clothes to caress the soft skin of her stomach.

"Cade. I need to talk to you." Weston leaned over, his voice low. He slid his phone over to me, and I stared at the screen.

From: roland@hydeconsultings.co.uk
To: j.hyde@alstonecollege.ac.uk
Subject: FW: Agenda

Joseph

Please see note re meeting. You are expected to attend.

ORIGINAL MESSAGE

From: cliff442@gomail.com
To: unknown recipients
Subject: Agenda

Dear All

Payments made as agreed. Moving ahead with the final stage of the plan. The contract is due to be signed in 11 days. Proceed as agreed, and prepare to meet in 10 days to discuss any last-minute arrangements: Alstone Castle 9pm.

CC

Talk about a fucking breakthrough. This could be the chance we needed.

I slid the phone in front of Winter. "Read this," I murmured in her ear, before turning my attention to my brother. "Where did you get this?"

"Ever since you told me about James' involvement, I've been working on getting into the Hydes' emails. I hadn't had any luck getting into his dad's, but Joseph uses his university email for everything, from what I can tell. It was easy enough to get into the uni email system, especially since I got a job."

"A job? What do you need a job for?"

"It's to add to my skills. I'm doing a couple of afternoons doing IT support here, and just like that, I now have clearance to access everyone here without even having to hack." He gave me a smug smile.

"I'm impressed. Good thinking." I grinned at him. "This is great. Anything else?" I leaned even closer, mouthing the words so Winter didn't hear them. *Did you check Granville's?*

He nodded. "He's clean. Everything there's uni-related. This is the other stuff I have from Joseph—he must've deleted most of the emails, but the few I've found give us more of an insight." He took his phone from Winter, who had frozen on my lap.

She turned her body as he took the phone, lining up her mouth with my ear and sitting sideways on me. "We need to do something. This could be our chance."

I nodded. There was only one fucking chance, and we had to take it. A thought suddenly occurred to me, and I opened my messaging app to the chat thread between me, my dad, and my brother. "Look at the date on that message. The deal between the De Witts and Alstone Holdings is due to be signed the day after this meeting Christine's having."

"Oh, fuck," she breathed. "This must be what my mother meant in the email when she mentioned a contract being signed. We *have* to be there."

"I know. We'll cause a distraction. I want everyone prepared. You need to train."

"Ooh, like ninja skills?" She kicked her leg out in front of her, accidentally kicking Weston's chair, and he gave her a dirty look while I laughed.

"Yeah, just like that, baby."

"I don't know what we're going to do, but we need to plan everything. It's time we put the rest of this puzzle together so we can get all the evidence and take it to your dad."

"Here." Weston interrupted our conversation again, handing Winter his phone. "These are the other emails. Just evidence that he was keeping tabs on you, Winter. Forwarding stuff to your mother."

She scrolled through, her face darkening. "I can't believe he actually sent these photos to my mother." There were only a few emails, but attached to each were pictures of my girl around the campus, taken without her knowledge. He'd also sent her details on Winter's assignment grades, the fucker.

Enough.

Fucking *enough*. Our time was running short, and I needed to step up.

I raised my voice. "House meeting tonight."

Everyone stopped what they were doing and looked at me.

"Does that include me?" Kinslee broke the sudden silence.

"Yeah. Lena, too, if you can get hold of her, Cass."

He nodded. "Guess we have to start speaking to each other again sometime."

"She giving you trouble?" I eyed him curiously.

"Nah, we had a bit of a falling-out over her bad decisions. She knows how I feel about her getting involved in all that shit down at the docks, but she can't see that she's been putting herself in danger." He groaned. "Why are women so fucking stubborn?"

Winter and Kinslee both gave him identical unimpressed looks, and I smirked at him. "Best not to even go there, mate."

He sat back, muttering to himself, and Winter twisted around to face me fully.

"What about James?" she asked softly, her blue eyes staring into mine. As if I could deny her anything.

"Fuck," I muttered reluctantly. "Give me his number."

She gave me a bright smile and kissed my cheek. "Coming right up."

I tapped out a text to Granville. *Fucking Granville.*

Me: Time to pick a side. Are you with us or against us?
Granville: Who's this?
Me: Who do you fucking think it is?
Granville: Did Winter give you my number?
Me: Irrelevant. One more time Granville. Are you with us or against us?
Granville: What's going on? I need more info

I growled, already irritated. "West? Forward me a screenshot of that email, will ya?"

I waited impatiently as he tapped at his phone, and finally the new message alert appeared on my screen. I saved the screenshot and sent it to Granville, then sat back to wait for his reply. Almost ten fucking minutes passed before he finally decided to respond.

Granville: I'm assuming you have a plan?
Me: OFC I have a plan
Granville: Good. Are you going to catch me up on everything I need to know?

I blew out a frustrated breath. "Are you sure we can trust him?"

My girl nodded, reading the messages I was exchanging with Granville. "I'm sure we can."

"Okay."

Me: Yes.
Granville: I'm in.
Me: There's no going back.
Granville: I know.
Me: If you're with us, don't fuck it up. No second chances.
Granville: *eyeroll emoji*

I growled, again. "Why does he have to be such an irritating fucker?"

Winter laughed, then nuzzled into my neck, scraping her nails lightly across the back of my neck, and my irritation disappeared just like that. Mostly. "Need some stress relief?" she suggested, and kissed my jaw.

"Yes, I fucking do."

"I'll sort you out. After the house meeting," she promised, her tone low and suggestive.

"You'd better. I'm gonna need a lot of stress relief after dealing with Granville."

She pulled back to look at me and rolled her eyes. Between her and fucking Granville, there was way too much eye rolling directed at me. "Play nice," she warned. "Then I'll reward you."

I lunged forward, pulling her to me and sinking my teeth into her neck. She shrieked, laughing, making me laugh in turn.

"Can you two give it a fucking rest?" Zayde muttered.

"Sorry, mate."

My phone buzzed again as I released Winter, and I saw yet another message from Granville.

Granville: What's the plan?
Me: Be at my house at 7pm. We'll discuss it then.
Granville: I'll be there

I threw my phone down, sick of seeing his name on my screen. Still, I'd rather put up with it than have him sending messages to my girl. The thought made my arms tighten around her. "Has Granville been sending you messages?"

She stared at me. "Why?"

"I don't like it."

"Of course you don't." She rolled her eyes again. "So fucking possessive," she muttered, but then she took in the expression on my face. "I'm not hiding anything from you, Cade."

"Yeah, I know." I did know, just still fucking disliked the guy.

Still, he was single, and me? Winter owned my fucking heart, and I was sure I owned hers. So maybe it was time to leave the past in the past.

For now, at least.

"I love you." She kissed me. "Can we talk about something else?" I nodded, and she raised her head, focusing on Cassius. "Operation Snowflake begins tonight."

He grinned widely, showing me all his teeth. Better than the mouthful of food he showed me earlier. "Fuck, yes. Operation BCD you mean, though."

"BCD? What's that supposed to mean?" Winter stared at him.

"Bring Christine Down." He winked.

"That doesn't exactly roll off the tongue, mate," Weston interjected.

"Yes, it does. It's fucking awesome."

"Operation Andromeda," I suggested, and Cassius gave me a surprised, pleased smile.

"Finally giving your opinion on the code name thing, are ya mate?"

"I can't let you fuckers come up with a shit name."

"I hope I'm not one of the 'fuckers' you're talking about." Winter pretended to be mad, giving me a weak punch in the arm.

"We need to work on your punching skills." I grinned at her.

She returned my grin. "We need to work on your manners."

"Excuse me? My manners are fucking fine."

"Maybe if you didn't use the word 'fuck' in every sentence."

"What? I like the word."

"I'd never be able to tell."

"Just for that, I'm gonna fuck the rudeness out of your mouth later."

"Behave, or I'll bite."

"That's a low blow, baby."

"As much fun as it is watching your verbal foreplay, we need to break this up. We've got a seminar starting in five." Zayde's dry tone cut through our banter, as he stood, cocking his head at me. I glanced at my watch.

"Shit, I'm gonna be late. See you back at the house, later." I lifted Winter off me, waiting until she sat back down in my vacated chair before I placed a quick kiss on the top of her head. Swinging my bag over my shoulder, I sauntered out of the cafeteria with Z, feeling her eyes on me every step of the way.

The atmosphere in the kitchen was tense. Everyone was here, sitting around the kitchen table, looking like they'd rather be anywhere else. In summary, it was awkward as fuck.

I looked across the table and caught Cassius' eye. I could practically see the thoughts flying through his head; then his expression cleared and he nodded once, decisively. He tapped on his phone, and then he sat back, waiting. Seconds later, the opening tune of "Unstoppable" by The Score blasted out of the speakers that were discreetly placed around the room.

"Operation Andromeda begins now!" he shouted, banging his fist on the desk dramatically, then he winked at Winter. *For you,* he mouthed to her, before he shot me a huge grin.

Just like that, the tension in the room dissipated. My girl

laughed and sang along, and even Granville was smiling, looking marginally more relaxed than he had been when he turned up with Lena in tow. Not that he should be.

I let the music blare from the speakers for a couple of minutes, before asking Cass to turn it down enough to hear myself think. Grabbing the large pad of paper that was sitting in front of me, I flipped it open to the first page, staring at the blank paper and gathering my thoughts.

Winter's hand touched mine, sliding a pen in front of me.

I took the pen, my mind overflowing with ideas. Staring unseeing at the Alstone College logo on the side, I tried to make some fucking sense of what was going on in my head.

Time to do this shit.

I put the pen to the paper, and began writing.

OPERATION ANDROMEDA

"Okay, let's get a fucking plan together."

20

winter

"I'm not sure about this." Zayde stopped dead on the pavement, standing outside the doors to a large, towering office block.

"We've come this far. We can't give up now," I urged. He sighed, and instead of leading me into the building, he headed around the side, into a tiny side street that was more like an alleyway, all cobblestones and large rubbish bins clustered in front of plain metal doors. Cameras were mounted everywhere, and I had the sense of being watched. He stalked down the alley and stopped in front of a nondescript grey door, then pressed a buzzer mounted on the wall. I heard a whirr as a camera swung around, and Zayde lifted his head, lowering his hood so the camera could see his face. We waited for a couple of minutes, before the door swung open and we stepped inside. There was a long corridor with one door at the other end, and that was where we headed.

The door slid open as we approached, and I saw it was actually a lift. Zayde pulled out a black card from his pocket and inserted it into a slot on the wall, then hit the button that said "13." The lift began to ascend with a slight shudder, and I stood silently, concentrating on breathing in and out, trying to stop the nerves overtaking me. We came to a stop, and Zayde placed a hand on my arm as the door opened.

"Let me do the talking."

I nodded and followed him out of the lift. We were standing in a large corridor of what looked like an incredibly opulent office block. Zayde sauntered casually down the corridor, clearly having been here enough times to feel confident in these surroundings.

He reached a door at the very end of the corridor and knocked once. I heard a soft, feminine voice call, "Come in," and the door opened for us.

We entered a room that looked like an upmarket waiting room, all shiny, polished glass, potted plants, and a large desk where a stunning woman in what I'd guess to be her mid-twenties sat, eyeing us. I couldn't help staring at her as she rose from the desk and walked around to us with a smile. Her hair was beautiful.

"Your hair..."

I hadn't actually meant to speak aloud, but she gave me a huge smile. "You like it?" She tossed it, letting the waves cascade over her shoulders. Shades of blue shot through with sea greens and purples, it shimmered as it moved, the colours reminding me of a tropical ocean.

"I love it. It's stunning."

"Thank you so much. I love experimenting with hair colour." She smiled brightly again and briefly clasped my hand in greeting. "I'm Natalie Brooks, Mr. Pope's assistant. You must be Ms. Huntington. Mr. Pope has been expecting you."

"Please, call me Winter. Ms. Huntington sounds weird to me. Way too formal."

"Of course. Hello, Zayde." Her attention turned to him, and her cheeks flushed slightly.

"Natalie." He barely spared her a glance, but I saw the look she gave him. Irritation warred with lust and longing. Hmm.

"Mr. Pope is just finishing up another meeting, so if you'd like to take a seat, go ahead. He won't be long."

Zayde needed no more invitation, sprawling on a stylish grey sofa that looked really uncomfortable, while I sidled closer to Natalie, who had made her way back around the desk and was seated once again.

"What's the deal with you and Z?" Keeping my voice low, I leaned over the desk, curious.

She glanced up from the computer. "Nothing. A one-time thing, never to be repeated." Her gaze briefly flicked towards him, and then she rolled her eyes. "None of these guys know the meaning of the word relationship, or commitment."

"Yeah, I get that." Caiden appeared in my mind. How he'd been so anti-relationships when he met me.

"His piercings, though." Her voice turned breathy as she practically swooned. "Whoever manages to crack through the ice prince's façade is going to be one lucky woman."

Almost as soon as she'd stopped speaking, the door swung open and Creed appeared in the doorway, ushering out a huge, muscular guy that I definitely wouldn't want to meet down a dark alleyway.

"I'll be in touch. Go and take care of your woman problem," Creed was saying as they walked out. The guy snorted, shaking his head, before looking over to where I was standing with Zayde.

"Z." He nodded.

"Axel."

"I'll show Mr. Savage out," Natalie said, her professionalism snapping into place as she came back around the desk. She disappeared out of the doors we'd entered by, and I followed Creed and Zayde into Creed's office.

"Wow. This is impressive."

My feet sank into plush grey carpet, and I stumbled slightly on my heels. Steadying myself on the overflowing bookshelf lining one wall, I glanced around and found my jaw dropping. The room was huge—a corner office with two sides made up of floor-to-ceiling windows showcasing a breathtaking view of the river and the city skyline beyond. Two expensive-looking modern leather sofas intersected with a glass coffee table sat in front of the windows, alongside an oversized desk.

Creed strode across the office and stopped at the side of his desk, turning to face me. "Winter, it's good to see you again," he said smoothly.

"Y-you too," I stuttered, my gaze drawn to the skyline. This all felt so much more formal than the other times I'd seen him, and I was a little intimidated both by the surroundings and the large man in front of me.

"My empire." He indicated out of the windows, following my line of sight. "This is where I conduct most of my business. The first time you met me, you got to see a side of me that I don't allow many to see. Other than my close friends, that is."

I thought back to how he'd been dressed down in a hoodie and jeans, but the sight of him had still been enough to intimidate me. Here, in this setting, in a dark suit that stretched over his huge figure, Kinslee's words about being scared of him came to mind. There *was* something about him, something lurking under the surface.

Gathering my courage, I pushed my negative thoughts aside. He'd never been anything but nice to me, plus he was a close friend of Zayde, my boyfriend's best mate. That was enough for me.

"How do you two know each other, anyway?" I was suddenly curious as I stared between the two of them. Both dressed so differently, but they had the same look in their eyes. That same icy, deadly intent.

They exchanged glances. "That's a story for another day." Creed lowered himself into the tall leather chair behind his desk. "Have a seat, and tell me what I can do for you. Z says you want my help, is that correct?"

I nodded. "Yeah. I know you have...connections. You can get things done."

He eyed me, amused. "I can get things done. But what sort of things do you have in mind?"

"I have this email..."

By the time I'd finished explaining everything to him, he was reclined in his chair, deep in thought.

"You see, Winter, I have a problem here. While I can provide my services for you, in theory, this is a complicated situation. The involvement of the Strelichevo syndicate presents a...problem. You see, they have connections with the Volkovs." At my blank look, he added, "Russian Bratva." I nodded, not that his words meant anything much to me, and he continued. "The Volkovs...let's just say you don't want to make an enemy of them. And not only that, I've had certain dealings with Mikhail Strelichevo myself, and to put it bluntly, if I interfered in his business, it would have unwanted side effects both for me, and a number of my associates."

"So you can't help us." I couldn't help the defeated sigh that escaped me. "Can you at least tell us anything about the Strelichevos? What kind of dealings do you have with them?"

"I have my fingers in many pies. My dealings with them aren't exactly on the books."

Oh. I thought back to the pallets of cocaine we'd found at the docks.

"Are you working with my mother?"

He turned the full force of his golden gaze on me. "No. Absolutely fucking not. Winter, let me tell you something. Zayde here, he's like a brother to me. You were the first woman he'd ever brought to meet me, and that tells me something. He likes and trusts you." He glanced over at Zayde. "Z lets very few people in, and therefore you being part of his inner circle means that you, in turn, are part of *my* trusted circle. Do you see?"

I massaged my temples, my head pounding as I struggled to take in what he was saying.

"Okay. So what I'm hearing is that you can't directly do anything that affects your business dealings."

He nodded.

"But you can help us out in some way, right? Like you did when you sent the guys to watch the docks for us, and, uh, cleared away the security guard's body."

"What are you proposing?"

I took a deep breath. "This is what I was thinking..."

We talked through the plan, and by the end of it, both Creed and Zayde were in agreement with me. I had amazing negotiation skills, what could I say?

Creed stood, coming around the desk to us, a new respect in his gaze as he looked at me. "We have a deal. You ever want a job after university, I could always use your negotiation skills."

I laughed. As much as I liked him, shady business dealings weren't on the cards for me.

"I'll keep it in mind, thanks."

"Natalie will show you out. I've got plans to put in place, thanks to a certain dark-haired beauty who came in here batting her eyelashes at me and getting me to do things I didn't want to do." His eyes gleamed with amusement. "I can see why you like her so much, Z."

Zayde shifted next to me, clearly uncomfortable. "Yeah. Come on, Winter." He stalked towards the door, throwing it open.

I turned to follow him, before I paused and turned back to Creed. "Thanks for helping us. I appreciate it."

"Anytime. And I meant what I said about the job. There's always a place for you, if you want it."

"Thanks." I smiled and left the room, Creed already picking up his phone as I was walking out, ready to get started on our mission.

As I entered the reception area, I saw Zayde around the back of the desk. Natalie was leaning against the filing cabinet, and he was speaking to her, his head close to her ear. His voice was too low for me to hear.

Hmm. "Am I interrupting something?"

Zayde stepped back, his face a blank mask, as usual. "Nothing." He emphasised the word, making Natalie's eyes darken with anger. She closed her eyes briefly, and when she reopened them, she'd regained her composure.

"I'll show you out." She swept around Zayde and over to me. "It was lovely to meet you, Winter. Have a great day." Smiling, she held the door open for us, and with one last goodbye, I left, following Zayde who had brushed past me.

"What was all that about with Creed's secretary?" I watched as Zayde inserted the card into the slot, and the lift began its smooth descent.

"Nothing."

"Didn't look like nothing."

"Nothing, as far as I'm concerned. Women want too much. Always getting the wrong idea. They're never satisfied," he muttered. At my frown, he added, "Except you, of course." Then he smirked at me.

Right. "Well, I'm glad our trip wasn't wasted. I feel like we have a real chance now."

"You did well." Zayde sounded slightly impressed, and I smiled widely. "Don't look so pleased. You cost me a hundred quid."

"What?" The lift doors opened, and I followed him out into the cobbled alleyway.

"I didn't think you'd be able to persuade Creed to help. He's very particular, and he takes care to stay neutral—particularly when it compromises his business interests. Cade made a bet with me, though. He thought you could do it."

My smile grew even wider. "He had faith in me?"

"Enough to bet on." He grinned at me, letting his mask crack, and I stared at him.

"You should smile more often."

His smile disappeared. Oops. We were silent for a moment, as we turned onto the busy street, and then he glanced down at me with a puzzled expression. "What is it about you, Winter, that makes people want to follow you into crazy situations?"

I shrugged. "No idea. Maybe I'm just really likeable?"

He smirked. "Maybe." Gripping my arm lightly, he steered me around the crowds of people that had started pouring out of the office buildings around us. "Let's get home so I can listen to Cade gloat about how he was right and I was wrong."

"Can't wait."

21

caiden

"I asked everyone to leave us." I pressed up against my girl as she stood at the kitchen sink, staring out of the window. I watched our reflections in the glass, her, barefoot in some tiny blue cami top and shorts set, and me, in my sweatpants. Fuck, we looked good together. Sliding my arms around her waist, I lowered my head to kiss her neck, and she shivered, responding to my touch like she always did.

"Why?" Her breathy whisper made my dick jump, and I continued kissing her soft skin, my hands moving under her top to caress her waist, and up to cup her tits. I brushed across her nipples, feeling them stiffen beneath my fingers. Fuck, she felt so good. So fucking perfect. And all mine. She moaned, and I nipped her neck, before moving my mouth to her ear.

"It's our last night before we carry out this plan. There's a massive chance of everything fucking up, and I wanted to have one more night with my girl, forgetting everything else, before shit goes down. We don't know how Christine will react, and yeah, we have some resources from Creed, but that might not be enough. This whole situation has the potential to blow up in our faces."

"Oh." She tipped her head to the side, grinding back into me, and I stifled a groan. "One last night before everything changes. I'm definitely on board with this plan."

"The question is…" I lowered my hand, sliding it into the tiny shorts she was wearing. "Can you manage to cook the dinner without fucking me?"

"What?" Her voice was barely audible as I slid my hand even lower, my finger slipping through her wetness, then coming up to circle her clit.

"I love how you're always ready for me." I kept up the slow movements, and she tried to press down on my hand, a tiny whimper escaping her lips.

"Cade…"

"Cook the food, baby, and I'll reward you if you can manage to resist me from now until we've finished eating." I removed my hand from her shorts and stepped away from her. She slumped against the sink, breathing heavily, regaining her composure, before she turned to face me.

"So you're saying, you want me to cook the dinner while you torture me until I give in and beg for sex?"

"That's exactly what I'm saying." I flashed her a wolfish grin.

She stared pointedly at the hard-on clearly visible through my sweatpants. "Or will you be the one begging to fuck me? I bet between us, you'll crack first."

"I don't make bets I can't win," I told her confidently.

"Hmm." She raised a brow. "We'll see. If you beg to fuck me, then I'll be winning this bet." Crossing to the fridge, she pulled out the ingredients for a quick pasta dish with a tomato sauce and carried them to the island.

"Careful with that knife, Snowflake," I cautioned as I

came up behind her while she was chopping the herbs for the sauce. Caging her in from behind, I heard her breathing hitch as she felt me close to her body. I stood still, my torso lightly pressed against her back, because as horny as I was, and as much fun I was having playing with her, I didn't want her cutting herself.

She carefully placed the knife down and spun in my arms. She went up on her toes, pulling my head down, and kissed me like she needed me to fucking breathe.

Fuck, I loved this girl. I shoved the chopping board to the side and scooped her up, depositing her on the marble island. She hooked her long legs around my waist, her hands sliding into my hair.

Pulling her into another kiss, I tugged her forwards so she was right on the edge of the counter, grinding her body against mine. "Do you give up yet?" Breaking the kiss, I spoke breathlessly against her lips, feeling her chest rise and fall.

"No." Her pupils were blown, and her pouty lips were swollen from our kisses. Fuck. My restraint was nowhere near as good as I thought. I was about ten seconds away from saying "fuck it" and burying myself inside her.

She pushed against my chest, a determined glint in her eye. "No," she said again. "I'm not losing."

I let her push me backwards so she could jump down from the counter, amused by the way she thought she could win this bet.

"Go and make yourself useful and boil the water for the pasta," she instructed.

"Whatever you want, baby." I pressed against her again. "Deny it all you want, but we both know you'll be begging me to fuck you before this meal is over."

"I like a challenge." Licking her lips, she ran her hand

down my chest, her eyes lowering as she followed the movement of her hand. She stopped at the band of my sweatpants, then gripped my cock through the material.

"Fuck," I hissed as she stroked her hand up and down my length, before she suddenly pulled away.

"Go. I've got food to chop." She pushed at my chest again, more insistently, and I grinned, despite the fact that my dick was almost painfully hard at this point.

"I fucking love playing with you, Snowflake. I'm not about to lose this bet, but if you wanna get on your knees and suck my cock, I won't complain."

"Nice try. Go."

Laughing, I left her to her food prep and went to fill the kettle with water to boil.

Ten minutes later, the sauce was cooking and Winter was carefully tipping the spaghetti into the pan. I had around ten more minutes until the pasta would be cooked and the food was ready, and I needed to up my game.

I waited until she'd finished with the pasta, then stalked over to her, spinning her around and lifting her up, walking us over to the wall at the side of the oven. She held on to me tightly as I pressed her into the wall, her body all soft and hot against mine.

This girl. "You want me inside you, don't you?" I swallowed thickly, my dick throbbing as she ground her pussy into me, desperate for the friction.

"Ye—no." She moaned the word, her head falling forwards. She scraped her teeth across my shoulder, her nails digging into my skin as she moved against me.

"No?" Fuck. This was more difficult than I thought. I

pulled her into a frantic kiss, and she ground on me, her grip on my back tightening as she returned my kiss, moaning into my mouth.

"No, no, no." She was moaning the words desperately. "I..." She took my lip between her teeth, biting down, and I growled low in my throat. Releasing my lip, she managed to get the rest of the words out. "Not...losing."

I did the hardest fucking thing I'd ever done in my life. I lowered her to the floor, then let her go. "Too bad," I said hoarsely. "I'm not giving in."

"Neither am I," she panted. "This is so fucking hard. Why are you torturing us both like this?"

"Fuck knows. Seemed like a good idea at the time." I shrugged, and her lips curved into a smile, before she winked at me.

"You're gonna lose, Cade."

"Someone's confident."

Unfortunately, she somehow managed to resist me. Both of us had taken a step back, neither wanting to lose the bet, and I think we both knew how close we were to just saying "fuck it" and giving in.

Damn it. Why did I make this fucking stupid bet? Oh yeah, to try and keep both our minds off tomorrow.

I sat down at the kitchen table, resting my elbows on the smooth wood as I admired my girl plating up our food. She carried the steaming bowls of spaghetti over, the smell of the rich tomato sauce making my stomach growl.

"Parmesan?" She leaned around me, purposely brushing her tits against my arm, and grated the cheese onto my food. I had to clench my fists to stop myself from touching her.

"I've decided you're sitting on me to eat." My dick was begging to be inside her, and it would be fucking torture having her on my lap, but it might just get her to give in.

"You've decided, have you?" Her voice was a sultry purr. I moved back to allow her to slide onto my lap, and we both gasped as her ass pressed into my cock.

"Hang on a minute, baby." I shuffled her around, adjusting my dick, and she gave a soft moan of approval.

"I'm going to sit on you sideways," she decided, her voice hoarse, swinging her legs around. Guess she couldn't handle the feel of my dick against her pussy. I smiled to myself.

"Whatever you want." Resting my arm around her waist, I scooped up some of the spaghetti and sauce, twirling it around on my fork.

"One-handed, and you didn't even spill any," she said, as I brought the fork to her lips.

"I can do a lot of things with one hand."

"I know." She opened her mouth, allowing me to slide the fork inside. While she was eating, I took the chance to grab a mouthful of my own food.

"Feeding me, making me sit on you..." She tilted her head, looking at me. "Is this all part of the plan to make me give in?"

I didn't answer, because I was distracted by the sauce on the side of her lip. I brought my thumb up to wipe it away, and she opened her mouth, taking my thumb into it and sucking it.

"Fucking hell," I ground out.

She released my thumb, and pressed her lips to mine. "Do you give in?"

"No. Eat your food, Snowflake."

For a couple of minutes we were both quiet as we ate, until I moved my hand from her waist and down between her legs. She let out a soft gasp, as I stroked my finger down over her silky shorts, feeling how soaked she was for me. I hadn't expected her to hold out for this long.

I kissed her shoulder, then moved to her neck, scraping my teeth up her throat as I continued my slow torture of her pussy, keeping the pressure light and teasing, knowing that she'd become desperate for more.

She wriggled against my hand, trying to increase the pressure.

"Still hungry?" I asked roughly, my lips skimming over her ear.

She moaned.

"Feed me."

Obediently, she picked up the fork, her hand shaking slightly, and aimed the fork at my lips. Her eyes met mine, all dark and lustful, and she sucked in a breath at the look on my face.

I opened my mouth, and she stopped dead, dropping the fork back down with a clatter.

"Fuck it, you win," she suddenly said, swinging herself around so she was straddling me, attacking my mouth with a desperate kiss.

Finally.

I opened my mouth for her, kissing her back just as fiercely, gripping her hips as she moved against me, driving both of us wild. Breaking the kiss, I pulled her top off over her head, then pushed the plates aside.

"You're so fucking beautiful." I took a minute just to drink her in. All tousled dark hair and wide eyes, her nipples standing up and begging for attention, she looked at me with so much fucking lust that I needed to be inside her more than anything. But first... I lowered my head, taking a nipple into my mouth, lightly biting it as I caressed the other.

"Cade," she moaned, throwing her head back. I sucked, nibbled, and caressed her gorgeous tits until she was panting under me, rubbing herself all over my cock.

Enough.

I had to have her right now. "Clothes off." I raised my head to look at her, my tone low and commanding.

She immediately obeyed, standing in front of me and peeling the rest of the clothes from her body. She stretched, bared to me, and my dick hardened even further. How did she always make me feel this way?

"You" was all she managed to say, and I ripped my sweatpants down in one easy movement, kicking them under the table, before I tugged her towards me.

"Come here."

She straddled me, then sank down onto my cock.

Fuck.

I'd never get used to this feeling. "Ride my dick, baby."

She moaned, gripping onto my shoulders as she moved against me, her mouth all hot, fiery kisses, as we lost ourselves in each other.

"Cade. Fuck," she panted. I buried my face in her neck, biting down on her soft skin, and slid my hand between us to touch her.

"Don't stop," she pleaded desperately. "I'm so close." I kept up the movements of my fingers and she kissed me harder, raking her nails down my back. Breaking the kiss, I watched her as she let go, falling apart against me. The sight of her coming? Sexiest fucking sight I'd ever seen in my life.

I pulled her head to me again, slowing the pace and kissing her as the aftershocks of her orgasm wore off, and then I lifted her off me and stood, shoving the chair away. "I need to fuck you harder, baby. Hold on to the table. Legs apart."

She gripped the table, raising her ass in the air. I stopped dead, drinking in the sight of her. With her body bared to me like this, I could see the wetness between her legs, and I needed to touch her. My dick was aching to be back inside her, but I wanted to feel her around my fingers first.

"You have no idea what you do to me." I swallowed hard. "You look so fucking sexy." Moving to stand right behind her, I slid my finger into her soaked pussy, then added a second, feeling her tighten around me.

She threw her head back, pushing back against my hand. "Cade…"

I removed my fingers as she turned her head to watch me and sucked them into my mouth. Her eyes darkened and she licked her lips.

That was it.

I gripped her hips, thrusting inside her in one movement, and we both moaned at the sensation. My thrusts became more frantic, and she gripped the table harder, sliding forwards to rest her cheek on it. I grabbed a fistful of her hair, pulling back as I pounded in and out of her, and she let out a growl of pleasure.

"I'm gonna come." The sound of our bodies against each other, and our pants and moans echoing through the kitchen was so fucking erotic, and I knew I couldn't hold out much longer. Releasing my grip on her hair, I pressed my thumb to her clit, and she shattered around me, crying out my name. Her pussy gripped my dick so fucking tightly, pulsating around me, and moments after her I came, hard, spilling my cum deep inside her.

She collapsed against the table, breathless and spent, as I pulled out of her, and I leaned forwards, moving her hair aside. I kissed down her spine, running my hand down her back, before gently tugging her up and into my arms.

"I love you so fucking much." My voice was thick, full of emotion, as I held her.

"I love you, too. More than anything." She wound her arms around my neck, kissing me softly.

"Let's get you cleaned up, then maybe we can reheat the rest of this food." I picked her up, carrying her towards the stairs.

"I'm not hungry anymore." She nuzzled into my neck, and lightly scraped her teeth across my skin. "I just want you."

"When you say stuff like that to me..." My arms tightened around her body, my cock hardening again at the feel of her mouth on me. "Forget the food. I want to make love to my girlfriend."

22

winter

Tonight was the night.

We were as ready as we could be. There was so much potential for things to go wrong, since none of us knew exactly what we were walking into. All we could do was try to cover every eventuality we could think of.

I'd spent the last week training, mostly with Zayde, and sometimes with Lena, working on the basic knife skills Zayde had taught me, and going through self-defence moves designed to help overthrow a bigger attacker and give me a chance to get away. Not that I wanted it to come to that, but we had to be prepared for anything. Zayde was fairly confident in my ability, and that in turn gave me confidence. Still, I hoped that I didn't actually have to use any of my newly acquired skills.

Lena had been a surprise during our week of training. She'd told me that ever since an "incident" when she was younger, she'd been training in martial arts, learning various disciplines, and it showed. She was extremely intelligent, another thing I'd come to realise the more time I spent with her, with an aptitude for numbers that I envied.

According to her, the key to becoming skilled in a discipline was to train your mind to keep it sharp, and she had me doing focusing exercises and all sorts of random brain training that made my head spin.

Anyway, we were ready and prepared. Our basic plan was simple and straightforward, but it was actually carrying it out that would be the problem. We'd agreed that Allan and Joseph were the weakest links, and therefore we needed to isolate them, preferably without drawing any attention to ourselves, and get them away so we could question them. We were running out of time—the Alstone Holdings deal was almost complete, the board due to sign it off the following day, and we needed answers.

Of course, the plan hinged on both of them actually attending this meeting, but we'd agreed that the chances were high. Arlo was at Alstone Members Club for the evening, so it would be easy enough for Allan to attend without arousing suspicion.

I sat in the back of the van, which from the outside looked like an ordinary, nondescript van. Inside, though, it was incredible. Like something out of a movie, complete with surveillance stuff and all sorts of gadgets I had no clue how to use. The boys and Lena had spent twenty minutes drooling over it, and I couldn't help smiling at their enthusiasm.

As per the email we'd intercepted, the meetup was at Alstone Castle. Why there, I had no idea. Maybe because it was generally deserted at night, and out in the open. Glancing through the open hatch to the front windscreen, I saw we were turning onto the familiar road, and nerves overtook me. My leg bounced restlessly, and I attempted to breathe deeply in and out to calm myself.

The plan had to work.

It *had to*.

I was so thankful that Creed had come through for us. He'd stayed away from being personally involved, but he'd provided us with the goods. We had Mack, and this van, and thanks to Mack, a place to take Allan and Joseph to question them. Obie, one of Creed's other guys, was also with us. He sat in front of the screens, monitoring surveillance. When I'd first seen him as I'd entered the van—a huge, hulking guy, all massive defined muscles, dark, intense eyes, and close-cropped black hair—I'd been completely intimidated. That disappeared the second introductions were made and he threw me a wide, genuine smile, completely disarming me.

We'd agreed that me, Mack, and Kinslee would cause a distraction. While they were doing that, Caiden, Zayde, Weston, and Cassius would sneak around and get Allan and Joseph. James was the getaway driver—it was too risky for him to be there in case Joseph saw his face. As it was, he was currently wearing a balaclava.

Lena had to stay in the van, since Cassius had put his foot down, so she was helping Obie monitor the screens, and had a direct link to the tiny mics that Cassius and I had pinned on our clothing. She'd be our primary source of communication once we were outside.

I'd wanted to be part of getting Allan and Joseph, but the boys point-blank refused to let me have anything to do with it. I could sense Lena's frustration, too. She wanted to be out there with us, although she seemed slightly pacified by all the equipment she was getting to use.

My gaze fell to the bag that rested at my feet, and my lips

curved into a smile. Despite not being part of the extraction, between us, we had a good bag of tricks to play with.

The van slowed. "Almost there." James' voice came through the hatch.

"Come here, baby." Cade pulled me into him for a kiss. I could feel his heart racing, and the worry in his eyes shook me. He gripped my face, stroking his thumb over my jaw. "Don't get into trouble. I couldn't fucking handle it if anything happened to you. Stay safe. If it all goes wrong, get out of there."

My stomach flipped. "I promise I'll stay as safe as I can." *I hope.* "I want you to stay safe, too. Please don't take any unnecessary risks." I kissed him again, putting everything I had into it. Around us, the others talked in low voices, giving us a semblance of privacy as I enjoyed the last moments wrapped in the arms of the man I loved.

The van came to a stop, and Caiden reluctantly released me. "I love you." He picked up the balaclava from the seat next to me and pulled it over my head, rolling it down until it covered my face. We both slid our gloves on, covered from head to toe, other than our eyes.

"I love you, Cade." My voice was muffled by the material of the balaclava. I squeezed his hand, then reached down to pick up my bag as the van doors swung open.

Showtime.

23

winter

Time for part one of the plan. Weston turned on the drone and, using the controls, sent it up into the air, hovering above us. The feed appeared on the screen in front of us, and we could see the dim outline of the van on the monitor.

"You sure you know what you're doing?" Weston reluctantly handed the controls over to Obie. He rolled his eyes.

"Mate, this ain't my first job. I've got this handled." He expertly sent the drone soaring towards the castle. We watched silently as the large courtyard came into view. A large fire had been lit in the pit in the centre, and grouped around it were shadowy figures. We counted six as the drone hovered undetected. I assumed that Christine, Joseph, and Allan were part of the group, and from the email West had intercepted, it was likely that one of the others was Joseph's dad. The remaining two I wasn't sure about, although I was betting that Petr was one of them.

They didn't appear to be moving around much. Most of

them were seated on the large rocks that were used as makeshift seats. That made our job easier.

The drone soared higher, and I noticed a shadow detach itself from the wall at the edge of the courtyard. "Look," I breathed, pointing at the screen.

"Yeah. That'll be a lookout. I'm betting they're not expecting any trouble, so it's likely that he's the only one," James said, having climbed into the back of the van with us so he could see the screen. "Let's hope so, anyway."

The drone did one more circuit of the area, and once we were satisfied that we knew where everyone was and there was nothing we'd missed, Obie sent it back to the van. "I'll send it up again when you're out, keep an eye on you," he told us. "Better go now."

We climbed out of the van and split into two groups. The combination of excitement and nerves was almost unbearable as I watched the Four slink away, silent shadows in the night, ready to carry out their part of the plan.

Once they'd disappeared from our view, I turned to Mack and Kinslee. "Ready to wreak havoc?"

"Fuck, yeah. Let's light it up." Mack grinned, before he tugged his balaclava down and picked up his own bag.

We made our way silently to an area just past the castle, close to where Mack had hidden his car earlier in the day. We wanted to be on the opposite side to the boys so that they could hopefully sneak in from behind while we caused a distraction. Then we'd flee in opposite directions and meet up afterwards at Mack's place. Mack assured us that we wouldn't be caught, but if we were, we had Creed as our last resort.

"Group one is in position." Lena's voice sounded quietly in my ear. Each group had an earpiece so we could stay in communication and make sure we timed everything correctly.

"Group two is in position," I whispered into the tiny mic that was pinned to my jacket.

"Group two, are you ready?"

"Hang on." I pulled the first item from my bag, placing it down on the cold ground, watching as Kinslee and Mack did the same. We continued until everything was in place, and I reached into my pocket, grasping the small metal object and lifting it out. "Ready."

I flicked on the lighter I held in my palm and held it to the bottom of the small bundle of fireworks, all connected by one long fuse.

The end caught instantly, the spark licking straight up the fuse, and Mack pulled me back, out of the way. We turned and ran into the shadows of the trees that outlined the area, hearing the bangs and pops as the fireworks caught alight.

Wow. The sky lit up in a haze of colourful sparks, illuminating the whole area clearly. I saw the guard rushing over from the other side of the courtyard, and we retreated further into the trees, hoping that our distraction technique would buy the boys enough time to get Allan and Joseph out of there. My heart was beating wildly, and my palms were damp. Anything could go wrong. Anything. I just had to hope and pray that they could do it.

"Hyde acquired." Lena's voice in my ear, only a couple of minutes later, sent a shock of relief through me.

"They have Joseph," I whispered, glancing over at Mack and Kinslee. I could only just about make out their eyes thanks to the balaclavas they wore and the fact we were in the shadows, but the relief was clear in both.

We waited, and waited. Nothing else.

"Lena?" I spoke into my mic. "What's happening?"

Her voice came through the earpiece a moment later, anxiety bleeding through her tone. "I don't know, I can't get hold of them."

My stomach flipped, and I relayed the message to the others, my voice shaking.

"Fuck. Something's not right. I'm gonna check it out. Kins, you go to the car. Get in, keys in the ignition ready to go." Mack handed her his car keys, and she nodded, already moving towards the car's hiding place.

"Winter, you ready to buy us a little time?"

I nodded, too worried to speak, but knowing that our distractions could be the difference between the mission working out and failure.

"Rich boy will murder me with his bare hands if I let anything happen to you, so if shit goes down, get the fuck out of here, alright?"

I nodded again, already feeling in the bottom of my bag for the other items we'd added as a last resort. The whole thing took place in the space of a minute or so, but time seemed to slow down as Mack and I quickly put together our makeshift petrol bombs and moved towards the castle. To get closer we had to go across open ground, but we were in the dark, and I was hoping with everything I had that this would be enough.

Mack stopped me with a hand on my arm, still a safe distance from the castle. The sounds of shouts could be heard from the courtyard, but all I noticed was the loudness of my heartbeat in my ears. Mack moved his head right next to mine, his voice barely discernible. "Stay. Count to thirty, light your baby up, then run. Don't stop. Don't look back. I'll be right behind you." Then he was gone, and I slowed my breathing, so fucking scared to be left alone in the dark but prepared to do whatever it took. My thumb was poised on my lighter ready to go, and I counted down in my head.

Four...three...two...one...

I lit the end of the alcohol-soaked rag, and threw the bottle with all my might, sending it soaring towards the castle.

Everything happened in slow motion.

There was a loud boom as the Molotov cocktail exploded, followed half a second later by another boom. Shouts of rage carried through the air towards me, and I saw a shadow detach itself from the crumbling castle wall.

Shit.

Another guard we'd missed.

He was looking straight at me.

I turned, and ran.

Faster than I'd ever run before, my lungs burning, I raced blindly towards the safety of the trees.

Almost there.

Then a huge body was gripping me around my middle with a crushing pressure, and I couldn't breathe, couldn't think.

Fuck fuck *fuck.*

What had we practiced? Every thought seemed to have left my head, as I struggled to control the panic.

The kubotan! I could have cried with relief as I remembered Cade showing me how to use the tiny self-defence item Arlo had given me for my birthday. I lowered my arms, stopping my flailing, and let my body stop struggling as the guard began to drag me back towards the castle. As quickly as possible, desperately trying not to let the panic overtake me, I worked my hand into the zip pocket of my jacket and pulled it out.

Inhaling a huge breath of the smoky night air to bolster myself, I jabbed it into the back of his hand as hard as I could. He let out a howl of pain, loosening his crushing grip on me. I gasped for breath, relieved tears filling my eyes, but then he was there again, ripping the kubotan from my grip with an angry roar and pinning my body in place. Fuck, he was too strong; I couldn't stop him.

Suddenly, his weight was gone, and I was falling backwards. I landed on top of him with a grunt, momentarily stunned. Scrambling to my feet as fast as I could, I saw Mack standing behind the guard, a large rock in his hand.

"You looked like you were having a bit of trouble there." He pulled up his balaclava, grinning at me.

"I had it handled." Relief filled every fibre of my being, as he grabbed my hand and we jogged through the trees to the car. I was dimly aware of Lena's voice in my ear saying, "Allan acquired," as we broke through the treeline. I yanked the car door open, throwing myself in the back seat as Mack slid into the driver's side and started the engine with a roar. My whole body started shaking.

"Group two accounted for. We're leaving," I managed to hiss into the speaker, before I lay back against the seat, closing my eyes.

"This'll help." I heard Mack's voice coming from the front and Kinslee's low reply, followed by the sound of her coughing and spluttering. Then a metal flask was being pushed into my hand by Kinslee, and I opened my eyes, pulling my balaclava off and tipping the flask to my lips.

"Fucking hell," I managed to choke out as the fiery whiskey burned a path down my throat, heating me from the inside.

"Fireball." Mack glanced at me in the rear-view mirror with a grin, before returning his attention to the road. As I took another small sip of whiskey, the second going down more easily than the first, I noticed his eyes flicking back and forth between the road and the rear-view mirror.

My breathing slowed, and I tugged off my gloves, before pulling my earpiece from my ear. We were out of range now, and we'd meet up with the others later. I remembered that my phone was stashed at our final location, so I couldn't contact the others until I'd seen them in person. As Mack took us through the empty roads, I hugged my body, all my thoughts with Caiden and the others. I hoped they were okay. I needed them to be okay. I couldn't stop the rising panic racing through me. What had taken them so long?

"First stop." Mack slowed the car, turning into the industrial estate where Kinslee was parked. As the car came to a stop, she turned in her seat to face me.

"Are you okay?"

How could I answer that? "Yeah, I'm good." I gave her a small smile, hoping she'd buy my lie.

"Call or message me as soon as you can." She reached out and squeezed my hand. "They're going to be okay."

"Thanks," I whispered. She slipped out of the car, and I clambered across to the passenger seat, contorting my body to move through the small gap between the seats. We'd agreed that she didn't need to be there for questioning Allan and Joseph—the less people that were around them, the better, but she was on standby in case we needed anything. Weston had set up an alert system on the apps on our phones, so that we could send an SOS message with one tap. Of course, I didn't actually have my phone at this point in time, so I had to hope that nothing would go wrong between now and the rendezvous point.

Mack started the car up again, taking us away from the Alstone area and onto the motorway.

"What do you do? Like for a job, I mean?" I felt a sudden need to make conversation, to take my mind off the panic bubbling up in me as I thought of everything that could have possibly gone wrong.

He glanced over at me. "This and that. I'm a tattoo artist, among other things."

"Oh. That sounds fun."

"Yeah, it is. I did most of your boyfriend's tatts."

And there went my plan to get my mind off Caiden. I thought back to him, peeling off his T-shirt and watching me notice his new tattoo. That look on his face, the combination of nerves, excitement, and love... fuck, he slayed me. I still found it bizarre that he even had any kind of nerves or was unsure around me. He was so confident, so commanding, that when he bared his soul to me, it took my breath away.

Mack continued speaking, shaking me out of my thoughts of my boyfriend. "Hit me up if you want any ink done."

"Thanks, I will."

We turned off the motorway. "Not far now." Our surroundings changed from fields to industrial as we drove, and my body thrummed with a mix of fear and anticipation.

I kept talking to take my mind off my nerves, as I twisted my hands together in my lap. "Have you ever had to do any really bad tattoo cover-ups?"

"Loads. Normally names. Never get anyone's name tatted on you. Bad idea."

"I wasn't planning on it." Although, now I thought about it, it might be nice to get some kind of tattoo to represent Cade. Momentarily lost in thought, I jumped when Mack's voice sounded again.

"We're here."

24

caiden

Earlier...

We stole through the night, fucking armed and ready. I was confident we'd get the job done; my concern was with my girl. I had to trust Mack to keep her safe. Kinslee, too.

I pushed all thoughts out of my mind and focused on the job. Get in, get the targets, get the fuck out.

Cassius murmured into the headset as we got into position, ready and waiting. Once we were in place, Z slipped through the shadows towards the guard, and I watched from my position behind a crumbling pillar as the guard crumpled silently to the ground. Good. It might not be long till they noticed him gone, but with luck on our side, we'd be able to get in position to grab the targets before anyone noticed.

I breathed deeply in and out. So much of this mission relied on fucking luck. I didn't like it, but we were almost out of time, and this whole thing could be the difference between my dad living or dying.

Z rejoined us, appearing next to my shoulder. "Guard down."

Weston scanned the area in front of us with the night-vision binoculars. "Right. Allan's sitting down on the stone." He pointed, still scanning the courtyard. "Hyde's over that side." Lowering the binoculars, he pointed in the opposite corner of the courtyard. "Uh, ten o'clock and two o'clock."

I would've laughed if the whole situation hadn't been so serious, but it was hard to find humour when so much hinged on what we were about to attempt. "Wait for the signal. You know what to do." I glanced around at the others, and they nodded. I held out my fist, and one by one, we bumped fists. "Stay safe," I cautioned, then Zayde and Cassius were gone, swallowed by the shadows, heading in the direction of Allan. "Ready, bro?" West nodded, and we prepared to make our move to grab Hyde.

Not even thirty seconds later, the sky lit up with fireworks, sparks raining down everywhere, loud booms echoing around the courtyard. We slunk inside the courtyard, noting the shouts as everyone ran around like headless chickens in a fucking panic. Yeah, we'd caught them unaware.

Looked like luck was on our side. Hyde had stayed at the back of the courtyard, close to where we were, probably expecting everyone else to do the work for him. Lazy fucker. Smoke from the fireworks filled the space, hanging in the still air, meaning it would be harder for them to make out what was happening.

I came up behind Hyde, throwing my arms around him and pinning him, while Weston clapped a rag over his mouth, muffling his cries, before injecting the tranquilizer into his neck. I doubted anyone would've heard him, anyway. Dragging him into the shadows so we wouldn't be seen, we kept him pinned, West holding the rag over his mouth while the sedative worked its way through his system.

After the longest couple of minutes of my life, Hyde suddenly went limp in my grip, sending me staggering back. Without a word, I nodded at West, and he picked up Hyde's feet. Together, we carried him out of the courtyard, moving as fast as we could with his dead weight.

"Heavy, isn't he?" Weston panted as we left the castle behind us, moving across the stubby grass towards the van.

I grunted in reply, concentrating on not tripping over. Of course the grass couldn't be flat. No, it had to have fucking lumpy bits and rocks and shit everywhere.

Finally, we were close to the van, and the doors swung open, Obie jumping out and helping us get Hyde into the van. We bound his wrists and feet tightly and threw a bag over his head so he wouldn't be able to see what the fuck was going on if he regained consciousness. I glanced over at Lena. Her face was pale, her eyes wide as she met my gaze, before returning to stare at the screen in front of her.

"Where's my brother? I can't see anything!" she hissed, scanning the monitor desperately. Smoke from the fireworks filled the entire courtyard, making the visibility from the drone pretty much zero.

I put a finger to my lips, indicating Hyde. He was unconscious for now, but it didn't mean he'd stay that way. "Shh. He'll be okay." I made eye contact with Weston, and he nodded, moving to sit next to her and placing his hand on her arm.

I lifted the balaclava. *I'll be back*, I mouthed, before slipping out of the van, trusting the others to keep an eye on Hyde. Not like he was going anywhere. I smirked, thinking of how fucking satisfying it was to have him bound and at my mercy.

Stalking back around the castle wall, I got to the courtyard just in time to see a shadow rush in from the other side through the haze of smoke, sending a flaming item hurling through the air, exploding close to the feet of Hyde Senior. He let out a roar of rage, jumping backwards, before spinning around and running in the direction Mack had disappeared to. In my periphery I saw Christine cowering behind Petr, who was raising his hand.

I saw the glint of the barrel and the direction he was pointing the gun in.

Fuck!

Z and Cassius had Allan in their grip, carrying him out.

I did the only thing I fucking could, unzipping my jacket and whipping the throwing knife from the bandolier strapped across my body.

I aimed and threw.

I willed it to reach him, to land where I wanted it to.

It soared through the air and tore through the material of his jacket, embedding itself in his forearm.

Direct hit.

He let out a bellow of pain, the gun falling from his grip as he clutched his hand to his side. I didn't stop and wait around. Cassius and Zayde needed me. Running over to them, I swiped one of Zayde's knives from the sheath on his belt since mine was now lost somewhere in the courtyard. Fuck. That blade was a gift.

"Faster," I urged them as they staggered across the grass, while I kept eyes on the courtyard in case we had any more trouble.

"Going as fast as we can," Cassius grunted, his eyes focused on the van.

We finally reached it, and Lena leapt out of the back, throwing herself at Cassius. He dropped Allan's feet down to the floor, capturing her in his arms.

"I was so fucking worried!" she was crying as Zayde and I bundled Allan into the van.

I stopped, just staring at Allan, the feeling of betrayal coursing through me as I took in his unconscious form. Weston stared over at him, and I watched the same thoughts I was having play across his face. The betrayal was still fucking strong.

"I'll take care of him." Z nodded to the seat opposite Allan, and I collapsed down gratefully as the van started up, swinging around and moving away from the area. Obie threw me a bottle of water once I was seated, before returning his gaze to the screen where he was monitoring the rear camera of the van to check if we were being followed.

Pulling off my balaclava and gloves, I watched as Z carefully bound Allan's hands and feet, nowhere near as tightly as we'd done Joseph's, and slipped an identical bag over his head. He threw Allan's phone to Weston, then came and sat next to me.

I handed him the water. "What happened? What was the hold-up?"

"We couldn't get Allan away from the others. Had to split up and cause a distraction over the other side." He glanced over at Cassius, who had his arm around his sister, comforting her. "It was all good. I did what I had to. You got my blade still?"

"Oh, yeah." I handed him the knife I'd shoved in my bandolier and passed it over. "Blood, huh?"

He grunted, carefully cleaning it.

I dropped the subject, raising my voice. "Everyone

alright?" At this point, it didn't matter if Allan or Joseph woke up and heard me speaking. They'd know I was there, soon enough. What we didn't want was for them to hear any of the others speak. Other than Z, that is.

They gave me thumbs ups and nods. I heard my girlfriend's voice in my head, telling me to check on Granville, and I groaned, moving across to the open hatch.

"You alright?"

He jumped, before nodding. "Yeah. I don't think anyone's following us. I'm taking the long way, though, just in case."

"Good." That was enough conversation with him for one day. Collapsing back on the seat, my thoughts returned to my girl. I trusted Mack, but she had a habit of getting herself into trouble. Fuck. I had no way of communicating with her, either.

"Did you hear from Winter?" I looked over at Lena.

She glanced at the unmoving forms of Allan and Hyde, and nodded. "I heard from them just as they were leaving," she whispered, her voice sounding odd. Relief filled me at her words, although I still couldn't fucking relax. Wouldn't be able to, until I could see her with my own eyes.

"What's wrong with her voice?" Z muttered from next to me, and I shrugged.

"I'm disguising it," Lena hissed, glaring at him. He rolled his eyes, not bothering to reply. We all lapsed into silence, lost in our own thoughts.

After about twenty minutes of driving, the van came to a stop. We were dropping Granville and Lena off, and Obie would take us the rest of the way to Mack's place, a warehouse on an industrial estate. Once we were there, he'd leave us with Allan and Hyde. The fewer involved in the interrogation, the better. Cassius wasn't even getting involved—the plan was for him to wait with Winter and my brother, listening in from outside the room, where we'd set up all the shit we needed to record them.

Not that things ever went to plan.

After the longest fucking journey ever, we finally pulled up at the warehouse, piling out of the van and leaving Hyde and Allan inside for now. No fucking sign of Mack. Where was he? Where was my girl?

"Cade." Z put his hand on my arm. I swung my head around to his, following his gaze. A car was turning into the lot, empty other than mine and Cassius' cars, which we'd parked there earlier. Headlights shone on us, temporarily blinding me. The car came to a stop, and the passenger door was thrown open. Huge eyes, filling with tears, met mine, and she flung herself into my arms.

"*Cade.*"

25

winter

I clung to Caiden, afraid to let go, wrapping my arms and legs around him. "I was so fucking worried. I had no way of knowing if you were okay," I cried.

"I'm okay, baby," he soothed. "Everything's fine." I buried my face in his shoulder, regaining my composure, feeling his steady heartbeat under me.

Lowering me to the floor, he cupped my chin in his hand, and kissed my tears away. "Are you okay?"

"I'm fine." I managed a tremulous smile.

"You didn't get into any trouble?" He raised a sceptical brow.

"Um...there was this one guy that came from nowhere and grabbed me. But it was all okay. I took him down."

"With a bit of help from yours truly." Mack swaggered over, throwing me a wink.

"Yeah." I grinned at him, then took in the look on my boyfriend's face, the muscle ticking in his jaw. "Honestly, it was fine. He didn't see who I was or hear me speak."

"Knocked him out with a rock, didn't I?" Mack

interjected, before he moved away from us to unlock the garage door we'd parked in front of.

"That wasn't the part I was worried about." Caiden pulled me closer. "I couldn't handle anything happening to you."

I threaded my arms around his neck, pulling him into a kiss, and he relaxed against me. "I'm fine. He didn't get a chance to hurt me properly. How did it go with getting Allan and Joseph?"

He gave me a brief rundown as we waited outside the garage while the van reversed in, ready to unload our passengers. When it reappeared, Obie driving away with a nod at us, Mack drove his car inside, and Cade took my hand. We followed Mack into the garage, dimly illuminated by a single bulb hanging from the ceiling. The door closed behind us, and I turned my attention to the figures at the far side.

I sucked in a shocked breath at the bound, hooded figures slumped on the floor, their backs propped up against the wall. I shouldn't have been surprised, since they'd have to be restrained, but this was suddenly starting to feel like I was in an episode of *Criminal Minds* or something.

"We didn't hurt them," Cade murmured in my ear, then flashed me a frankly evil-looking grin. "Not yet, at least. I can't say Hyde won't be getting hurt tonight."

I rolled my eyes at him, and he dropped a kiss on my forehead. "He deserves everything that's coming to him."

"I know," I conceded. "But can we at least try and get some useful information out of him at the same time?"

"That, I *can* promise you. Come on." He led me over to the others. "Ready?"

We ended up in what looked like some kind of small warehouse. "Supplies," Mack told me, when he caught my curious glance at the shelves running all down the walls, piled high with boxes. I nodded, accepting his answer, because he clearly wasn't about to elaborate, and followed him over to the door at the side of the warehouse. The door led to an office-style room with a window overlooking the main floor of the building. The first thing I noticed as we entered was the recording equipment set up on a desk, along with three chairs. A large, slightly battered monitor sat on the desk, a blinking cursor on the screen. There was a group of phones laid out haphazardly in front of the monitor, and I recognised mine and Caiden's.

I breathed out a sigh of relief. Honestly, I hadn't realised how much I'd taken my phone for granted until I couldn't use it to contact Caiden.

Mack touched my arm, interrupting my thoughts. He nodded in the direction of a thing that looked like a cross between a chair and a bed, which was sat in the corner of the room. "Might be a long night. Brought that over from my shop in case anyone needs to catch some sleep. There's drinks and snacks in the top drawer, too."

I smiled at his thoughtfulness. "Thanks."

"No problem. I'll leave you to it." He disappeared out of the door.

I walked to the edge of the room and stood in the doorway, watching as Caiden and Zayde manhandled Joseph into a chair in the centre of the warehouse space, tying him to it, then pulling up a couple of chairs in front of him. He still had the hood covering his head, but he was facing away from me anyway.

Cassius and Weston brought Allan in, seating him in a

chair in the far corner of the warehouse, facing the wall. They came over to join me in the office, and we watched as Zayde and Caiden strapped him to the seat.

Caiden stood behind Allan, removing the hood, and Zayde placed a pair of headphones on him. Working quickly as a team, silently communicating, Caiden passed him what looked like a roll of tape, and Zayde used his knife to slice off a strip, before carefully taping over his mouth. At least, I assume that was what he was doing.

"The headphones are noise-cancelling." Weston answered my unspoken question. "It'll stop him hearing anything Hyde decides to share with us."

"Or stop him hearing the screams." Cassius smirked. "Just kidding...maybe."

Job done, Caiden and Zayde joined us, and I was taken aback by the dark look in Caiden's eyes as his gaze found mine. "Listen, baby. We're gonna question Joseph now. We might do or say things that you won't like, depending how agreeable he is. I want you to remember that this is necessary. We're almost out of time, and we need answers."

Stepping forwards, I reached up to kiss him softly. "You don't need to explain. I understand. Do what you have to."

He tugged me into his arms. "I just don't want you to look at me differently if I end up having to do something you don't like."

"I love you. I won't look at you differently." I moved my mouth to his ear. "If you wanna rough Joseph up a bit for me, I won't mind."

I felt him laugh into my hair. "Just when I thought I couldn't love you any more, you have to go and say something like that."

His words made me smile, too, and I hugged him to me more tightly.

"Cade." At Z's voice, Caiden released me, dropping one last kiss on my head. "Let's do this."

As they left us, I took a seat at the table next to Cassius, and Weston dropped into the chair next to me, adjusting the monitor and turning some dials on the little pad in front of him.

"Okay, I think that's it." Four images of the warehouse appeared on the screen, the cameras each showing a different view. Weston adjusted it so that only the two feeds from the cameras facing Joseph, Caiden, and Zayde were showing, and did something to zoom in on the images. Lit by a single strip of lights from the ceiling, Caiden and Zayde both appeared shadowed and menacing, towering over Joseph.

"Testing." Zayde's voice came out of the speakers in front of us, the sound slightly crackly but clear enough to easily make it out.

"Glad the sound quality's good. I'm recording everything," Weston told me, still messing around with the controls.

"I don't get why I have to sit here instead of being out there," Cassius muttered, tearing open a bar of chocolate he'd pulled from the desk drawer and breaking off a square.

"We discussed this. Joseph and Allan don't need to know you're involved. The less people, the better." Weston glanced over at him, and he pulled a face, before breaking off another square of chocolate.

"Yeah, I want to be out there, too, Cass. I know it makes sense, but it's frustrating sitting here not being able to do anything." I squeezed his hand, and swiped a piece of his chocolate.

He turned to me, about to say something, but was interrupted by Zayde's voice coming through the speakers again as he spoke to Caiden. "You want to do the honours?"

Joseph had woken up.

26

caiden

"Fuck, yeah." I grinned at Zayde, and he returned my grin. In front of us, Hyde struggled against his restraints, his indignant shouts muffled by the hood. Stepping forward, I ripped the covering from his head, leaving him blinking at the sudden light.

He fell silent, staring between us open-mouthed, momentarily stunned. Then a dark rage came over his face.

"Untie me right now, you assholes! If this is some juvenile prank, I—"

I ended his rant with my fist to his face, and his head swung round at the impact.

"Fucker." He spat in the direction of my feet, blood flying out of his mouth. I glanced down at the floor—was that one of his teeth? Didn't really matter. He deserved it.

"That was for my girlfriend," I told him.

"Jessa? Why?"

His confusion matched mine. "Jessa is *not* my fucking girlfriend, you dick."

"But James told me..." He trailed off. "Doesn't fucking matter, just untie me right now! The joke's over."

"It's not a joke." Z stepped forwards, the blade in his hand glinting. Hyde's gaze was drawn straight towards it, and he paled, finally realising the serious shit he was in.

"We want answers. You'd better start talking, otherwise it's going to hurt."

"What the fuck is this all about?" His voice came out hoarse, a tremor of fear running through it. Here, bound, unable to go anywhere, he was completely at our mercy.

"First question. Why did Christine pay you to split me and Winter up, and why was Granville involved?"

He glared at me, temporarily defiant. "I'm not telling you anything."

"Z."

Zayde was there before the word had even left my mouth, the knife slicing through Joseph's hoodie and into his skin. Hyde roared in pain, his eyes wide and glassy. "You cut me, you fucking sadist! What's wrong with you?"

"I barely scratched you," Zayde said dismissively, giving Hyde a blank look. "Next time, though, I'll cut deeper, if you don't answer my friend's questions."

"Psycho bastard," Hyde muttered under his breath but immediately shut his mouth at Zayde's icy stare.

"I'll say it again." I dragged my chair towards him and straddled it, my boots almost touching his. We'd bound his legs to his chair—there's no way he wouldn't have tried kicking me otherwise. "Why did Christine pay you, and why was Granville involved?" The last part of my question was more for my own peace of mind. As much as Granville had proven to be of some use lately, and despite the fact he'd saved my girl, I still didn't like the guy.

Hyde stared at me, before he let out a defeated sigh. "Fine. She didn't want you together. She can't stand you. I hate you, I dislike Winter, thanks to her obsession with you and your friends, and I got paid to fuck with your relationship? Easiest money I ever made." He smirked, and I clenched my fists, the need to take another swing at him so fucking strong that it was only Z's presence next to me that helped me keep it together.

"And you didn't give a shit that you were fucking up our relationship? Didn't even question why?"

He shrugged. "Not my problem."

"Are you fucking serious?" I lunged forwards, and he shrank back in his chair. Before either of us could make a move, we were stopped in our tracks.

"Why, though?"

The voice came from behind Hyde, and I raised my gaze to see Winter standing there, hurt clear in her eyes.

For fuck's sake! Why hadn't the boys stopped her coming in here?

I shook my head at her, pleading at her to leave with my eyes, but she set her mouth stubbornly, coming around to crouch next to Hyde so she was at his eye level.

"Why?"

Her one softly spoken word had him opening his mouth without any more prompting.

"You're back together." It wasn't a question. He eyed her with a mixture of guilt and contempt. Yeah, he should feel fucking guilty after what he did to her.

She nodded, and he returned his gaze to mine. After a loud huff, he spoke through gritted teeth. "She didn't tell me why, but I'd imagine it has something to do with the not-so-secret fact that you've never seen eye to eye, and it's clear to everyone with eyes that you hate her."

"Can you blame me?" I muttered.

"Whatever, don't give a shit about your family

problems," he said, and my girl actually bared her teeth and growled at him, fire in her eyes.

"Put a muzzle on your bitch."

Winter jumped to her feet, her hand coming out so fast it was almost a blur. It connected with his face, a loud smack echoing across the room.

I was so fucking proud of her in that moment. Just in case he hadn't got the message, I added, "Insult my girl again, and I'll do more than knock out one of your teeth." My words were low, but full of intent.

"Think it's fun to knock me around when I can't fight back?" he sneered, but I could see the tears filling his eyes. I knew Winter had noticed, because she sucked in a breath, visibly composing herself, then unexpectedly came and sat on me.

"Snowflake, you know I love you near me, but I'm kind of in the middle of an interrogation here," I whispered in her ear.

"I know" was all she said, not moving from her position.

I groaned, defeated. So fucking stubborn.

"So she hates Cade. What about me?" Winter probed, using the same soft tone she'd used before, but her body was thrumming with tension, and I knew it wouldn't take much for her to fly off the handle again. Weirdly, her tension was actually calming me, and I could think clearly. I slid an arm round her waist, and she relaxed incrementally.

"I don't know. I do recall her saying that you having a relationship with your stepbrother was distasteful, and it would affect her reputation. You're clever—I'm sure you can put it together."

"Hmm." She nodded, deep in thought. "Yeah, I can see that. She alluded to it before, actually. Maybe in her own misguided way, she thought she was doing me a favour.

What about James, though? How did he end up being involved?"

A smug smile flitted across his face briefly, before he caught himself. "It was an easy way to drive a wedge between you, and I knew it would work. I knew Cavendish was a jealous, possessive hothead and would jump to the wrong conclusion—well, the right conclusion, for the outcome I wanted."

I stiffened, the rage that had disappeared just a minute ago back in full force. "Why is it that every fucking word out of your mouth makes me want to put my fist through it?" I gritted out.

He rolled his eyes but wisely didn't say anything else.

"How did you persuade James?" Winter spoke carefully.

"A pile of guilt about family loyalty and our rivalry with the Cavendishes. A well-timed black eye when that didn't work."

I looked at him closely, noting the shifty look in his eyes. He was holding something back, I could tell. Z must've noticed, too, because he stepped forwards, brandishing the knife. Joseph shrank back. "Okay, okay! I'll tell you the rest." He took a deep breath. "The black eye didn't work, either, so I had to get creative, and he realised he'd have to give in. The threat of me using my TA position to alter the records for the class you had with me so you'd fail was enough to persuade him. Oh, and fail your friend Drummond, too."

Winter gasped, and I stared at him. "You—you're a despicable person. Who abuses their position like that?" Her voice shook slightly, and I tightened my arm around her, pulling her against my chest.

"It's nothing personal. We're just on different sides."

"That's the weakest excuse I ever heard." Her voice was flat.

He stared at her unrepentantly. Next to me, Zayde cleared his throat, and I decided to move it along. We were running out of time, and we needed our answers before it was too late. "Next question. Why were you and your dad meeting with Christine tonight?"

"I can't answer that."

"Can't, or won't?"

He shook his head, and Z stepped forwards. The shallow cut on Hyde's arm, barely even a graze, had stopped bleeding. Zayde touched the tip of his blade to the cut, and a small drop of blood appeared on Hyde's skin. He flinched, mumbling a stream of expletives under his breath, but no answer was forthcoming. Z applied light pressure, and a thin trickle of blood made its way down his arm.

A hiss of pain escaped from between his gritted teeth. "Fine! I'll tell you. And you'd better make sure this doesn't get back to anyone. Not to Christine, and especially not my father, because my life won't be worth living." Raw fear was rolling off him in waves, and Z suddenly straightened up with a muttered curse, throwing the knife down with a clatter.

What the fuck? Pretty much shocked into silence, Winter and I watched as he used the torn sleeve of Hyde's hoodie, pressing it down on the cut to stem the bleeding.

"What's going on?" Winter ventured.

"His dad isn't a nice person" was all Z said, and I frowned but continued on with my line of questioning, aware that time was moving on. Over in the corner of the room, I could hear Allan's struggles as he fought against his own bonds.

"Tell us what you know."

He took a deep, shaky breath. "She's been working with my father for a long time. They've been plotting to take over

Alstone Holdings. I've never been privy to the ins and outs, but I know that there's the deal going down tomorrow with the De Witts, and she was going to make a move after that." Glaring at us, he added, "I probably would have found out more, if you hadn't interrupted the meeting tonight and fucking kidnapped me."

Fuck. Working together for a long time? I shouldn't have been surprised. That woman was a snake, pure and simple.

"What move was she going to make?" Winter asked softly.

"I honestly don't know. My father keeps all his cards close to his chest."

I let out a growl of frustration. "Is there anything else you can tell us?"

He shook his head. "Nothing, except those guys at the meeting tonight? I know she's paying them a lot of money, and I know they don't like her very much. I picked up that much from the short time I was there."

Fucking great. Information we already knew. "Why were you at the meeting, anyway?"

"I don't know exactly, but my father wants to bring me into the business. Not that I'd have anything to do with it if I had any choice in the matter." His words were bitter, but he stared at me defiantly, his lip curled. "I'm sure you can appreciate being groomed for the family business, being the son of the almighty Arlo Cavendish."

"Fuck you." I moved Winter off me, standing up and glancing at Z. "Tape?"

Zayde handed me the roll, and I had the immense satisfaction of slapping it over his mouth, silencing him.

"You've said enough tonight." Together, Z and I lifted him, chair and all, and carried him the short distance to the side of the room, where we arranged his chair facing the wall. I smirked, watching his eyes bulging and his cheeks puffing as he tried to speak. "Something you wanna say, Hyde?"

He glared up at me, defiant to the end. I could almost admire him for that, if I didn't loathe him so much.

"You ready to do this?" Zayde brought my attention to the next task at hand. I swallowed hard, staring over at the familiar figure slumped in the chair against the far wall. Clenching and unclenching my fists, I made my way towards his chair. This was going to be fucking tough.

"Let me try. Please?"

27

winter

After making my request, I held my breath as Caiden stared down at me, his gaze conflicted. I hadn't planned to get involved when I'd come here, but when I saw the look in his eyes...it could end up breaking him, if he had to do anything to hurt Allan. Despite everything, he'd pretty much grown up with him, and I could see that he still cared for him. Allan's betrayal had cut him deeply, and if I had to push past my own discomfort and misgivings to save him beating himself up over this, then I would.

"I want to try it my way, first," I said firmly. "If it doesn't work, Zayde can help me. Right, Z?" I glanced over at him, and he nodded silently.

"Okay," Caiden finally said. "For the record, I'm not fucking happy about this, but we're running out of time here, and I don't wanna waste time arguing about it."

I nodded. "Good. Come on, then. Bring him into the light." I waited, seated on Caiden's chair as the boys manoeuvred him into position. Caiden had been behind him, and when he came around to the front of Allan's chair and Allan took in both of us in front of him, his face drained of all colour, panic clear in his watery blue eyes.

"This will hurt," Zayde warned, but I don't think Allan was listening, too busy staring at me and Caiden in dismay. He flinched as Zayde ripped the tape from his mouth in one swift movement, his jaw working.

"Be right back," I murmured, hopping up from the chair and jogging over to the room where Cassius and Weston waited.

"Water," I explained, pulling the drawer open and grabbing a bottle.

"Hey, Winter." Weston's voice stopped me in the doorway. "Thanks for doing this."

I gave him a small smile, before I rushed back over to Allan. Both him and Caiden were frozen in position, the air between them thick with tension.

"Allan? I have some water for you. I'll have to tip it into your mouth." His pale, teary eyes swung to mine, and he gave a slight nod.

I pulled the cap off the bottle and carefully tipped it up, letting it trickle into his mouth. He swallowed and gave me a grateful look. Placing the bottle back on the floor, I took my seat once again.

Then I got up. "Zayde? Can I borrow your knife, please?"

He raised a brow but handed it to me. I walked around behind Allan and carefully cut through the restraints binding his hands. He sighed with relief, flexing his hands and rubbing at his wrists. As much as I should feel anger at him for what he'd done, and I did feel anger, I also felt an overwhelming sense of sadness.

"Would it be okay if I asked you a few questions?" I returned to my seat in front of him.

"What questions? What is going on here?"

"I was wondering what you were doing at the castle tonight. With my mother, of all people."

"I'm afraid I'm unable to tell you that." Allan shook his head slowly, his expression exhausted.

Taking a deep breath, I decided to take a gamble. "Does this have anything to do with your family connections?"

"*What*?" His shocked intake of breath told me everything I needed to know.

Mentally crossing my fingers, I continued. "I know. I know about my mother, about your Strelichevo connection."

He swayed in his chair a little, his face going from white to a deathly grey. For the first time, I was truly worried for his health.

Caiden must've been thinking along the same lines because he rushed over and placed his hand on Allan's back. "Bend down. Head between your knees," he instructed.

Allan obeyed without protest, holding the position for what felt like an eternity before he finally lifted his head. "I'm okay, now," he croaked. "I suppose I may as well fill in the rest of the details, since you seem to know so much already."

Finally. We were about to get some answers.

"I suppose I'd better start at the beginning..."

Caiden pulled up a chair next to me and reached out for my hand, threading his fingers through mine. Zayde rested his hand on the back of my chair as he came to stand behind us, his other hand on Caiden's shoulder, offering silent support.

Allan started his story, his words slow and halting, and the puzzle pieces began to click into place.

"I was born in a small village in Belarus. Mikhail Strelichevo's mother was my sister. Your grandmother was my best friend." He swallowed hard. "Not only my best friend, but the girl I'd fallen in love with. Unfortunately for me, my love was unrequited."

"My grandmother? I never knew anything about my grandparents," I said quietly.

"Yes. Her mother was English, and when we were both teenagers, she persuaded her family to move to England." He sighed, his eyes glazed as he recalled the details. "She was never happy in our village. It was only a matter of time. Anyway, we stayed in touch throughout the years, and we grew up. Your grandmother fell in love with an English boy, and I finally accepted the inevitable, that she'd only ever seen me as a friend.

"Your mother was born, and your grandmother asked if I would be her godfather. Of course, I accepted. It was an honorary title, more than anything, as we were in different countries. She would send me letters, with updates, and through her letters I began to fall in love with the idea of England myself."

Clearing his throat, he rubbed a hand over his face, lost in his memories. "My sister married into the Strelichevo family, Mikhail was born, and with that, things changed. You have to understand, they are a very powerful family. Not only in Belarus, but here, too. They have connections across Europe, and beyond. I knew I had to get out, before I became too entrenched in their criminal lifestyle."

"That didn't work out for you very well, did it?" I murmured.

He shook his head. "With the fall of the Soviet Union, I decided to take my chance and left the country. I went to Mikhail's father and made my case, and thankfully he was supportive of my decision. Unusual, perhaps, but he loved my sister very much, and she had a hand in persuading him. He falsified documents for me, allowing me to travel unchallenged. Upon my arrival in England, your grandparents found me a place to stay. I owed everything to them."

I felt Caiden's grip on mine tighten, and I stroked my thumb over his hand, a silent support. Not having known anything about my grandparents and having been estranged from my mother, I felt detached from the whole story he was telling us. Cade, though? Allan had been someone he lived with. Someone he trusted.

"I worked odd jobs here and there, constantly striving to improve my English, losing my accent. I ended up in the service industry and eventually fell into Mr. Cavendish's employment."

"How could you betray us?" Caiden's hoarse voice, full of pain, sliced straight through me, and I leaned into him, trying to provide whatever comfort I could.

Allan turned his eyes to meet Caiden's. "I never meant for it to go so far. By the time I realised what was happening, it was too late. I was...blinded to Christine's true nature. Blinded by my loyalty to her mother. I was in too deep, and there was no way out."

"You could have told my dad! He would have helped you."

He shook his head. "No. Don't you see? By the time I knew the depth of Christine's nature, too much had happened. Your father was in love with her, your mother had passed away, and your family was hanging on by a thread. All I could do was to prepare myself as much as I could, putting my own contingency plan in place, meeting with the Ivanov—"

His sentence was abruptly terminated by the door to the side room flying open with a crash.

Weston appeared in the doorway. Brandishing a phone in the air, his panicked gaze met Caiden's.

"Christine's calling."

28

caiden

I froze in shock. Christine? What the fuck? How?

"Allan's phone." His eyes, wide and guilty, met mine. "I'm sorry. In all the excitement, I forgot to turn it off."

Fuck. This wasn't good. Nothing we could do about it now, though. I stalked over to him, taking the phone from his outstretched hand. "It's okay. What's done is done. Wh —" The phone started ringing in my hand again, Christine's name flashing up on the screen.

I had to make a snap decision. Heading back over to Allan, I held out the phone. "I'm putting Christine on speaker. Answer it. Don't try anything stupid."

He nodded once, his eyes full of fear. I hit the button to connect the call and turned on the speaker.

"Allan?"

At the sound of Christine's voice, my jaw tightened, and I felt my girlfriend's hand from behind me reaching out to mine, holding on with a death grip. I curled my fingers around hers, as I held Allan's stare.

He closed his eyes briefly, then opened them. "Christine." His voice was steadier than I'd anticipated.

"Where are you?" Her words were harshly spoken.

I shook my head minutely at Allan.

"I'm—I'm okay."

"I didn't ask how you were, I asked where you were." There was a slight undercurrent of concern to her words, which I knew my girl was picking up on. She acted like Christine meant nothing to her, but I could see how she wanted Christine to have something redeemable about her. That was the thing about Winter. Despite everything, she always wanted to see the best in people.

What she refused to see was that some people were beyond redemption.

Allan blew out a shaky breath. "I—"

Before he could even finish the fucking word, she was addressing me. Us.

"I know you're listening in. I know it's you." She sucked in a breath, and spat out the next words as if they were acid. "Caiden Cavendish."

I felt the eyes of everyone on me, and bile rose up in my throat. How? How the fuck did she know I was involved?

I didn't have a chance to think about it, because she continued speaking. "Bring Allan, alone, to Alstone Docks within the next hour. No tricks. If you don't do as I say, Miss De Witt will meet an unfortunate end." She punctuated her words with the sound of a high-pitched scream, which I assumed was from Jessa.

I heard Winter gasp next to me, immediately clapping a hand over her mouth the second the sound escaped.

My head was fucking messed up. How the fuck did Jessa get involved in this shit? And why was Christine using her to threaten us?

She knew I was there, so there was no point hiding.

"Christine." I drawled her name, my tone completely indifferent. Inside, though, I was fucking raging.

She laughed, if you could call it a laugh. Acerbic, setting my teeth on edge. "I knew you were involved. Not so clever now, are you?"

"What do you want?" I got straight to the point.

Her words seemed to echo around the warehouse. "Be at the docks with Allan." There was a pause and the sound of a muffled voice, and then she added, "Bring the Hyde boy, too. No one else."

The call abruptly ended.

Fuck.

This was it. Our time was officially up.

I sank into the chair behind me, running my hand through my hair. Shit, how could I do this? How the fuck could I keep anyone safe? How had I fucked up so badly that she knew who I was?

"I'll go on my own," I finally said.

"No."

The voice came from behind Allan, and I jerked upright to see Cassius standing there, arms folded across his chest.

I shook my head. "You heard her. I have to go alone. Not only that, it's too dangerous."

He came around Allan to stand next to me. "Allan's seen me now, anyway. I'm coming."

"Me too." Weston joined him. "Hi, Allan." A brief expression of hurt flashed across his face, but he masked it. Allan winced at the sight of him, his face falling.

"And me." Winter's grip on my hand tightened.

"Same." Zayde's tone was uncompromising.

They were fucking insane if they thought I was going to

let any of them get within reach of Christine, but I went along with it for now.

I indicated with my head towards the office, and the others followed me in. After closing the door, I swiped my phone from the desk, powering it on. "We're out of time. West, can you forward everything we have to Dad? I'm gonna try and get hold of him."

My call went straight to voicemail. Fuck.

"Cass, Z? Can you try your dads?"

"They're at AMC. No phones allowed." My brother's eyes met mine. "Leave Dad a message. I'm sending everything to him now."

I pulled up the message thread with my dad, tapping out a new message.

Me: DO NOT IGNORE!!! Check your email as soon as you get this. Leaving you a voice message too.

I hit the Call button again and left a message. "Dad. Christine's planning to take over Alstone Holdings. West has sent you all the evidence we have. We're heading to the docks—we have Allan, and she has Jessa De Witt." I paused, then choked out, "In case everything goes wrong, I want you to know, I've forgiven you. And I'm sorry for the way I acted, too."

Winter grabbed my hand as I ended the call. "I'm proud of you," she whispered, kissing my jaw softly. I gave her a small smile, keeping hold of her hand as I turned to the others.

"I'll take Allan and Hyde. We've only got my car and the SUV here, so we'll split up, and when we get near to the docks, we'll pull over and I'll go on in with them. I don't want any of you in danger."

I took in the identical expressions of grim determination on their faces. Fuck, they weren't going to listen to me. "Z, can you get hold of Mack on the way? We don't have any time to lose."

He nodded. "On it."

I leaned closer to my girlfriend. "Baby, can you get hold of Granville? See if we can get him to go to AMC if we can't get hold of Dad."

I continued to bark out orders, not that we had time to do much. It was fucking pissing down with rain outside, it was going to take us long enough to get to the docks as it was.

"Everything's sent." My brother looked up from the computer.

"Good. Let's go."

29

winter

Caiden followed behind Cassius' SUV, our speed much slower than usual on the rain-slicked roads. I could just about make out the taillights in front of us, the wind sending the rain lashing at the windows faster than the wipers could clear it away.

"If anything happens to me..." Caiden's voice trailed off, white-knuckling the steering wheel, his jaw set.

"Don't talk like that," I begged him. I couldn't let myself think about anything going wrong. Somehow, we had to get through this. My fingers closed around the sheathed knife I'd liberated from Zayde before we left. I knew that Caiden would try and keep me away from my mother, but there was no way I was letting him face her alone. We'd thought we'd been so prepared, but now here we were, our only protection a few knives, and no backup.

My phone battery was low, but I made the call.

"Winter? What's happening?" James' concerned voice came through the speaker.

"Christine found out we had Allan." I hurried to continue, interrupting his shocked exclamation. "She has

Jessa. Why would she have Jessa? And why does Joseph think she's Caiden's girlfriend?"

"Oh, fuck. I told him that they were together. Trying to throw him off the scent, make him think his plan worked. What do you mean she has Jessa?"

"I don't know. But we're on our way to the docks. She said if we don't bring Allan back, she's going to kill Jessa."

"What the fuck!"

"She sounds pretty desperate. No idea how and when she got her, but at this point, that's not important. We have to get her back."

"What can I do?"

"Can you get to AMC? Try and get hold of Arlo?"

"On my way." I heard the sound of a door slamming. "Should I call the police or something?"

"No. No police. Remember, we kidnapped two people. Not to mention the petrol bombs. Oh, and Zayde torturing Joseph."

"He what?"

"Just a bit. Only a tiny cut. It couldn't really be classed as torture, but...you know. The police won't see it the same way."

"Right. Anything else?" The sound of his car engine starting up came through the speakers.

"No. Just get hold of Arlo, and get him to check his phone. Thanks." I ended the call and turned to Caiden. "Do you have a plan?"

"No." That one word was loaded with despair, and my stomach flipped.

"Cade..."

"What the fuck am I supposed to do? If I don't hand over Allan, I'll have Jessa's death on my conscience. I hand him over, and best-case scenario, she takes me and her henchmen get to enact their revenge on me. Worst case, they decide to kill me. Either way, I'm fucked."

His voice cracked at the end, and it broke me. Tears filled my eyes, and I bit my lip, hard, to stop them falling. I reached out and placed my hand on his thigh, unable to speak, needing to touch him. I couldn't let myself think about what might happen. There had to be something I could do. I wouldn't allow her to take the man I loved away from me.

We slowed, and I could just about make out the docks up ahead. Cassius pulled the SUV off the road, and we stopped behind him. This was it.

Caiden climbed out of the car without another word, slamming the door behind him. I climbed out after him, pulling my hood over my head to try and provide some protection from the pouring rain. Lightning flashed overhead, illuminating his face in stark relief as we stared across the car at one another. Then I ran to him, and his arms were around me, and his lips were on mine, hard and desperate. I could taste the rain, and the salt of tears. Mine or his? I couldn't tell. All I knew was, I didn't want to let him go. I wouldn't let him face this alone.

He pulled back, cupping my face in his hands, his gaze holding mine. Neither of us spoke aloud, our eyes saying everything we couldn't put into words.

Then he let me go.

My whole body began shaking, the severity of the situation hitting me as Cassius, Weston, and Zayde came to stand at my side. Cassius tugged me into his arms, and I leaned into him, letting his strength support me. Caiden had point-blank refused to let us go in with him. He was going to drive Allan and Joseph into the docks, alone, and wing it. He had to know we wouldn't wait outside though.

The rain was easing up slightly. The lightning still flashed, and there was a distant rumble of thunder in the distance, but it was no longer driving against my face.

"Let's go." At Zayde's low command, I spun to face him. "We go in, avoid being seen, get Cade and Jessa out of there. Mack's on his way, but we don't have time to wait for him. Everyone ready?"

We nodded, slipping into formation. As the entrance to the docks came into view, I saw the entrance barrier was open. Inside, three cars were parked in a kind of U shape, and Caiden had stopped in front of them. Under the floodlights, I could see my mother, and off to the side, Petr holding a struggling Jessa.

We drew nearer, keeping to the shadows, before splitting up. Cassius and Weston took one side. I started to follow Zayde, but he pushed me back. "Go. Hide behind the SUV. I don't want anyone seeing you." Then he was gone, slipping away into the shadows, and I was left alone.

Before I could figure out what to do, the SUV door opened, and Caiden got out. "Give me Jessa," he called. I couldn't make out Christine's reply through the sound of the rain and inched closer, dropping to a crouch and coming around the side of the car. Now I could see my mother clearly. Her face, distorted with hate as she stared at Caiden, a gun in her hand. My boyfriend, holding his head high, facing her down.

I didn't stop to think. I couldn't take the risk of her shooting him. I shot around the side of the car and threw myself in front of him. He cried out, and I felt his terror for me break over me in a suffocating wave.

My mother staggered backwards in shock at my appearance, dropping her hand and pointing the gun at the ground.

"Winter? What are you doing here?"

The relief of the gun no longer being pointed at us gave me the strength I needed. Out of the corner of my eye, I saw Cassius and Weston inching closer to Petr and Jessa. Distraction.

I answered her question with one of my own. "Why did you kill my dad?"

Her face paled. "What? I—"

"Don't lie to me!"

Our eyes met, and hers narrowed. "How did you know?"

And there it was. She'd admitted it. A spark of white-hot rage ignited inside me, rushing through my blood, turning it to fire. It fuelled me. "Why do you think I came to Alstone? I knew there was something suspicious about his death."

Her face hardened. "He deserved it—poking his nose where it didn't belong. He knew too much. Thanks to my connections with the Strelichevos, I was able to arrange an 'accidental' gas leak." A smug, satisfied smile spread across her face. "He really should have been more careful."

The fire raged inside me, and I dug my nails into my palms so tightly, I felt the skin break. Tiny pinpricks of blood heated my chilled fingertips. "You killed the only parent I ever knew. The only one who ever cared about me." My words were calm, measured, though it was costing me *everything* I had to keep the fury from bleeding through my voice.

Caiden's breath ruffled my hair, and I felt his body tense behind mine. I hoped he'd stay in place—Christine seemed to have temporarily forgotten about him, and the longer I could keep the attention on me, the better.

"You were better off without him. Look at you now. Attending one of the most prestigious universities in the country, a guaranteed legacy, countless riches once you join me on the board of Alstone Holdings."

"Once I join you?" I focused on the final part of her speech. "How, exactly, is that going to happen? I'm not a Cavendish."

She laughed. "The Cavendishes will cease to be an issue, as of tomorrow."

My stomach flipped, and everything seemed to still. "What do you mean by that?"

"I may as well tell you. The De Witt deal that Arlo has been working on? It will be signed tomorrow morning, and after that, Arlo will no longer be of use to me. Your stepbrother, here, he will pay tonight."

"What do you mean?" My words were a breathless whisper.

She directed a poisonous smile in Caiden's direction. "Imagine my surprise when Allan and Mr. Hyde were taken from right under our noses this evening. I had no idea who could have done such a thing, until Petr came to me, bleeding from the arm and holding a knife. One of the very knives that Arlo had purchased for his eldest son, the Christmas before last, in an attempt to worm his way into his good graces. He had them custom made, you know."

"Fuck," Caiden muttered from behind me. I didn't dare to move to comfort him; I didn't want anything to set Christine off.

"I knew that the game was up. It was then a case of sending a message to Miss De Witt's phone, to say that Caiden wanted to meet with her. She didn't question it—stupid girl."

She sighed. "I have to say, I'm extremely disappointed to

see you here, Winter. I knew you had feelings for him, but I never imagined you'd be so stupid as to follow him into something like this. Especially not where his girlfriend is concerned. Don't you have any pride?"

"Never mind that. What did you mean by Caiden paying tonight?"

She raised her arm. The arm holding the gun. "One Cavendish down, three to go. I was originally going to let the boys live, but after tonight...no. I'm afraid I can't risk keeping them alive."

"One Cavendish down?" Bile rose in my throat.

"Arlo's wife was easy. The right words whispered in her ear, the open bottle of pills...I barely had to do anything. Arlo will have a car accident tomorrow, on the way back from signing the contract. Weston will go mad with grief, once he finds out every member of his family is dead, and it'll be a simple matter to stage his death to look like a suicide. Now, be a good girl and step aside so I can eliminate one of them here and now."

"No." I stared at her, never faltering.

She waved the gun threateningly.

"Move, or I will shoot you. I'd hoped you'd join me, but if you refuse to see sense, then you are of no use to me."

Her eyes glittered maniacally. She really was insane.

"I would never join you," I hissed. "Never, ever."

"Have it your way." She squeezed the trigger.

Several things happened at once.

Time slowed down to a crawl.

Caiden shoved me with all his might, sending me flying across the docks. There was the sound of two gunshots and shouting. Someone screaming.

My only thought was Caiden. Nothing else mattered.

Winded, I struggled to my feet, crawling towards the

SUV as more gunshots sounded, the noises rebounding off the buildings, echoing all around me.

Where was he?

My eyes were drawn to the figure on the floor, unmoving, the rain soaking through his clothes.

I took in his unnatural stillness, the blood pooling at his side.

No.

No.

No.

Reaching him, I fumbled for his pulse with shaking hands but couldn't feel it. I tried, and tried again, my fingers slipping over his soaked skin as I tried desperately to feel for anything. *Anything* that would tell me he was still here with me.

Nothing.

I curled myself over his lifeless body, stretching my arms around him and laying my head on his chest.

His heartbeat, always so strong and steady, was silent.

"Don't leave me," I sobbed. "Wake up. *Please*, wake up. I can't live without you."

The pain in my chest was so immense that I could barely breathe through it.

"You won't have to."

I looked up, through my tears, the rain falling on my face and fizzing on my skin. My mother stood over me with a gun in her hand.

"You killed my boyfriend!" I screamed. "You killed my dad!"

"And since you refuse to join me, you can join them." She smiled.

Reaching down, I pulled the knife from its sheath and lunged forwards, slipping on the wet ground. Zayde's words echoed in my head—*stick and twist*—and I channelled every single piece of my rage and heartbreak into my strike. I stabbed it through her leg, and twisted it.

She toppled backwards, her shrill scream of pain echoing around us, and the momentum tipped me over the edge. I was falling with her, still holding on to the knife, landing on top of her with a thud.

There was blood coming from her forehead. Why was there blood coming from her head?

I shook my own head, blinking, then rolled off her body.

"Winter." I was being scooped up, someone carrying me.

"*Caiden!*" I cried his name over and over, desperately struggling against the person carrying me.

"Shhh. We need to get you out of here." The sound of sirens drew closer, and then I was being bundled into a car, and we were moving.

Without Caiden.

I left my heart behind, shattered into a million pieces.

aftermath

"Even the darkest night will end
and the sun will rise."

— *VICTOR HUGO, LES MISÉRABLES*

AFTERMATH

winter

I slowly blinked my eyes open, screwing them up against the light. The sun was streaming in the window, the rays falling across my arm. Where was I?

"I wondered when you were going to wake." I turned my head to see the speaker. Arlo's face creased into a smile when he saw me.

"Where am I? Wh—" I stopped dead as everything came rushing back to me. A cry tore from my throat. Utter devastation tore through me, leaving me gasping for breath.

Caiden.

I curled into a ball, the pain too much to bear. I sobbed into the pillow, my heart breaking all over again.

A warm hand touched my head, brushing my hair back gently. "Shhh. It's okay," Arlo soothed, the mattress dipping as he settled on to the side of my bed.

"How can it be okay when he's gone?" My words came out as an incoherent sob.

"What?" His voice was suddenly alarmed.

"How can you be so calm after everything that's happened?" I choked out, turning my head to meet his eyes.

"Take a deep breath. Maybe I'd better fill in the blanks."

arlo

Something wasn't right. Call it a gut instinct. I glanced across the table at Lars De Witt, engaged in casual conversation with Michael Lowry. He was relaxed, swirling the whiskey in his glass absentmindedly. Nothing wrong there. The official signing of the deal tomorrow was only a formality; this would benefit all of us greatly. These drinks were a chance to show him that we'd accepted him as one of our own. Of course, he already belonged to Alstone Members Club, but here, in our inner sanctum, we only allowed a trusted few.

Still, I couldn't seem to shake the unease gnawing away at me.

"Sir?" At the low voice of my security guy, I sat up straight. "We have a gentleman at the door of the club. He wishes to speak to you, and he's refusing to take no for an answer."

I frowned. "Who?"

"The Granville boy. James. He's, uh, rather agitated."

"Right. Leave it with me." I turned to address the table. "Excuse me, gentlemen. Something has come up that requires my urgent attention." With that, I strode from the room, making my way out to the main floor of the club. At the doorway, I paused. James Granville stood, being held back by the doorman, his face desperate and panicked.

"Let him go," I commanded the doorman, before turning

to James. Before I could say anything, urgent words were tumbling from his lips.

"Do you have your phone? You need to come with me, now."

I reached into my pocket, pulling out my phone and turning it on. "What's this all about?"

"Caiden and Winter. They're in trouble."

A sudden, sharp pain pierced my chest, and I immediately reacted, not wasting a second. I barked out an order as I headed in the direction of my Range Rover, James Granville hot on my heels.

"We'll take my car. You drive."

There was no time to do more than take a quick glance at the emails Weston had sent me, but my heart broke for my eldest son as I listened to his voicemail. The sheer desperation in his voice, his words of forgiveness. I *had* to get to him. I hoped and prayed we weren't too late.

As we drove, I made calls, barking out orders over the speaker. I'd never been so grateful for my connections, as I threw everything I had into this. I didn't allow myself to think of the double betrayal of both my wife and butler; that could wait until afterwards. Once I knew my son was safe.

James Granville was silent next to me, other than giving brief answers to my questions. I knew there was no love lost between him and my son, but I had the distinct impression that there was respect there between them. Afterwards, once this was over, maybe I would find out what had happened to change their relationship. My money was on my stepdaughter.

Now wasn't the time to think about that, though.

As James brought the SUV to a careful stop, I unsnapped my seat belt and dragged my finger along the side of the centre console, feeling for the button that opened the hidden compartment where I kept a small pistol, loaded and ready. It had always been a precautionary measure, advised by my security team, and I'd never dreamed I'd actually have to use it.

Easing the pistol from its cradle, I grasped the smooth, cool metal in my palm, and turned to James. "We're here. Everything is in place, on my end, but I have no idea what kind of situation we're going into. Stay in the car."

"I'm coming with you." James' words were uncompromising, and I nodded in acceptance.

"Fine. Do you know how to fire a gun?"

He hesitated briefly, then shook his head. "No, but I have this." He brandished an innocent-looking small metal tube.

"Retractable baton?" I raised a quizzical brow. "That'll do."

We exited my Range Rover and crept through the entrance to the docks, sidling down the side of the SUV blocking my view. James Granville disappeared, off to the left, and I hoped he'd stay out of trouble.

I stopped dead, hearing Christine's voice. "Arlo's wife was easy. The right words whispered in her ear, the open bottle of pills...I barely had to do anything. Arlo will have a car accident tomorrow, on the way back from signing the contract. Weston will go mad with grief, once he finds out every member of his family is dead, and it'll be a simple matter to stage his death to look like a suicide. Now, be a good girl, and step aside so I can eliminate one of them here and now."

It was like the scales suddenly fell from my eyes and I could see properly for the first time in years. I staggered backwards at the venomous words spewing from her lips, clutching my heart.

At the sound of gunshots, I leapt into action. Lives

depended on me keeping a cool head, and I needed to stay focused.

The back door of the SUV abruptly sprang open, and Allan fell out at my feet. Two things happened in quick succession—he scrambled to his feet and saw me; then he looked over my shoulder, and raw fear filled his eyes.

Throwing himself at me, he pressed me into the side of the car. Temporarily stunned, I froze in place as his body jerked against my chest to the sound of another gunshot.

Suddenly his weight was gone, and he fell to the ground, the life draining from his unseeing eyes.

What?

How could he be gone? So suddenly? Before we'd even had a chance to talk?

Sorrow washed over me in a heavy, suffocating wave. Despite Allan's betrayal, despite everything, he'd saved my life.

He'd chosen to give up his life for my own.

Behind him stood a man I vaguely recognised, gun raised, staring down at Allan in abject horror. He whispered something that I couldn't understand, his face turning ashen as the realisation dawned that he'd shot Allan instead of me.

As if in slow motion, the man's head swung to the side with a blow from James' baton, followed by Zayde Lowry leaping onto him, a blade glinting in his hand.

Heaving a sigh of relief, I turned away, my focus returning to my son. They were capable enough.

Edging around the car, I was greeted with a sight that filled me with dread. My son's lifeless body, Winter over him, and Christine pointing a gun at her head.

I didn't hesitate.

I lifted my hand and rained down chaos.

The bullet struck straight and true, embedding itself in Christine's skull. The sound of sirens filled the air, the ambulance I'd called on a hunch almost here, as I dropped to my knees in front of Caiden.

A hand came to my shoulder, and Weston was there, his eyes wild and afraid as he stared down at his brother's body.

"Take your sister, please." I spoke calmly, although inside the storm was raging. I would *not* lose Caiden. I would not allow it.

I performed CPR unceasingly until the paramedics forcibly pulled me away, and then I had to watch as my son flatlined twice in the ambulance on the way to the hospital. I was overcome with total and utter despair, as the paramedics battled tirelessly to save him.

They say your life flashes before you when you die; mine flashed before me during that ambulance ride to the hospital. I prayed with everything I had that Caiden would make it.

I never got a chance to tell him I loved him and I forgave him, too.

winter

"Eventually they managed to stabilise him. He lost a lot of blood, but he's going to be okay."

My heart stuttered, and I stared up at Arlo through my tears. "He—he's not dead?"

He smiled gently. "No. He had us worried there for a

while, but he's a fighter. He hasn't woken up yet, but he'll be alright."

I bolted upright, throwing my arms around Arlo. "Thank you. Thank you for..." I couldn't get the rest of the words out, I was crying so hard.

His arms came around me, and he rubbed my back in soothing motions. "I know. I know." His voice broke on his next words. "For a moment, I thought I was too late."

Then I was the one comforting him, and we cried together.

Eventually he released me, wiping his eyes. "That was a long time overdue. I want to personally apologise to you, Winter. I have a lot of making up to do once Caiden is awake."

"Let's start afresh. A brand-new start." A thought occurred to me as he smiled down at me, looking so much like an older version of Caiden at that point, that it made me ache for my boyfriend. I *needed* to see him. "I guess we're not related anymore, huh? Since my mother is gone."

He squeezed my hand gently. "You're family. That will never change. Now, what do you say we go and find Caiden?"

"Yes."

As we walked, I asked Arlo why I was in a hospital room, and he told me that I'd basically flipped out and had to be sedated. Physically, I was fine, but emotionally, I'd shut down.

I didn't care about any of that. All I wanted was to see Caiden with my own eyes, to see that he was alive.

He'd been so still in my arms.

And the blood. So much blood.

If I'd ever wondered exactly how much he meant to me, I knew now.

"Here we are." Arlo indicated towards a door. "I've paid for the best private treatment possible. You can go in, talk to him. The doctors say it helps to hear familiar voices, and I'm sure yours will be the one he most wants to hear.

I entered the room, my eyes going straight to the bed where my boyfriend lay, all sorts of tubes and machines surrounding him.

"*Caiden*," I whispered, my lip trembling as I took in his still form. I collapsed into the chair next to his bed, gently threading my fingers through his, careful not to disturb anything. The only thing that helped me keep it together was the machine showing his steady heartbeat. Proof he was alive and he was going to come back to me.

I bent my head to whisper in his ear. "I love you. So, so much. Wake up for me, *please*, Caiden." I brought my free hand up to run it through his hair, the strands soft under my fingers. I ran it over the scratchy stubble on his jaw, every touch feeling like a privilege after coming so close to losing him.

"He's going to be okay." At Weston's voice, I turned, to see him, Cassius, and Zayde grouped around the end of the bed. I hadn't even been aware of them; my entire focus had been on Caiden.

"What happened?"

Over the next few hours, we discussed and analysed what had happened, and the boys each took turns to fill in the blanks. Cassius and Weston had managed to get Jessa away from Petr. While they were doing that, Zayde had taken out another one of Christine's men. Hyde Senior had managed to escape during the chaos, Joseph in tow, but Arlo apparently had a plan to pin some stuff on him that would get him locked away.

I listened carefully, asking questions when I needed

clarification, Christine's words about the death of Caiden and Weston's mum coming back to me. It didn't appear that Weston had heard her—too far away and too busy with Jessa and Petr to pay attention. I was so thankful—he deserved better than to hear the news second-hand from her, and I knew Caiden wanted to tell him in his own time.

The gunshots I'd heard? Petr had a gun, and I gathered from what Arlo had told me that he had been the one to shoot Allan, as well as shooting at the boys. Mack had made it there at the same time as the ambulance, and he'd been the one to organise the clean-up while the rest of us were en route to the hospital.

Caiden had been lucky. The bullet had struck his abdomen, but miraculously there was no major damage. He'd passed out from the blood loss, but the doctors weren't worried—they were confident he was going to make a full recovery. When I'd been panicking, thinking the worst, he'd still had a pulse, but it must have been too faint for me to feel.

I never, ever wanted to go through that again.

Once I was completely up to date, the room fell silent.

"It's really over, isn't it?" I said at last. "After all this time."

"At last." Cassius gave me a small smile.

"Yeah." The hoarse, scratchy word from behind me had me spinning around, as something happened that I'd thought only happened in movies.

Stormy eyes met mine, and Caiden's lips curved into a smile.

My heart jumped, and tears of utter relief and joy filled my eyes as his fingers curled around mine. He winced, staring down at the dressing covering his wound, as the memories rushed back to him.

"Christine?"

"Gone," I told him, and he looked at me, his gaze searching.

"Are you okay?"

I nodded, running my thumb over the back of his hand, and leaned down to kiss him softly. "I'm okay. You...you got shot because of me." My lips trembled, and the tears that were filling my eyes spilled down my cheeks. When I thought about how close I'd come to losing him...I choked back a sob, desperately trying to hold it together.

His grip on my hand loosened, and he reached up to brush my tears away. "I told you I'd take a bullet for you, baby." He held my gaze, his voice lowering to a croaky whisper. "I'd do anything for you."

"Please don't get shot again."

That smirk I loved so much played across his lips. "I'm not planning on it."

"Cade." I smiled through my tears as I stared down at the man who owned my whole heart. "I love you so much."

The depth of the love I felt for him was reflected in his eyes, shining out of him, taking my breath away.

He tugged me closer.

"It's over now. But you and me? We're just beginning."

EPILOGUE 1

winter

Fourteen days later...

"You okay?" I squeezed Caiden's hand, and he nodded, followed by a slight wince as we stood, the hard pew behind us. His hand automatically went to his abdomen, and I eyed him, concerned.

He grinned at me. "Never been better."

"Don't smile, we're at a funeral." I squeezed his hand again, then stepped closer to him and placed my other hand on top of his, over the scar that remained. "I love you. You don't have to be strong all the time, Cade. You can lean on me, too."

"I know." He dropped a kiss on my head. "Thanks," he added quietly.

It was a simple service. Private, family only. The press had come sniffing around, but one well-placed call from Arlo and they'd disappeared as soon as they'd arrived.

Creed and Mack had worked overtime with the clean-up crew in the two weeks since everything had happened. We'd had to bring Arlo in on the discussions, because the docks belonged to Alstone Holdings, after all, and what Mack was proposing was going to have an effect on the company. The official line was that Christine had been inspecting one of the cargo boats docked at the harbour. She'd taken Allan with her, as she'd done in the past, which wasn't anything unusual. Unfortunately, there had been a gas leak on the boat while she was on board, and...*boom*. Gone, just like that.

I didn't know all the details, but it kind of felt like poetic justice, since she'd had my dad killed in a gas explosion. The actual blast that Mack and Creed had orchestrated had obliterated the boat and taken out part of the dock, leaving the building I'd been held in structurally unsound.

According to Creed's sources, Petr had fled the country, badly injured, and the Strelichevos had pulled their operation out of Alstone. They'd already been on the verge of leaving, and with Christine gone, there was zero monetary incentive for them to stay. We still had loose ends to tie up, such as the Hydes plotting against Alstone Holdings, but those were worries for someone else. Finally, I felt free. Able to breathe properly. Knowing that no one was lurking around the corner waiting for me. Knowing that my dad could now rest in peace.

Arlo stood, silently, his head bowed, as the ceremony concluded. We had no bodies, so there'd be no cremation or burial. I knew today had been hard on him—despite everything, he'd loved both Christine and Allan in his own way, and the shock of their betrayal cut deep.

"Arlo." I pulled Caiden forwards, and then Arlo was gripping us both in a hug. I reached blindly behind me, tugging Weston into our circle. No words were spoken as we held each other.

"I love you. All of you," Arlo said hoarsely. "We're going to be okay."

I smiled, his quiet affirmation filling me with warmth. Every word he spoke was true.

We were going to be okay.

We had each other.

The day after the funeral, Caiden got a call from Arlo, asking us to meet him at the docks. I was really sick of the place, in all honesty, and I'd be glad if I never set foot in it again, but Arlo had insisted we both be there. When we turned up, parking just inside the open entrance barrier, I saw Cassius' SUV, along with Arlo's car. What was going on?

"There you are." Arlo waved us over to where he was standing with Cassius, Weston, and Zayde. He clapped his hands for attention. "I called you all here today to make an announcement. This has been signed off by the board already, by the way. The docks are officially on the market."

On the market? Did that mean—

"You're selling the docks?" Cassius stared at him.

He nodded. "Yes. I think we can all agree that this place holds some rather...unpleasant memories for all of us. Alstone Holdings will belong to the five of you one day, and—"

"The five of us?" I whispered. "But I—I'm not—"

"I had Christine's shares transferred into your name." He waved a hand. "Plus, I get the impression that one day, in the future, my son might like to marry you." My cheeks heated, and I chanced a quick look at Caiden, who was watching me with a smile on his face. "Preferably not in the near future."

Arlo winked, and I blushed harder, Caiden tugging me into his arms with a chuckle.

"Stop embarrassing her, Dad."

"Sorry." He wasn't sorry. "As I was saying, Alstone Holdings will belong to you, and I want you to feel comfortable with every aspect of the business. I know that this will be a sticking point, therefore, the land is being sold."

"What will you do instead?" Cassius asked the question that I'm sure was on all of our minds.

"It's already been sorted. We've acquired new premises, just ten minutes down the coast, with much more convenient road connections, and room for expansion we never had here. With our additional cargo from the De Witts, we were at a breaking point. It came at the right time, in all honesty."

"I for one will be glad to see the back of this fucking place," Zayde muttered.

"Me too," I murmured. Caiden kissed the top of my head, his arms tightening around me.

"Now, Winter. I have something I wanted to share with you personally. Follow me, please."

What now? I obediently trailed after Arlo, rounding the long, low storage building that hid the building I'd been held captive in from view. Caiden stayed close to me, a silent support, as I stared at the scene in front of me.

My mouth fell open in shock. "What...where..." I couldn't think.

He smiled at me. "Caiden and Weston told me a little about what you went through. I know you gave them permission to, and I want you to know that it goes no further."

I nodded. I'd wanted the boys to be open with him about

what had happened, and part of that included telling him about my time in captivity. We hadn't given all the details, but enough to give him a cohesive story.

"After they'd told me, I was...I think 'horrified' would be the appropriate word. I did some digging, made a few calls to your friend Mr. Pope. By the way, he speaks very highly of your negotiation skills, Winter." He gave me a grin that was so infectious, I couldn't help returning it.

His smile faded. "What I managed to glean was that the Strelichevo syndicate had been using our docks to transport drugs, thanks to Christine's underhanded techniques. That would have been bad enough—after all, if it had come to light, Alstone Holdings would have been liable. That wasn't the most concerning news, though." He scrubbed his hand across his face. "At some point, that building you were held in had been used for people."

"What do you mean?" Nausea rose up inside me.

"Human trafficking. Girls."

"*No.*" I gripped hold of Caiden's arm, needing his strength.

He smiled sadly. "I'm afraid so. In cutting the head off this operation, so to speak, it's ended with us. But cut the head off in one place, and another will grow elsewhere."

"That's just..."

"I won't let it lie, Winter. Listen to me. I am going to donate a considerable amount of my own personal funds and resources towards hunting this operation down and ending it for once and for all, I can promise you that."

"Thank you." What else could I say?

"As for the building..." He indicated to the empty area where it had once stood. "I had the basement filled in and the entire building demolished. Even if the future buyer keeps the docks as they are, it's gone, never to be seen again."

"Thank you," I said again, a lump in my throat and tears in my eyes.

"You're welcome. I hope it makes some small difference, at least."

It did.

I gave him a grateful smile and he nodded, before glancing at his watch. "Better get going. The estate agent is due in half an hour to take photos."

Caiden took my hand. "Come on, baby. Let's go home."

We drove away, and I never looked back.

EPILOGUE 2

caiden

Twenty-nine days later...

"What's going on?" Winter's gaze was suspicious as she took in the four of us standing in front of her.

I grinned. "Do you trust me, baby?"

Her eyes narrowed. "You know I do, but why does it feel like a trick question?"

"No tricks." I took her hand, leading her towards the door. "Come with us."

We split into two cars so I could drive my girl, needing to be alone with her. It had only been just under a month since everything had gone down, but with all the shit that had been going on, it felt like we'd barely had time to be alone together. Not only that, she'd refused to have sex with me because of my bullet wound. Oral wasn't out, but she wouldn't let me inside her, saying I needed to heal. So fucking stubborn. Yeah, getting shot had really fucking hurt, but I was fine now. As fine as I was gonna get, anyway. I still had twinges of pain, but it was nothing I couldn't handle.

I was tired of waiting, and I knew she was, too, so I was planning on using all my powers of persuasion later.

My phone rang as we were pulling onto the motorway, and I connected the speaker so I could answer my dad, pushing all thoughts of sex from my mind.

"Alright, Dad?"

"Caiden. Just wanted to touch base and give you an update." He was silent for a few seconds. "Also... Do... Do you want me to talk to Weston with you about Christine and your mother?"

I sighed, feeling conflicted. Next to me, Winter placed her hand on my leg to let me know she was there for me. "Yeah. I'd appreciate that. Let's just give it some time. Wait till things calm down a bit. We've all been through a lot of shit, and half of it still hasn't sunk in yet. You know?"

He sighed, too—one of relief. Neither of us were looking forward to that conversation. "Good plan, son. I'll be there for you, whenever you decide to tell him." His voice lightened. "The main reason I was calling was to pass on some good news. I pulled some strings, and thanks to my connections, my lawyer's managing to build up a decent case against Roland Hyde."

Hyde's dad, I mouthed to Winter and she nodded.

"So what's gonna happen?"

"We don't know, yet, but it'll go to court. We've got plenty to throw at him, and some of it's bound to stick. Fraud, embezzlement, blackmail—even if nothing comes of it, his name will be forever sullied in this town."

"That's great. Keep me updated, yeah?"

"Will do. See you both tomorrow for dinner." He ended the call, and I passed the time with my girl, talking about everything and nothing. Every day, I felt lighter. Finally getting answers, and being able to share stuff with my dad like I was now, and my relationship with Winter going from strength to strength? Yeah, I'd go as far as to say life was really fucking good.

As we entered the suburban area that led to our destination, Winter's phone buzzed. She swiped it open and laughed at something on the screen. Fuck, I loved to hear her laugh. All I wanted was for her to be happy. "Something funny you wanna share, Snowflake?"

She grinned. "It's just a meme Cass sent to our group chat with Jessa."

What the fuck? "Did you just say *Jessa*? As in Jessa De Witt?" We came to a stop at a red light, and I stared at her in shock.

She peered through her lashes at me, biting her lip, making my dick fucking jump.

"Snowflake," I growled in warning.

"Sorry." Her eyes sparkled with mischief. Yeah, she knew exactly what she was doing. "It's just a group chat Cass set up that he added me to." Her voice lowered, turning serious. "After everything that happened at the docks...well, he said Jessa took it really badly. She was so scared, Cade. Did you know that they threw her in the boot of the car, in the dark, all tied up and gagged? And one of the men, um...touched her. Inappropriately."

"Fuck," I breathed.

"My thoughts exactly. Yeah, so anyway, when he got her away from Petr, she was in a really bad state, and she wouldn't let go of him or anything. He drove her home and she was so scared of being left on her own. He was kind of worried about her, you know?" She paused. "He said to me that he kept thinking what if it was me or Lena? What if he'd been too late? All these 'what ifs' he was pretty much torturing himself with. So he told her to text him anytime."

"How did you get involved? You two hate each other." I raised a brow.

"Yeah, I know." A sigh escaped her lips. "Cass added me because he thought she should have a girl in the chat. You know what he's like. He can't help flirting, even if he's just trying to be friendly. Since I'm his best friend—"

"One of his best friends," I interjected.

She rolled her eyes. "Yeah, one of them, whatever. He added Lena and Kins to the chat, too. Anyway, she's not so bad in the chat. Not like in real life. She never really says anything—it's mostly just been Cass sending memes to make her smile. We don't like each other, like *at all*, but every time I think about what happened to her, it makes me feel sick." She shrugged.

"Baby, you have such a big heart. I'm so fucking lucky to have you." Out of the corner of my eye, I saw her give a shy smile that made my stomach flip.

We entered the small car park, and I brought the car to a halt in front of the garage door, beeping once. We rolled inside once the door lifted, and the second the engine was off, I gripped the back of her neck and pulled her mouth to mine.

"I love you so fucking much." I punctuated my words with kisses, and she melted against me, her lips sliding against mine as she opened her mouth for me.

"I love you, too," she said breathlessly against my lips, when we finally drew apart.

I slid my fingers through her hair, pushing it back from her face. "You ready?"

"How can I be ready if I don't know what's going on?" She gave me a kind of exasperated smile, and I grinned back at her.

"Trust me."

I led her into the tattoo shop where the rest of my boys already waited, along with Mack. Glancing around her, her eyes finally sparkled with excitement as she took everything in.

"We're getting tattoos?"

"You are." Cassius grinned at her, pulling her into a hug.

"Just me?" She stared between us, chewing her lip, looking all fucking cute and confused.

"Yep." I glanced at Cass' arm around my girl, pointedly, and he released her. After he stuck his tongue out and threw up his middle finger at me.

Yeah, I returned the gesture.

"You two are so mature." She rolled her eyes at us both, smiling.

"That's why you love us, babe." Cassius winked at her.

"Sure it is."

"Stabby. You wanna follow me?" Mack cocked his head at Winter.

"Stabby? Did you just call me *Stabby*?" Winter frowned at him.

"Yeah. You got all stabby with your mum, or so I heard. Wouldn't wanna cross you when you're holding a knife."

The room fell silent, Winter's mouth set in a flat, unsmiling line.

"Too soon to joke about it, huh?" His face fell.

My girl kept up her façade for about five seconds before she cracked, a huge smile spreading across her lips. "You should've seen your face. Fucking hilarious," she laughed. "But can't you think of a better nickname? Like, I dunno, Blade or something?"

"That's the name of that vampire guy," Weston interjected helpfully.

"Wonder Woman," Winter suggested.

"I'd like to see you dressed as Wonder Woman" was Cassius' helpful input.

"I'm gonna pretend I didn't hear that," Winter said to him, and I tuned out their banter, knowing from experience they'd be there all day. I tilted my head at Z, reclined on the sofa with a coffee in front of him.

"Alright, mate?"

He looked up at me, his usual mask down, emotion glittering in his icy eyes. "Yeah. Just been thinking about shit. You and Winter. I—" He stopped himself. Then he dropped his gaze and sighed. "There was—fuck. Things got fucked up for me. Just...take it from me. You've got a really fucking rare thing with Winter. Hang on to her, okay?"

I stared down at him. He was staring into his coffee mug. Fuck, there was so much I wanted to ask him, but I knew him. If he didn't want to talk, there was nothing I could say, and if I pressed him, he'd just walk out. "I will," I said instead. "You know I'm always here for you though, right? I've got your back."

"Yeah. I know." A small smile flickered across his lips, and I squeezed his shoulder, before clearing my throat and deciding to change the subject.

"Thanks," he added, his gaze flicking up to mine briefly before returning to his mug.

"Anytime. You thinking of getting any new ink?"

He seized onto the subject gratefully. "Thinking of it, yeah. You want to see how your girl's doing? Does she have any idea what we've planned?"

I shook my head, grinning. "Not a fucking clue."

"Rich boy! Get over here," Mack called, at that exact moment.

"Guess that's our cue."

We moved to stand in front of the tattoo station. Winter

lay back, Mack sitting next to her. Cassius had his phone out, high-pitched exclamations coming from the screen, and I peered closer to see Lena's and Kinslee's excited faces as they both watched what was going on.

"Your wrist, yeah?" Mack said.

Winter nodded. "Yeah. You're sure it won't look weird there? I just thought it might be nice there, since I have the other one on my other arm."

"It's the perfect place," I reassured her, giving her a soft kiss.

"I can't believe no one will tell me what's going on. You do realise this is permanent, right? It's not like I can just wash it off if I hate it."

I lifted her wrist and kissed it. "Baby, I wouldn't let you get anything marked on your skin that wasn't going to look fucking perfect. Trust me."

She smiled. "I do. Okay, go for it."

"Close your eyes," Mack instructed, cleaning the area, before applying the stencil he'd prepared earlier. The familiar buzz of the needle filled the space, and I grinned.

"All done." Mack wiped over the area he'd tattooed, and my girl's eyes flew open.

"Can I look?"

Mack glanced over at me, and I nodded. "Yeah."

She lifted her wrist, and stared in silence for the longest fucking minute of my life, before her eyes filled with tears, and the brightest smile lit up her face. Fuck. She was so beautiful, like the sun coming out after a storm.

"What does this mean?" Her voice was all shaky as she

sat up, studying the Roman numerals inked on her skin, identical to mine, Cassius', Weston's, and Zayde's.

"It means, you're officially, one hundred percent, permanently one of the Four. An unbreakable bond. You're ours, and we're yours, and we'll protect you with our fucking lives." I spoke the words hoarsely, the significance of the moment affecting us all, as we all stepped closer to her. Mack moved away to give us our privacy, and I took her hand, placing it on top of mine. The boys placed their hands on top, one by one.

"We love you. We're family," Weston added, throwing his arm around her.

"Forever. Ride or die, babe." That was from Cassius, who flashed a quick smile at me, before kissing her head.

"You're one of us." Zayde gave her a smile, allowing her the rare glimpse of emotion in his eyes. The tears spilled down her cheeks, and she smiled at him, mouthing *thank you*.

"I—I don't even know what to say." Her words were choked, and she brushed her tears away with a smile. "I never expected this. Fuck. I love you all, you know that, right?"

"We know." Cassius grinned at her. "Wonder if we'll get some shit at uni for being known as the Four still, even though there's five of us now."

I smirked. "Like we give a fuck. I say we get home and celebrate our new fifth member."

Yeah. Everyone was in agreement.

Later that night, I watched Winter as she talked and laughed with Kinslee and Lena, happy and carefree. She'd invited them over to celebrate with us, and everyone was a bit worse for wear. Everyone other than me, that was. And my girl, since I kept watering her drinks down. I wanted her to be aware for every moment of what I had planned.

My eyes raked over every inch of her. Dressed down in her yoga pants and tiny, tight white top, her hair tumbling down her back, and her eyes shining, she was so sexy that I'd had a semi all fucking evening looking at her.

She caught my eye, and her gaze drifted down to my sweatpants. Her eyes darkened, and she licked her lips, tilting her head suggestively.

Enough.

I jumped up, stalking straight over to her and scooping her into my arms. "We're going to bed," I announced, just so none of those fuckers got any ideas about following us. Although I think it was pretty obvious what my plan was.

She laughed and buried her face in my neck, clinging on to me tightly. I carried her out of the room to the sound of cheers and borderline inappropriate comments, heading up the stairs to our bedroom.

"You're fucking mine, Snowflake." I dropped her onto our bed, moving over her, sliding between her legs.

"Always," she moaned, hooking her ankles around me. "You're the only one I want. The only one I'll ever want."

My girl. She owned every single piece of me. I stopped grinding against her and met her eyes, meaning every word that came out. "I see you." I kissed her. "Only you." I kissed her again. "You're *mine*. My whole world."

"Yours."

After that, there was no more talking.

THE END

THANK YOU

Thank you so much for reading Caiden and Winter's story!

Want a bonus epilogue? Download it now from http://bit.ly/waiden

There's also a little bonus Christmas catch up with the Four at http://bit.ly/cavxmas

Weston's book (The Four, book 4) is available now at http://mybook.to/tfiu

Feel free to send me any and all abuse/love/comments, and spoiler-free reviews are always very appreciated!

Want even more? You can catch up with both Lena and Cassius in my Alstone High standalone bully romance, Trick Me Twice! Get it now at http://mybook.to/tmt

ACKNOWLEDGMENTS

First of all, thank you so much for reading the conclusion of Caiden and Winter's story. I know we still have some unanswered questions, but those will be answered in other stories.

I have to thank my amazing friends/betas for dealing with everything I've thrown at them! Ashley, Claudia, Jenny (thank you for coming up with the perfect title and being an amazing PA), Kat and Sue - seriously couldn't have done this without you!

Thank you to Sid for your proofreading skills! And to Veronica for all your help with the cover (and general motivation!), and to Ivy for our writing sprints and encouraging me to write every day. Sandra, my editor, how you put up with me, I'll never know! But hey, you're stuck with me now.

Huge thanks to my fantastic street team for all that you do. And my ARC team, you're awesome, and I thank you for taking the time to read and share things for me!

All the bloggers, bookstagrammers and readers that have supported this series in so many different ways... I see and appreciate you!

Thanks again for reading! 🤍 Look out for Cassius, Weston and Zayde!

Becca xoxo

ALSO BY BECCA STEELE

LSU Series

Blindsided (M/M)

The Four Series

The Lies We Tell

The Secrets We Hide

The Havoc We Wreak

A Cavendish Christmas (free short story)*

The Fight In Us

The Bonds We Break

Alstone High Standalones

Trick Me Twice

Cross the Line (M/M)

In a Week (free short story)*

Savage Rivals (M/M)

Boneyard Kings Series (with C. Lymari)

Merciless Kings (RH)

Vicious Queen (RH)

Ruthless Kingdom (RH)

Other Standalones

Mayhem (a Four series spinoff)*

Heatwave (a summer short story)*

London Players Series

The Offer

London Suits Series

The Deal

The Truce

The Wish (a festive short story)*

Box Sets

Caiden & Winter trilogy

*all free short stories and bonus scenes are available from https://authorbeccasteele.com

**Key - M/M = Male/Male (gay) romance

RH = Reverse Harem (one woman & 3+ men) romance

ABOUT THE AUTHOR

Becca Steele is a USA Today and Wall Street Journal bestselling romance author. She currently lives in the south of England with a whole horde of characters that reside inside her head.

When she's not writing, you can find her reading or watching Netflix, usually with a glass of wine in hand. Failing that, she'll be online hunting for memes, or wasting time making her 500th Spotify playlist.

Join Becca's Facebook reader group Becca's Book Bar, sign up to her mailing list, or find her via the following links:

- facebook.com/authorbeccasteele
- instagram.com/authorbeccasteele
- bookbub.com/profile/becca-steele
- goodreads.com/authorbeccasteele

Milton Keynes UK
Ingram Content Group UK Ltd.
UKHW041427090224
437562UK00002B/372

9 781915 467058